I0451100

Deadly Seizures
Death Agents Book Two

G. L. Didaleusky

Dedication

To Muffin, our Yorkie-Poo, who had been by my side in the computer room for over ten years while writing my novels.

Chapter One

Detective Janet Bennett sat a round table in front of Federal Medical Investigators' ten-passenger jet. Janet didn't like riding in airplanes, not because she was afraid of heights or had motion sickness. No. Her reason stemmed from a friend of hers dying in a plane crash five years ago. She knew the odds of an airplane crashing with her in it was extremely low.

Agent Frank Littlefield of the Federal Medical Investigators, who now sat to her right, said, "I noticed you appeared anxious after taking off from Ocala International Airport a few minutes ago. After we released our seat belts and walked over to this table, you still appear anxious."

The table sat in an opened area at the end of the row of seats.

Janet glanced down, then turned toward Frank. "A friend of mine died in an airplane crash a few years ago. I know it's irrational thinking."

"Not at all," Frank reassured her. "You're not the first person to experience this fear. Let me put your fear in perspective. You and the rest of us have a one in eleven million chance of being involved in a plane crash. Our odds to become president of the United States are one in ten million, and are one in seven hundred thousand to being killed from a meteorite."

Janet grinned. "Thanks. Those facts make me feel a little better."

Agent Jean Cliftwood, sitting to Janet's left, added, "Flying in airplanes isn't one of my favorite things in life, either. I'd rather take a car or bus. Time is essential when we need to investigate mysterious, unexplained deaths in the United States. Too much time can be our foe."

Janet still couldn't believe she'd accepted the position as an agent for the newly formed Federal Medical Investigators' team. She was getting complacent as a detective for the Marion County Sheriff Department. Besides, she didn't have any responsibilities as a divorced woman with no children.

Simon Woods sat across from Janet. Several manila folders sat on the table in front of him. "I'm going to give you FMI's oath. All you need to do after I read it to you is to say, 'Yes. I agree to uphold FMI's oath.' Frank will be video recording the proceedings on his iPhone. There's no formal ceremony."

Frank glanced around as if looking for something. "Dang. I don't see it."

Simon frowned with a puzzling expression. "See what?"

"The champagne to celebrate and toast this event."

Simon chuckled as he shook his head back and forth. He stared at Janet. "There isn't any pomp and circumstances, including champagne."

"I figured that," Janet responded.

She already knew Frank was a jokester at times.

Simon read the oath. Less than a minute later, he asked Janet, "Do you, Janet Bennett, accept FMI's oath?"

"Yes. I agree to uphold FMI's oath."

"You are now an official member of our team."

He picked up the manila folders and handed one to Jean, Frank and Janet. "Reach into the folder and remove its contents."

Everyone complied.

Janet removed several papers and photographs. She stared at pictures of six people with backpacks, along with headlamps attached around their heads. They were inside a cave. The victims were lying down without any apparent trauma to their bodies. The cave explorers appeared as if they were all sleeping, either on their sides, stomach or back. In fact, each of them was deceased. "It looks like they're sleeping."

"That's what it looks like, doesn't it?" Simon said, staring down at the photograph in his hand. "Each diagnosis on the autopsy reports from Franklin County Medical Examiner, which each of you have a copy of, states, Undetermined Death."

"This is something new for us," Frank said, with a grin.

He was obviously being facetious, thought Janet.

"I'm assuming the toxicology report didn't show anything, such as an overdose of drugs, poisoning or any abnormal levels of a chemical?"

Simon chuckled. "Spoken like a true major crime detective."

Janet stared up at Simon. "Ex-major crime detective."

Jean said, "It says in the autopsy report two of the victims had urine saturated on their underwear. Three of the victims had bitten their tongues. You can see these conditions after a person has a seizure."

"Very good, Jean. You're right. Some or all the victims could've had seizures. This is what's so puzzling. If in fact they all had a convulsive episode, what caused the six people to have them simultaneously? Plus, having a seizure doesn't mean you're going to die from it. A seizure is a brief episode of signs and symptoms. They can be due to abnormally excessive or synchronous neuronal activity in the brain. We need to find out what caused their convulsions, which will determine if their deaths were accidental or deliberate."

"This is why they pay us the big bucks to solve mysterious and unsolved deaths," Frank said. "We're FMI Death Agents."

Jean sighed. "I hate that name, Frank."

"We are FMI agents investigating deaths. Aren't we?"

Simon stood. "You all can go back to your seats. We'll be landing in Hagerstown in about ninety minutes. For our newest member of our team, Janet, there's a refrigerator at the back of the plane stocked with sodas, water and juices." He glanced at Frank. "No alcoholic beverages."

FMI's ten-passenger jet plane landed at Hagerstown, Regional Airport in Maryland a few minutes before nine-thirty in the morning. An unmarked black SUV awaited them on the tarmac. They got onto I-80 and headed to Chambersburg, Pennsylvania.

"It's twenty-four point one miles to Chambersburg. It should take us about thirty-three minutes, depending on traffic conditions," Frank announced, sitting behind the driver seat, after glancing down at the vehicle's GPS on the dashboard.

Janet sat in the back seat with Jean. Simon sat in the front passenger seat. Janet thought about her five years as a detective for the Marion County Sheriff's Office. She had formed a relationship with her partner, Bill Matters, and…

Simon interrupted her reminiscing as he turned toward the back seat and said, "We'll be going to the Franklin County Sheriff's Office. Detective Spurrier will be taking us to the site of the six deaths."

An amorous chill bolted up Janet's spine as she stared into Simon's eyes. *Get hold of yourself, woman. Yes. You like Simon. Yes, he's good looking with brains.*

She grinned, then said in a serious tone, "Have all the victims' pasts been looked into regarding anything possibly connecting their deaths?"

Simon smiled. "Probably. You'll need to ask Detective Spurrier this question when you meet him."

Janet frowned. "Why are you smiling?"

"It's a-a-a compliment. What I mean. You're a great asset to the FMI's team. None of us have your detective prowess."

"Thanks."

I'm not so sure that's what he was smiling about.

~ * ~

Simon turned back around and thought, *I gotta be more careful in my expressions when I'm with Janet. I know she didn't believe my answer.*

He did state the truth to Janet, although it wasn't related to her question.

His smile reflected his admiration toward Janet for both her beauty and intelligence. He didn't want to spoil their working relationship as FMI agents. There was no FMI policy about agents having friendships. Of course, his feelings about Janet infringed upon an amorous perspective. His previous serious relationship with a woman had ended up in turmoil and heartache, something he didn't want to go through again.

"If I may interject," Jean said. "I've noticed since first meeting Janet how easily she can read a person's body language, including expressions. I'm sure part of this attribute she learned from being a major crime detective." Jean raised her eyebrows as she glanced at Janet.

"Thanks for all these compliments. Does this mean I'll be getting a raise?"

Everyone chuckled. Frank then added, "I guess some of my fast and witty tongue has worn off onto our newest agent."

"I'd never take that honor away from you, Frank."

Simon knew he made the right decision asking Janet to join their team. Each agent had a different personality and ESP ability. Even with these differences, everyone got along together. Frank with his super sense of smell. Jean with her vision of a yellow glow around a person or persons who were about to face an ominous event within the next twenty-four hours. Janet with her forewarning feeling prior to opening a door, turning a corner, or prior to her answering a ringing phone. Finally, his visions of people in ominous events taking place within twenty-four hours, including his ability to visualize objects surrounding a person when talking to them on the telephone.

Janet asked, "What are the circumstances or criteria directing us to unexplained deaths in the United States? Who makes these decisions?"

"Good questions," Simon answered. "First of all, there are many unsolved deaths in the United States. One of our criteria is unexplained multiple deaths. We must investigate these deaths within seven days of their occurrence."

"That's two reasons. Isn't it?"

Simon rolled his eyes and chuckled to himself. "You got me there. Yes, I gave you two criteria. Since we're a division of CDC, it gives us jurisdiction when there's a possibility of a contagious factor in multiple, unexplained deaths. To answer your next question, Brian Littlefield determines our cases following FMI's criteria. Do you have any other questions for me?"

"No. I can't think of any more right now."

Jean nodded and smiled as she nudged Janet's elbow. She leaned toward Janet and whispered, "That-a-girl." Jean apparently agreed with Janet's assertiveness.

The remainder of the ride to Chambersburg was uneventful without any other significant statements or questions from anyone.

The GPS announced, "You've arrived at 157 Lincoln Way East." Frank pulled in the parking lot of Franklin County Sheriff's Office.

A moment later, the FMI's team walked up to the front counter. A deputy stood behind the counter.

Simon cleared his throat, then said, "We're here to see Detective Spurrier."

"I assume you're from CDC," said the deputy.

Simon glanced at his name plate on the front of the deputy's gray shirt. "Yes, we are, Deputy Olson."

"I'll call him and let him know you're here."

"Thanks." Simon, along with his agents, walked over to across from the front counter and sat.

"Oh, my God," Jean whispered, as she stared at a female sheriff deputy walking through a doorway to her right.

"Does she have a yellow glow?" Simon asked Jean.

"Yes. I need to get her name."

"Deputy, can I talk with you a minute?" Simon asked walking up to her.

The deputy stopped and faced him. "What can I do for you?"

Simon glanced down at her name plate, M. ROBINSON. "We're new to Chambersburg. Do you know a good restaurant nearby?"

"Sure. Aunt Sarah's Restaurant is down the street about two blocks. You'll make a left when you get outside."

"Thanks. Appreciate it, deputy."

Deputy Robinson walked up to the front counter and began talking to Deputy Olson.

Jean touched the palm of her hand against her cheek and breathed in deeply. "How are we going to tell the deputy about her possible deadly fate in the next twenty-four hours?"

"Not sure," Simon answered, glancing at each agent. "There's gotta be something we can do. Think people. Detective Spurrier is going to be here any minute."

"We need to alter her routine today, change her assignment or somehow delay her from doing her normal duties. Any of these things will change the timeline, preventing her from serious injury or death."

"I have an idea," Janet said getting up from the bench. She turned toward Frank. "Give me your cup of coffee."

"I didn't know you liked iced coffee."

"I don't."

Frank handed her a sixteen-ounce paper cup.

Janet removed the plastic lid. The cup was half filled. She gave the lid to Frank. She walked over toward the front counter and said, "Deputy Robinson,"

The deputy turned around. "Can I help you?"

Janet stumbled forward, throwing at least eight once of cold coffee on the front of the deputy's shirt and pants. "Oh…I'm so sorry."

The deputy's jaw dropped, and her eyes widened as she gazed down at her coffee soiled uniform. She then stammered, "I-I-I don't have a clean uniform in my locker. I'll have to go home and change my uniform. I'll also probably have to take a shower to get the coffee smell off my skin."

"I'll pay for any dry cleaning. It's the least I can do. Again. I'm so sorry. My shoe must have struck something sticky on the marble floor."

"No need to dry clean. I'm sure the coffee stain will come off in the washing machine. Accidents happen. That's why they call them accidents. I was about to go out on patrol. I'll have to let the duty officer know."

"Good thing you live a couple of miles away," Deputy Olson stated. "Your patrol car will be here when you get back."

"I'll be back as soon as I can."

The deputy turned and walked back toward the door she'd come through earlier. She stopped and opened a locked door with a plastic card by swiping it in front of a security scanner. She then stepped into a hallway.

Janet turned around and walked back over to her FMI comrades with a smile. She handed Frank the empty cup. "I owe you a cup of iced coffee."

"You don't owe me anything, Janet. I'm glad I brought my iced coffee with me. I don't know if we would've had a plan B."

Before anyone could respond to Frank's question, the door to the left of the front counter opened. A man, who stood about six-foot four inches, of medium build and wearing a gray suit, walked through the opened doorway. The man looked at the FMI's agents and said, "I'm Detective Steward Spurrier. I'm glad you all got here safely. Our department appreciates your help in these tragic deaths."

Simon stepped up to him, reached out and shook his hand. "We're pleased to help in every way we can. I'm Agent Woods." He continued to introduce Frank, Jean and Janet. "Everyone has reviewed the file you sent to our director, Brian Littlefield."

Detective Spurrier looked at Frank. "Are you...?"

"He's my older brother," Frank interrupted.

"Oh, I see." Spurrier turned to Simon. "Are you ready to see the site of the six deaths?"

"Yes. We'll follow you. We're driving a black Chevy Suburban."

Spurrier chuckled. "Don't all federal agency guys drive black SUVs?"

Simon raised his eyebrows and shrugged his shoulders. "Not sure. Most TV crime shows seem to display this type of vehicle."

Detective Spurrier led the FMI team out of the sheriff department's parking lot. Jean leaned forward toward the front seats and said, "I'll be anxious to know if Deputy Robinson will have an uneventful next twenty-four hours."

Janet reached over and briefly touched Jean's forearm. "Thanks to your ESP ability, I'm sure the deputy will avoid any tragic event."

About forty minutes passed before they reached the area of the cave. They parked their vehicles on a meandering one-lane dirt road. On both sides of the road stood densely spaced evergreens and deciduous trees. Simon couldn't see any visible path through the denseness of the forest. They were about a quarter of a mile from the base of Black Mountain. Wrapped around a tree to his left was a red ribbon marking the direction of the cave.

Detective Spurrier told them about the ribbon before leaving the parking lot. Detective Spurrier summoned them to come over to him as he stood in front of the opened trunk of his car. He handed each of them small LED circular lamps. "You'll need them to light your way through the cave."

Spurrier removed a long, metal cane from the trunk.

"I didn't know you needed a cane," Simon said to the detective. "I didn't see you using one at the sheriff's office."

"The cane isn't used for helping me walk. It's to defend myself against any crawling creature on the ground. I've walked from here to the cave a few times and haven't encountered any snakes yet."

"It's the 'yet' that bothers me," Jean said, reaching up and wiping off sweat cascading down her forehead.

Detective Spurrier grinned. "I'll lead the way, so there shouldn't be any problem."

Spurrier led the way through the forest. Red ribbons tied around saplings, every twenty feet, marked their way to the cave.

About ten minutes past where they had reached a small opening void of trees, a cluster of bushes at least six feet tall encompassed the area. Someone had recently cut down bushes in front of them at the base of the mountain, exposing an opening to a cave. The irregularly shaped crescent opening measured about six feet wide by seven feet high. Vines had once draped down, partially concealing the cave entrance. The recently cut vines lay on the ground to the right of the opening.

"This is the place. The cave had been inconspicuously hidden from human eyes. No one knew the cave existed until the six cave explorers found the concealed cave five days ago. Some people felt maybe methane or ammonia gas killed them. Of course, this theory proved false. The medical examiner didn't find any cause of their deaths. That's why your team was called to find the cause of their demise."

"I assume," Janet said, "you looked into the background of each caver to see if there were any grudges or conflicts between them which could've motivated one of them to commit an evil act?"

"Yes."

He peered down at Janet, pursed his lips and flung his shoulders back in a defiant manner. "You should know what normal police procedure since you were a previous major crime detective."

"I didn't mean to insinuate you don't know how to do your job. I understand you have an outstanding detective department."

Detective Spurrier's shoulders slumped as a smile appeared. "Thank you. We try to do our best. I'm sorry I offended you. I know you're trying to find answers to these unexplained deaths." He looked around at the team. "Turn your lamps on. I'll show you the spot where the cavers were found."

He turned and faced the opening to the cave.

Simon stared at Janet. "Anything?"

He wanted to know if she had an ominous premonition feeling about entering the cave, as she did a few days ago at the parking structure in Greek Town. If she did, they'd wear protective equipment, N95 masks, googles and a body suit.

She whispered, "Nothing."

Everyone turned on their LED lamps and followed Detective Spurrier into the cave.

Simon walked beside Janet while Frank and Jean walked behind them. A musty smell overwhelmed Simon. "I wonder if all caves smell like this?"

"According to my research of caves along the Black Mountain range near Chambersburg, there usually is a musty odor. Most of them in this mountain range are comprised of sedimentary rock mainly limestone with a mixture of numerous minerals. Depending on moisture and if a water source is near them, there can be a variety of smells inside of them. Different species of fungus can grow in a cave's environment. Another name for cave explorers is 'spelunkers.' There's…"

"Thanks for the information, Frank," Simon interrupted his dissertation on the composition and environments of caves.

"No problem, boss."

Simon had stopped correcting Frank's use of the word "boss" when addressing him. Simon knew he used the jargon with no ill will or disrespect. He relied on Frank's expertise with the computer, and of course, his ESP ability of smell.

Their LED lamps lit up a cavern with a height of about twenty feet, a width of approximately sixty feet and a depth of about two hundred feet before the cave began to narrow. "Up ahead is where we found the six dead cave explorers," Detective Spurrier announced, as his deep voice echoed through the cavern.

In a couple of minutes, they stood at the point where the cavern narrowed to a height of six feet. Roots hung down, resembling a curtain covering the back wall.

As Frank looked up and around the cavern in a three-hundred-and-sixty-degree scan, he said, "I don't see any bats nesting in here. I'm not an expert on bats, but from what I've read, there should be bats in here."

"You would think there should be. A medical examiner employee who helped remove the bodies, who also was a cave explorer, stated the reason there weren't any bats in this cave was because there wasn't any significant opening at the entrance to the cave for the bats to enter or leave. Made complete sense to us. We also invited Shippensburg University's Geology Department to explore the cave in a couple of days. We're hoping they'll find something unusual in the cave. Anyway, here's the spot where we found the six dead cave explorers." Detective Spurrier pointed down at the rock floor to his left.

"From what I read in your investigative report, the bodies laid here for at least twenty hours before they were discovered by one of their friends."

"You're correct, Agent Bennett."

"Call me Janet. Agent Bennett sounds so formal."

Simon huffed to himself. *I've heard that line before. Instead of Agent she said Detective to me.* Simon sighed. *I'm not dating her. What's come over me?*

He couldn't believe a jealous feeling overtook his emotions. She was being congenial, not flirtatious. Simon turned to his left and stared at the wall covered with roots. "Strange all these roots are covering this wall."

Spurrier turned around, nodding. "Apparently the roots aren't uncommon according to the medical examiner's assistant. We'll be getting more information when Shippensburg's people explore the cave."

Frank walked over to the rooted wall, bent down, and inhaled a deep breath. "I smell the odor of almonds. I think the odor is coming from the other side of this wall." He began pushing the densely tangled roots aside. "There's an opening through this wall. The opening is large enough to squeeze through on my hands and knees." He moved forward. The front half of his body disappeared through the opening. "The odor of almonds is becoming stronger." A few seconds later, his body disappeared.

"What did you find, Frank?"

No answer.

Simon shouted louder, "Frank. Are you okay?" *Did he succumb to what killed the six cavers?*

"I'm all right." His voice was muffled. "There's another cavern about half the size of the one you're in. Bats are living in here. There're numerous stalactites and stalagmites throughout the cave. The odor of almonds is prevalent in here."

Simon sniffed in deeply near the opening. "I don't smell anything."

Of course, Simon wasn't going to smell anything. He didn't have Frank's ability of supernatural smell.

"Besides, not all people can smell the bitter odor of almonds."

"The odor of almonds can be present during cases of cyanide poisoning," Spurrier said. "Was cyanide responsible for the deaths of the cave explorers?"

"Cyanide is naturally present in bitter almonds and many other plants used as food, including apples, peaches, apricots, lima beans, barley, sorghum and flaxseed. Of course, a person would have to eat a tremendous amount of one of these foods to feel its adverse effects."

Spurrier removed his cellphone. "I'll call the ME and see if he checked for cyanide poisoning."

He pushed "call" on the medical examiner's phone number. A few seconds later, he glanced down at his phone. There's no reception inside the cave. I'll call when we get outside."

A thunderous roar crescendoed toward them as the cave's floor shook. Small rocks and dirt began to fall from the ceiling, striking them. "It's a cave-in," shouted Simon. "How is it on your side, Frank?"

"No problem over here."

"We gotta get out of here. Our only chance of surviving is through this opening. You go first, Jean"

She crawled on her hands and knees through the opening, followed by Janet and Spurrier.

Simon had difficulty breathing due to the increasing dust and dirt-filled air. He got into the crawling position as darkness enveloped him due to the rocks smashing his lamp. Larger rocks began striking the back of his legs. *I don't want to be buried alive.*

Chapter Two

Spurrier reached inside the opening, grabbed Simon's hands, and pulled him into the cavern. Simon coughed. His body from the back of his neck to lower legs was covered with small rocks and dirt.

"In a few more seconds, your body would've been crushed by the rocks and debris," Detective Spurrier said, as he helped Simon to a standing position.

"Thank God. You're all right," Janet said.

She couldn't believe it: her first day as an FMI agent and one of her team members was almost killed.

"If it wasn't for Detective Spurrier, I may not have survived."

"Call me Steward. Detective Spurrier is too formal."

Simon glanced at Janet and raised his eyebrows. He then turned to Spurrier. "Thanks, Steward, for pulling me through."

He nodded. "No problem."

Janet knew what Simon's eyebrow gesture meant. *Touché. Sounds familiar.*

Their LED lamps lit up a cave half the size of the other cave. Numerous stalagmites and stalactites covered the ceiling and floor of the cave. There was a crevice in the far-right corner measuring about eight feet wide and the same height of the cave, enough space for a person to easily walk through. In the far-left corner of the cave, bats hung from the ceiling while others nestled in cubbyholes near the ceiling. Below the bats' nest lay decaying bat droppings.

Frank sniffed. "Bat guano."

"What's bat guano?" Jean asked.

"Bat shit, to be exact."

14

"Did you know *Histoplasma capsulatum*, a fungus, can be found in this poop?" Simon declared. "Caves are the usual habitat of many species of bats and dimorphic fungus can be rich in bat droppings, which favor the growth of this fungus. The air in caves can contain spores of this fungus. Cave explorers may inhale these spores and get infected with this fungus. The fungus can cause histoplasmosis, a systemic infection involving internal organs, skin and mucous membranes, leading to a fatal fungal infection."

"Great," said Frank. "We were almost killed by a cave-in, but now we'll probably die from bat shit."

"Unlikely, Frank. We do need to get a sample of the bat guano and have it analyzed when we get out of here."

Frank put some of the bat droppings into a plastic Ziplock bag. He placed the specimen into a satchel hanging from a leather strap around his neck to the right side of his body. He raised his head and sniffed. "I smell something that shouldn't be in a cave. The odor is coming from the direction of the opening over there." He pointed to the opening between the two caves. Frank walked over to the opening and breathed in deeply through his nose. "Damn."

"What's wrong?" Janet asked.

"I smell the remnants of dynamite coming through this opening. I don't think the cave-in was Mother Nature's doing."

Janet turned and peered into Simon's eyes. "Do you think The Circle is responsible for this?"

"Anything is possible. If it wasn't them, who else would want us dead, preventing us from investigating the six cavers' deaths? Maybe whoever caused the explosion and cave-in are responsible for the deaths of the six cave explorers?"

"Maybe there was a different evil group or organization behind the cavers' deaths and cave-in?"

"What are you two talking about?" Spurrier asked.

Janet gave a short synopsis about The Circle and their probable involvement in the deaths of sixteen people in Ocala, Florida. "Neither the Marion County Sheriff's Office nor the Federal Medical Investigators had concrete evidence to prosecute them, only the speculation The Circle had something to do with the murders. No judge would've ever issued a search warrant against The Circle under those circumstances."

"Great story," Spurrier said. "If you couldn't find proof to prosecute The Circle in Ocala, what makes you think you'll find proof against them here?"

"All we can do is try," Janet answered. "That's if The Circle is responsible for the cave-in or possibly the deaths of the six cavers. One of the first things we have to do, once we get out of this cavern, is determine what caused their deaths."

"My first job," Spurrier declared, "is to find out who caused the cave-in. Once I find out, attempted murder charges will be filed against them. I don't like death staring back at me."

Janet didn't blame Steward for his vindictive thinking. She and the FMI agents had encountered the reaper of death during their investigation of the Whispers Before Death case in Ocala. "If there's fungus spores floating around, I don't think it would be a good idea to be exposed to the spores any longer than we should. If the bats are in here, they'd need an opening somewhere for them to fly in and out of the cave. Let's hope the opening is large enough for us to get through."

"You're right on both points," Simon said. "What we all need to do for a few seconds is to turn off our lamps. Hopefully, we'll see a light from the outside projecting into the cave."

Everyone turned off their LED lamps. Darkness stared back at them. They turned their lamps back on, lighting up the cavern.

Simon pointed to the right. "The crevice over there has to lead to an opening to the outside." He led the way through the narrow fissure in the cave.

Janet walked behind Simon, followed by Jean, Frank and Spurrier. Being a narrow space, their shoes clunked on the rock floor. The hard soles of their shoes created a marching cadence as if a military troop was marching over a cobblestone road. The crevice meandered for a least hundred feet before it ended at a solid rock wall.

"Turn your lamps out again," Simon ordered.

As the last lamp was turned off, a ray of sunlight above them shone down from the top of the crevice, illuminating them like a spotlight shining on stage performers. Unfortunately, the opening was twenty feet above the trapped investigators. The opening appeared to be about a foot and a half wide. Wide enough for flying bats or birds, but not wide enough for adult humans. *Even if we had a long rope, no one could squeeze through the opening,* thought Janet.

Frank grunted as he peered up. "One of us will need to go on a crash diet to make it through the opening."

Jean stared at Frank's midsection. "Speak for yourself, Pillsbury Dough Boy. If I was any lighter, I'd probably float up to the opening."

"Let's get serious, you guys," Simon barked. "Let's try using our cellphones. Maybe the reception is better in here?"

Everyone brought out their phones and dialed a number. No reception showed on each of their phones.

"Since Plan A was to easily climb or walk through an exit made by nature, Plan B was to try our phones again. We need to think of a Plan C to get out of here."

Janet remembered a time when she and a girlfriend were thirteen. They had gotten lost in Ocala National Forest. They came to a clearing in the woods. Her girlfriend made a comment that led to them being rescued: *"We need to build a signal fire."*

Janet turned to Spurrier and suggested, "We'll build a fire and the smoke will billow outside. I'm sure someone from your department will send a detective here when you don't return to your office. They'll see the cave-in, then the smoke. When they climb up the mountain, they'll come right to the opening above us."

She glanced at everyone else. "What do you all think about my idea?"

Spurrier put his hands on his hip and squinted as he cocked his head in a gesture of thinking. "I think it's a great idea. One major problem, though. We're not in the middle of a forest with burning material. We're in a cavern surrounded by solid rock."

"We do have cloth," Janet suggested

"There could be a problem with cloth," Frank added. "Synthetic fiber may give off toxic smoke and very little smoke. It would have to be nearly one-hundred percent cotton. Even then, the cloth probably wouldn't create enough smoke for a smoke signal that could be seen through the opening above us. Secondly, even if we found something to burn, does anyone have a lighter to start the fire?"

Everyone shook their heads back and forth indicating a negative answer, except Spurrier, who nodded as he removed a cigarette lighter from his pants' pocket. "I guess this is one of the rare situations where smoking is a good habit to have. Like what Agent Littlefield said a moment ago, there isn't anything we could burn to create enough smoke."

"We do have something to burn," Simon said. "Tree roots. We had to push them aside as we crawled into the second cave."

~ * ~

Simon crawled through the opening toward the other cave, stopping when he reached the curtain of roots. Spurrier had given him a pocketknife to cut through the roots. The roots were dry and easy for the blade of the knife to slice through. Many of the roots were halfway cut through due to the falling rocks during the cave-in. Thirty minutes past as Simon crawled backward sliding several roots measuring between one to three inches in diameter and about two feet long in front of him. A moment later, he scooted into the bat cave. "This should be enough roots for now. There's more roots I can get if we need them."

"Great," Spurrier said grabbing some of the roots from the floor. Frank also pitched in and grabbed a few roots.

They all walked back toward the crevice. Simon stared up at the bats. The small, mammalian creatures with wings seemed to peer back at him, wondering why these humans were intruding upon their domain.

Frank also glanced up at the bats and stated, "Did you know one bat can eat up to one thousand insects in an hour at night?"

"How do you come up with all these statistics?" Janet asked.

"Before we start our investigations, I try to get as much information about where we're going and what we might face. Since we were told we'd be investigating six deaths in a cave, I read up on caves in Pennsylvania, especially this area of the state."

"That makes sense."

"Don't let him fool you," Jean said. "He loves reading trivial material not even related to any of our cases. Never play for money when playing a game about trivial knowledge with him."

When they reached the end of the crevice, Spurrier removed his knife and cut lengthwise along one of the smaller roots, creating shavings. He then crumbled up paper from his pocket-size notebook normally used for taking notes during an investigation. The others also contributed paper from their notebooks. He placed the shavings on top of the paper. Spurrier then made a teepee-like structure with the roots over it. "Well, here goes," he said, lighting the paper with his lighter. The paper ignited the root shavings. The flames started the dry roots smoldering. In a few minutes, the roots began to burn, letting off a billow of smoke ascending through the opening above them.

Frank looked up at the rising billow of smoke. He inhaled a deep breath, then expelled it. "Ladies and gentlemen...we have a smoke signal," he shouted in the cadence of a circus announcer. Everyone chuckled.

Simon felt confident someone will see the smoke and investigate its source. He had noticed a fire tower on their way to the cave. He heard on the news about live action cameras were now being placed in these towers. The cameras video feed was sent to ranger stations' monitors.

"All we can do now is wait and hope someone sees the smoke. Also, to conserve the batteries in our lamps, we'll only need one lamp on at a time."

Simon was realistic, knowing if no one saw the smoke or the smoke dissipated before reaching above the treetops, they might not be rescued for at least two days when students and staff from Shippensburg University's geology class arrived to explore the cave. They would need a light source to feel psychologically safe, especially at night when there'd be no light coming through the hole above them.

Of course, this scenario would be highly unlikely since someone from Detective Spurrier's department would be sent here to investigate why he didn't return to the office, why he didn't answer his cellphone, or at least call someone in his office and inform them he wouldn't be coming back to the office today.

A couple of hours passed and no one came to the opening above them. The smoke from the roots continued to send up a substantial amount of smoke. They estimated the roots were burning for another three to four hours. Simon and Spurrier decided to go to the opening between the two caves to get more roots. Forty minutes later their outstretched arms carried a stack of roots as they approached the end of the cave's crevice. Janet, Jean and Frank sat about six feet from the fire.

Frank stood, cleared his throat, then said, "Okay, did you bring me a cheeseburger without pickles and fries?"

Simon chuckled. "Sorry, Frank. McDonald's was closed due to renovation of the building."

Jean said, "I have to use the lady's room. I'll be right back." She turned her lantern on and walked toward the cave.

About a minute later, a male voice from above the trapped group yelled, "Hello. Anyone there?"

The voice sounded familiar to Simon. How could that be? He didn't know anyone in Pennsylvania. "Yes. We're here and safe. Detective Spurrier, Agents Bennett, Cliftwood, Littlefield and me, Agent Woods. Who am I speaking with?"

"Danny Emerick."

Danny Emerick? The computer geek with a microchip analysis machine from Ocala, Florida? thought Simon. "Are you the same Danny whose farmhouse was blown up by a missile?"

"Yep. I'm the one," he shouted back. "I assume this opening is the only way out of the cave?"

"Yes. Someone blew up the front entrance to the cave."

"So, the unfortunate cave-in wasn't by the hands of Mother Nature?"

"No. Someone deliberately caused the cave-in. We're in a crevice at the far end of an adjoining cave. The other cave is impassable. Is anyone else with you? And why are you here?"

"To answer your first question, I'm all alone. Your second question, Director Littlefield of FMI sent me here. Once I get you guys out of there, I'll explain things in more detail. I'll be right back. I have to get something from my van."

"Did you call the Sheriff's office?"

Danny didn't answer. Simon looked at Janet.

"He's probably already left for his van. I wonder why the director didn't call me about Danny coming here?"

"Maybe Director Littlefield didn't send him? Maybe he was the one who caused the cave-in? When he saw the smoke, he wanted to see if someone survived the explosion."

Simon's lower jaw fell as his shoulders dropped in a forlorn gesture. "Do you think Danny went back to get more explosive material to collapse the opening above us and possibly cause a cave-in…killing all of us?"

"God. I hope not," Frank said. "I agree with Simon, why didn't my brother call to let us know Danny was coming here? Even if Danny sealed the opening above us without causing the rest of the cave to collapse in on us, we'd soon run out of oxygen. It'll take at least two days before a rescue team reaches us. By then we would've suffocated from lack of air. Since no one knows about the second cave, they'll assume we were all lying dead under the tons of rock in the first cave."

A light from a lantern shone down the crevice. It was Jean returning. A moment later, Simon peered at Jean, the one person who'd know if all of them were about to die in the next twenty-four hours.

"Do you see anything, Jean?"

Janet and Frank also stared at Jean, except Spurrier, who was stirring the fire with a root. The detective had no knowledge of FMI's agents' ESP powers.

No immediate response from Jean. The crackling sound coming from the burning roots created an eerily atmosphere inside the crevice. Jean stopped, almost dropping her lantern, as she stared at her colleagues with a worrisome expression.

Chapter Three

"Why's everyone looking at me?" She peered down at the front of her crotch. "Did I pee on myself?"

The FMI agents laughed except for Detective Spurrier, who had a puzzled expression as if wondering why they were laughing at Jean. The agents' laughter reflected their nervous energy built up in anticipation of Jean saying they all had yellow glows encompassing their bodies. Was death about to meet them at the pearly gate of heaven?

"No, Jean," Janet answered, "you look fine. Your statement about yourself touched our funny bone relieving the built-up tension we're all feeling. If you know what I mean?" Janet put her hands to the side of her face in an expanding gesture of glowing.

She set her lantern down of the floor. "Oh, now I know what you meant by your gesture and question, Janet. Everyone looks okay."

"This must be an FMI inside joke or something. Did I miss something? I didn't find it funny or understand Janet's gesture?"

"Yeah," Frank said, "it's an inside joke shared among us in our group."

"Good. I don't feel so bad now for not laughing or understanding."

Janet reached out and touched Jean's forearm. "Something happened while you were gone. Danny Emerick, the computer geek, whose house was blown up by the missile, showed up at the opening above us."

"Great. We'll be rescued then."

"We think we are."

"That doesn't make any sense. Danny's here to rescue us. Right?"

Simon explained to Jean their suspicion about Danny and why there may be a sinister reason he was here at the opening above them. She gazed up at the opening. "I'm an optimist. Let's hope Danny went back to his van for equipment to get us out of here?"

While Simon talked with Jean, Frank and Spurrier put out the fire by scattering the hot root coals and burning roots several feet from the opening. The smoke was reduced more than seventy-five percent.

Danny had been gone about twenty minutes when the light from the opening above them lessened in intensity. Simon gazed up and thought, *Had a cloud passed in front of the sun*?

"I'm back. You all will need to step back about twenty feet. A lot of rock and debris will be falling from up here. I'm going to widen the opening."

"Okay," Simon shouted. *Either Danny is lying to us and is going seal up the opening and trap all of us down here. Maybe he's going to rescue us? We'll know very shortly.*

Simon peered at Jean. "Anything?"

"Everyone looks good."

Spurrier who was talking with Janet and likely didn't hear his conversation with Jean. Otherwise, he would've responded to Jean's answer. An ominous thought crossed his mind: *What if Jean didn't see a yellow glow around everyone because they all would be dying after the twenty-four-hour period from suffocation? If, in fact, Danny was about to seal off the opening?* He decided not to tell anyone his thoughts because if in fact they were about to die, what good would it do to tell them?

Everyone hurried up the crevice about twenty feet and stopped. The moment of truth hung over them, literally. "It would be best we all turn our backs to the opening," Frank said. "Like Danny's warning, there will be a lot of rock and debris falling into the crevice. Need to protect our eyes."

"Here goes," Danny yelled through the opening above them.

Simon's muscles tightened as his heart rate and breathing increased, anticipating an explosion either to widen or seal the opening. The sound of falling rock thundered down the crevice toward them. No explosion. *What is Danny doing up there? Why wasn't there an explosion?* The thunderous sound of falling rock stopped within thirty seconds. A bloom of dust passed around them followed by clean air. He turned around and saw a large opening. *How could that be?*

"Everybody okay down there?" Danny yelled.

Simon along with everyone else walked toward the new, widen opening above them. "Everyone is fine." Broken rock, dirt and weeds lay beneath the opening. He peered up and saw a smile on Danny's face. The opening appeared to be at least four feet wide. "How did you widen the hole?"

"Laser. I used one of my inventions."

Danny disappeared for a few seconds and returned holding a long cylindrical object about three feet in length. "This is my laser here."

Frank and everyone else stood looking up at Danny. "I remember you telling me on the phone when we were in Ocala about how you loved to make electronic and electrical things. In that case, beam me up, Scotty. Or should I say, Danny?"

"I wish I possessed that capability, Frank. We'll have to rely on the old-fashioned way. A rope."

Danny tossed down a rope. Attached to the bottom of the rope was a metal foot plate wide enough to stand on with both feet. Jean stood on the plate. She slowly rose to the top of the crevice where Danny reached out and pulled her the rest of the way to the surface.

Simon was the last one to be rescued. He stood on the side of the mountain and stared at the nylon rope used in their rescue. He followed the rope to a strange apparatus attached to a tree about six feet away from the opening in the ground. "I've never seen a pulley like this one."

Danny smiled. "The pulley is one of my inventions. It works on the principal of weight distribution, torque ratio and spring tension. You don't need a lot of manual strength to pull an object, such as a person, out of a hole."

Simon was impressed by Danny's inventions. "Why don't we get off this mountain before something else happens?"

Everyone agreed.

On their way down the mountain slope, Spurrier called his

department and told one of the detectives what had happened. After getting off his cellphone, he announced, "They'll be doing a full investigation by my department and the forensic unit on the explosion causing the cave-in."

They reached the foot of the mountain. The FMI team and Spurrier stopped and stared at the debris of rocks blocking the entrance to the cave. "If there was any evidence in the cave on the six deaths, the evidence is now gone. I assume this will put a damper on FMI's investigation on the six cave explorers' deaths?"

"To some degree, yes," Simon answered. "You're right about any possible evidence in the cave being destroyed. This is just the beginning of our investigation." He looked up the mountain toward the area of their rescue. "At least the bats now have a larger hole to fly in and out of at night."

Spurrier nodded. "I guess some good has come from the cave-in. I'll call the ME and see if they checked for cyanide poisoning in the six cavers."

After a minute or two, he put his cellphone away into his belt holder. "I talked with the ME. He said there was a minuscule trace of cyanide in their bodies, but not enough to cause any symptoms or damage to their organs and health."

"Thanks, Steward." Simon turned to Frank. "You still have the bat guano, right?"

"Yeah. I got the bat poop. I wouldn't leave home without it."

Simon rolled his eyes, shaking his head back and forth. He'd never get use to Frank's comical responses. Although, his humor was refreshing during serious moments, either during or after their investigations. "We'll need to give it to the investigating sheriff detective when *he* gets here."

"It'll be a her," Stewart said. "A Detective Carla Collins, who'll be the lead detective in this case. As you and Agent Bennett already know, if a detective is part of a crime scene, they can't be the investigating detective."

His phone rang. He answered, "Detective Spurrier." He listened to the caller for less than a minute before putting his phone away. "I'll be heading back to my office. My captain needs to talk with me on couple of matters not related to what we went through in the cave. I have to say, this has been quite a harrowing day for me, one I'll have to put at the top of my list for 'hope this never happens again,' if you know what I mean?"

"We do, Stewart." He wanted to tell the detective, "This is a normal day for us." Instead, Simon added, "We'll keep in touch with you during our investigation."

"Thanks. I'll do the same, especially who caused the cave-in." Spurrier said his goodbye to the FMI team and walked through the clearing toward the forest.

As Detective Spurrier disappeared into the woods, Simon turned his attention to Danny, who was holding his laser cutter invention and explaining how it worked to Frank.

"Danny. Tell us why you're here in Pennsylvania?"

Janet and Jean stood next to Simon, directing their attention at Danny, waiting for his answer.

"I'm sure you all are curious. Director Littlefield called me yesterday evening and asked if I would like to join the FMI team. I told him I'd let him know this morning. I called the director early this morning and agreed to join your organization as an FMI agent."

They congratulated him as the newest member of their team. In twenty-four hours, the FMI team had grown from three agents to five agents. Simon wondered if Danny had any ESP capabilities and if he knew about each agents' special powers. "Did the director tell you anything about any of us?"

"Oh. You mean your ESP abilities? Yes, he told me. I told him, I didn't have any special powers. He didn't care. He wanted my expertise in computers and my ingenuity and talent of developing gadgets. You saw two of my gadgets…the laser gun and the pulley I call Danwinch."

"Danwinch? Sounds like something else."

"Yeah," Frank interjected. "It sounds like sandwich. Who cares? The Danwinch rescued us. That's all that matters as far as I'm concerned."

"You're right," Simon agreed.

His muscles stiffened as visions flashed across his mind. Several seconds later, the visions disappeared.

"Did you have a vision?" Jean asked.

She'd seen Simon have visions over the past few months. She recognized his sudden blank stare and statuesque posture.

"Yes. I saw a vision of three people with nystagmus or horizontal flickering of the eyes. There was a woman in her early thirties, a man in his mid-twenties and a man in his forties. All three of them were conscious. It appeared they were standing or sitting. I wonder if their eye condition was also present in the six cave explorers?"

"Quite possible," Janet answered. She glanced away toward the ground for a moment, as if she was thinking of something. Raising her head, she looked into Simon's eyes. "These visions could be unrelated to the six cavers' deaths five days ago. Don't you think?"

"No way of knowing since I only saw headshots of the three people. Although, all three of them were in front of a rock wall."

"Like in a cave?"

Simon thought a moment. "Could be a cave wall."

Danny frowned. "Do all your visions have to do with death? Also, are your visions of the future?"

"No, to your first question. Not all of them. I'd say at least ninety percent of them are related to people about to die or will be in perilous situations possibly leading to their death within twenty-four hours. The time frame of my premonition visions is the same as Jean's vision of yellow halos around people. To answer your second question, about ten percent of my visions occur the moment of my vision. For example, when I first talked with Detective Bennett on the phone a few days ago, I saw her name plate on the front of her desk and a small statue of a green frog on the right side of her desk."

Danny's eyes widened exposing the upper whites of his eye globe. "Wow. I'll make sure I don't have anything illegal around me when I talk with you on the phone."

Simon chuckled. Now they had two jokesters on the team, him and Frank. It must be related to their computer forte. He turned to Frank. "You may have competition with your jokester remarks."

"No problem. I don't mind sharing with Danny. Us computer

guys have to stick together."

"Let's get serious now. So far in our investigation of the six dead cave explorers there were traces of cyanide inside each of the victims. Which was why Frank smelled the odor of almonds in the cave. The paramount question is how did this small amount of cyanide, a chemical compound, show up in each of the cavers' bodies? The bat guano will need to be analyzed for *Histoplasma capsulatum* and any other potential deadly organisms, including cyanide. After we're done with Detective Collins, we'll need to interview the families of the six cavers." He glanced at his watch, it was four forty-three p.m. "We probably won't be done with the sheriff detective for a couple of hours. We've been through a lot today. Everything I said about what we need to do can wait until tomorrow morning. I believe a refreshing shower and some food in our bellies is our priority after we leave here."

Frank raised his hand, "I second the motion, boss."

"I figured you would. I'm sure you'll want to get on your computer and do a search on the six dead cavers. Plus, check what companies in the area use dynamite."

"I guess you know me, boss." Frank put his hand on top of Danny's shoulder. "Now I have an accomplice, I mean, a computer partner, to help me."

"Sounds like fun to me," Danny agreed.

Janet said, "What about your vision of the three people in your vision with nys...nys... whatever it's called."

"It's called nystagmus," Simon answered. "There's no way for us to know who the three people are and if in fact they were in a cave. I'd imagine there are many caves in a fifty-mile radius of us."

"There are more than twenty known caves in the area," Danny answered. "Which would include caves west of Harrisburg, the state capital of Pennsylvania, to Crystal Grottoes Caverns in Maryland. The Maryland border is about twelve miles away from us. There isn't any government or private company where a caver must register their intention to explore a cave. It would be a monumental, if not an impossible, task to find out this information. All we can do is wait and see if what you saw in your premonition vision causes their deaths or a life-threatening medical condition."

Simon grinned. "I suppose you also did research on caves in this area on your way to Pennsylvania from Ocala?"

"I did. How'd you know I did research on caves?"

Simon glanced at Frank then back to Danny. "Ask your computer geek friend. You two should compare notes on caves."

Franklin County Crime Scene Unit investigators and Detective Collins spent little over an hour to do their investigation and questioning. A CSU investigator snapped pictures of the collapsed cave entrance and samples of rock with scorch marks left by the explosive compound.

Frank told one of the investigators that he was pretty sure the explosive material would turn out to be dynamite and not TNT, amatol, a military explosive or ammonal, an industrial explosive. Each of the last three explosives had added ingredients different than dynamite.

The CSU woman asked Frank how he was sure it was dynamite and not one of the other types of explosive compounds. He told her he did research on all the types of explosives, including their composition and the odor left by each of the explosive compounds after their detonation. The response by the crime scene investigator was, "Oh. I never realized each of the explosives gave off a different odor."

After Frank talked with Detective Collins, he handed her the plastic bag of bat guano and told her what forensics needed to examine for in the specimen. She then gave a CSU investigator the guano with Frank's instructions.

The Crime Scene Unit investigators and Detective Collins left the clearing, heading back to their vehicles on the road beyond the densely wooded forest.

Simon stood and looked around, wondering if whoever the person or persons responsible for the explosion were peering down at them with disappointment that they hadn't killed the investigative team.

Janet, who stood next to him, noticed him looking around. "Do you think the culprits are watching us?"

"Quite possible. The denseness of the trees would hide them from plain view. Like we've said when we were in Ocala and Detroit, trouble seems to follow us…Pennsylvania is no exception."

"Isn't that the truth? Like I said earlier, I wouldn't be surprised if The Circle was responsible for the cave-in. All we need to do is prove it."

Simon removed his cellphone from his jacket. He needed to call Director Littlefield and tell him what happened in the cave, including his recent ominous vision.

"All we can do is use all our resources, detective work and maybe luck to solve the six cavers' deaths. With the addition of Danny Emerick, two FMI agents with computer expertise has made us more diversified and stronger."

He called Littlefield.

The phone rang three times before Littlefield answered, "I presume you're calling about Danny Emerick? I tried to call you earlier but was unable to get through to you."

"There isn't any reception inside the cave." Simon proceeded and told him what had happened.

"I'm glad no one was killed or injured. I guess recruiting Danny turned out to be a godsend. So, from what you just told me, you don't have any leads on the cause of the six cavers' deaths other than Frank smelling the odor of almonds inside the two caves and the bodies of the cavers having traces of cyanide in their system?"

"No. That's it so far. As for my recent vision of three people with nystagmus, we'll have to wait and see if it means anything."

"That's all you can do at this point. Keep me informed as things go on in the investigation as you normally do. Talk to you later."

Simon put his phone away. Frank, Jean and Danny walked over to him and Janet. "Are you guys ready to leave?"

"I'm going to ride with Danny," Frank said, as he handed Simon the keys to the Suburban.

"That'll be fine. We'll be staying at Chambersburg Motor Lodge. See you there."

The FMI team left the collapsed cave and the clearing, heading out of the forest to their vehicles on the meandering dirt road. A few minutes later, Simon sat in the driver's seat and turned the key in the ignition. Janet sat in the front passenger seat and Jean sat in the back seat.

Janet turned on the SUV's GPS. The GPS had already been set for their hotel after they had gotten off the plane in Hagerstown this morning.

Simon looked ahead and watched Danny close the windowless back door of his burgundy-colored van, then get into his vehicle. He turned around and drove past them, waving. Simon noticed there weren't any windows in the paneled section of the vehicle. No one from the outside would know what was inside the van even if they peered through the passenger or driver side windows and the windshield, since there was a solid wall behind the front bucket seats.

A man in his early thirties and a woman about the same age, dressed in camouflage clothes, stood inside the woods about twenty yards away and watched FMI's burgundy van and black Suburban drive away. A few yards away behind them sat two four-wheel drive electric ATVs on a wilderness trail. The trail was only wide enough to accommodate one ATV. They put on black plastic helmets with a plastic visor covering their faces, got onto their ATVs and drove away.

Chapter Four

Simon pulled into the parking lot of Chambersburg Motor Lodge. After everyone checked into their individual rooms and had their showers, they all met in the hotel's restaurant. There were a several patrons eating. The five FMI agents sat at a large round table in the far-right corner, away from people's probing ears. After ordering their drinks and being served by the waitress, Simon raised his bottle of beer and said, "Let's toast to our new agent, Danny Emerick."

Everyone raised what they were drinking and clinked glasses or bottles in the traditional toast gesture. "Welcome aboard, Danny."

"Thanks, everyone. I'm glad to be part of your group. One thing I know for sure, there's never a dull moment during the investigations. The noun 'boredom' and the adjective 'mundane' along with their derivatives aren't in your dictionary."

"I thought you were a science and technology type of guy," Frank said, putting his glass containing a whiskey sour mixed drink down on the table. "Not a student of the English language."

"Science and technology are my passions. I minored in English at Yale to get a break from all the mathematical and technological esoteric exactness being implanted into my mind daily from my science professors, including all the books I studied from."

Frank nodded. "So, if I need to do a lengthy written report on a particular matter for the home office in Atlanta, I now know where to come to have my report checked for grammatical errors and sentence structure."

"No problem, Frank. Since you're a team member of FMI, I'll give you a discount from my normal fee of one hundred dollars an hour for editing." He thought a moment. "I'll only charge you ninety-five dollars an hour."

A frown shadowed across Frank's face, then followed by a smile. "Man. What a great friend you are. I don't know what to say."

A roar of laughter erupted from the table of FMI agents. People from across the room stared at them, then went back to eating or conversing with one another.

After the laughter subsided, an ominous thought crossed Janet's mind: what if one or more than one of the customers were watching her and the other agents? Spying on them, trying to hear what was being said regarding the death of the six cavers and the cave-in. She stared at a middle-aged couple, then a table of three, a man and woman in their late-twenties with a girl who looked to be about nine years old, and finally a couple in their mid-thirties. Janet knew when she and Simon were in Detroit, Cary Gaines and Keith Nelson, members of the evil clandestine organization The Circle, were in the restaurant spying on them. Were they up against the same organization? Maybe their investigation had stepped on the toes of another evil entity?

Frank had checked all their rooms for listening devices and nanny cams before anyone took their showers. Nothing was found in any of the rooms.

Simon cleared his throat, then said, "We'll discuss what we'll be doing tomorrow in my room around seven-thirty. Afterward, we'll have breakfast. Once we eat, each of us will do our assignments. Tonight, we'll all relax and enjoy ourselves following our harrowing day. I'd say we deserve it."

Danny pushed against the back of his cushioned-backed chair. "Man. This is like a spy vs. spy scenario, James Bond and stealthy movies all put together. I told Frank the same thing when he checked my room for electronic bugs, listening devices and hidden cameras before I showered."

The waitress brought their food. They had begun eating when Janet asked Danny, "Are you rebuilding your house after it was destroyed by the missile?"

"No. After getting the phone call from Director Littlefield

yesterday, I decided to sell the property, including the shelter, to a computer friend of mine. It'll be put to good use by him and his friends. What's remaining of the house will be removed, leaving the reinforced underground concrete bunker. My friend plans on putting a double-wide manufactured home on top of the bunker."

They continued eating, discussing things not related to their investigation or the cave-in. Simon paid the bill for everyone on FMI's Visa card. Frank and Danny left together to do computer search for information about the six dead cavers, businesses in the area and surrounding counties that carried permits for explosives.

Frank already told Simon that computer searches were one of the ways he relaxed. Frank now had a computer comrade, Danny, who also enjoyed doing computer work besides developing new inventions. He looked forward in helping Frank do the searches this evening and in the future.

Jean left. She said she was looking forward to lying in her comfortable bed and watching a movie on TV.

After receiving the food and drink receipt from the waitress, Simon stood, as did Janet. "Would you like to get a nightcap at the bar?" Simon asked.

"Sure. Sounds good to me. But no peppermint schnapps."

Her mind raced back several years ago when she had first drunk several servings of the drink, not realizing its cumulative effects on the body and mind. She had to leave her car at her friend's wedding reception and take a cab home. Since then, she had never had another drop of schnapps.

"I think it was banned in Pennsylvania."

Janet chuckled, then said, "I got to say, since I've been associated with FMI, I haven't laughed so much in such a short period of time."

"As I said few times before, I'm glad you are part of the team." Simon reached out and touched her forearm.

Janet felt a pulsating warmth cover her body as his hand gently touched her skin. It had been a while since she was sensually aroused by a man's touch. In fact, Simon was a man with good looks, intelligence and self-assurance. "I'm glad I made the decision to leave the sheriff's department."

They sat at the bar for about forty minutes, talking about everything from politics to the latest trend in clothing before Janet said, "I think I'm going to call it a night. It's been another action-packed day."

"I agree. It's almost ten o'clock."

Simon walked Janet to her room. They stood in the hallway, outside her door, as she removed the room's keycard from her slack's pocket. She looked up into his eyes, waiting for a response from him. A grin appeared. What was she expecting, a kiss? *Get ahold of yourself, girl.* "I'll see you in the morning. Good night."

"Good night." He turned and walked down the hallway toward his room.

Janet opened her door and walked inside the room. She glanced down at a white letter-size envelope laying on the floor a couple feet in front of her. The envelope likely was pushed under her door after she left for supper around seven o'clock. Maybe it was from hotel management or the cleaning staff. Although both had keys to the room and would've placed the envelope on the TV counter or bed. She picked up the unsealed envelope without any writing on the outside of it. Janet opened the envelope. She removed a newspaper clipping folded a few times. After unfolding the clipping, she peered at the headline of the article, *Six Cave Explorers Die Mysteriously.* Written in blocked letters with a black felt pen at the bottom of the article, Janet read, *"It wasn't an accident."*

Why would the person want to be anonymous? How do they know the deaths were deliberate and not a misfortunate accident? Maybe it was one of the six victims loved ones who left the newspaper article with their opinion? Janet had three questions without answers. This bothered her and added more suspicion to the cavers' deaths. She thought about calling Simon and letting him know about the article.

There was a knock on her door.

Janet reached for her holstered Glock, removed it, clicked the safety off and let her right arm fall to her side as her hand clutched the gun. *Who could that be this time of the night? Was it the person who left the article who now wanted to meet face to face and discuss the killing of the cavers? Could it be the perpetrator responsible for the death of the six cavers?* She peered through the peep hole in the door. Simon stood outside the door with solemn expression looking back at her.

"I'll be right there, Simon," she said loud enough for him to hear. She put the safety back on her Glock and holstered it. She removed the chain, turned the deadbolt lock, then opened the door. Simon stood in the hallway, holding a newspaper clipping in his hand. "You got one too, I see."

"Oh. You also got one?"

"Yes. Come on in," Janet said as she stepped aside, allowing Simon's entrance into her room.

As he walked by her, the pleasant odor of Old Spice aroused the sensory nerves in her nose. She sighed.

"The clipping was in an unmarked envelope lying on the floor when I walked into my room."

"So was mine."

"What do you make of it being in our rooms? I assume Jean, Frank and Danny didn't get one. Otherwise I'm sure they would've notified us."

Janet walked over and sat at the end of the bed. "I'm sure they didn't since they left the restaurant about an hour before we did." She glanced down at the clipping. "I'd say the person who shoved the envelopes under our doors didn't want us to know who they are. Otherwise they would've approached us in person or at least called us on the phone. There's still the possibility it was a staff member from housekeeping or someone from the front desk who'd have access to the hotel's room keycards."

"Those are all possibilities. No one else can get into our rooms without a keycard. It isn't like they can pick our rooms' locking system with two metal wires anymore. You know, this somewhat reminds of when Keith Nelson came to my hotel room in Detroit and told me about The Circle. In this case, someone left us a clue in the deaths of the six cavers. If it was a person involved with the cavers' deaths, they would've likely stated how they died. Don't you think?"

"You're thinking like a detective, Simon."

"Did you call me Detective Simon, or did you mean detective," comma, Simon?"

"The latter. You're now sounding like Danny with his correct grammar and proper punctuation marks."

"I hope not. One is enough in our group. Anyway. You're the true detective of our team. Should we have the envelope and news clippings checked for fingerprints?"

"Yes." Janet grinned. "Good idea, Detective Simon."

He chuckled. "Frank and Danny's humor must be rubbing off on you."

"Between your humor at times, along with Frank and Danny, it's no wonder I'm starting to react that way. I think Jean is the lone agent not affected by the humor bug."

Janet almost never experienced humor between her and her ex-husband, Rick Ridder. She had changed her name back to her maiden name of Bennett after they were divorced, since they didn't have any children together.

"I'll give the envelopes and the newspaper clippings to Frank tomorrow morning. I'll have him take them to the forensic lab for analysis of fingerprints and DNA." He glanced at his watch. "It's late. I guess I'll get back to my room. We'll talk more tomorrow morning."

Janet stood. "Okay. Maybe we'll get lucky and get a person's name from a fingerprint or from their DNA? We deserve a break in this investigation from what we had to go through in the cave today."

She handed him her envelope containing the news clipping. Their fingers momentarily touched sending a sensuous chill through her body. *My God, calm down, girl. You only met the guy a few days ago.*

"Since we're not sure if someone was in our rooms, make sure you use the security bar and chain on the door. You can also prop the back of your desk chair against the doorknob for added security. The more I think about it, I'll call Frank, Danny and Jean, letting them know what happened. I'll make sure they secure their doors also."

"Good idea. It's better to be safe than sorry, as the saying goes. I have a feeling this won't be the last time we hear from our intruder."

Janet watched Simon walk down the hallway toward his room, which was across the hall and two doors down from her room. She closed her door, securing it as they had discussed a few moments ago.

Janet removed her Glock, along with its holster, and laid them on the nightstand next to the bed. After putting her nightclothes on, she walked over and laid in bed on her back. Reaching to her left, she turned out the light from the lamp on the nightstand. A quietness entombed her in the darkness. The day's events flashed across her mind, followed by sleep.

Ring. Ring. Ring. The hotel's landline phone on Janet's nightstand blared out its piercing sound. She awoke on her back with a startled jerk. She rolled to her left side, glancing at the blue numbers and letters on the clock next to the phone: two thirty a.m. *Who in God's name could be calling me this time of night?* She picked up the phone on the fifth ring. "Hello. This better not be a wrong number."

"Janet?"

The male voice sounded familiar to her. Her mind was still fogging after being awaken from a sound sleep. "Yes, this is Janet."

"This is Captain Robins from the Marion County Sheriff's Department."

Why would the captain be calling me at this time of the night? She was no longer a detective. Yes, when she was a Marion County Sheriff detective, she'd get calls in the middle of the night and early morning hours regarding a homicide. Bill Matters, her partner, would normally be at the crime scene holding a cup of coffee for her when she got there. "Captain. Why are you calling me?"

"It's about Detective Matters." Several seconds of silence, then, "He's in the hospital lying in ICU in a coma."

A cold wave washed across her body as she sat up in bed. Her partner for over five years rarely complained about being sick. His five children from ages seven to sixteen might be without a dad, and Karen, his wife, might be losing a husband of twenty years. Janet saw him for the last time a couple of days ago. His five-foot, nine-inch moderately overweight stature stood by his desk. They hugged. She told Bill that he was the best partner she ever had.

He replied, "I'm the only partner you ever had."

"Janet. Are you still there?"

"Sorry, captain. I can't believe he's in a coma. What happened?"

"Yesterday evening, about eight hours ago, Bill got a phone call from an anonymous woman caller regarding the bombing of Danny Emerick's house. She told him to meet her at Sullivan Park. She didn't want to talk over the phone. Bill didn't tell anyone about the phone call. Since all incoming calls to the office are recorded, we found out after the fact. The phone she called him on was an untraceable cellphone. No way to identify the woman caller. A passerby saw Detective Matters slumped over on a park bench. When paramedics got to him, he was unconscious and barely alive. He was taken to Ocala Regional Medical Center's emergency room. They did bloodwork, scans of his brain and an EEG. Everything was normal. According to the doctors there wasn't any trauma to the head or evidence of poisoning or a stroke. They don't have a cause for his coma yet. We don't know if Detective Matters met with the woman. If he did meet with her, did she or somebody else somehow cause his coma? Until a witness comes forward and states they saw them together on the park bench yesterday evening, we don't have any clues to go on."

Janet felt guilty. If she hadn't resigned as a detective, Bill Matters might not be in a coma, since more than likely both her and Bill would've met the woman at the park. On the other hand, if foul play had occurred, they both might be in a coma. "Thanks for calling me, captain."

"I knew you would've wanted to know as soon as possible."

"I appreciate you calling me and letting me know about Bill."

"The second reason I called you was to see if you had any ideas on who may have wanted to harm Detective Matters?"

"As far as I know, Bill didn't have any enemies. No one I can remember we arrested in the past five years had ever threatened either of us. Regarding the bombing of Danny Emerick's house, we thought The Circle was responsible. As you know, we didn't have any proof tying them to the missile. Were there any security cameras in or near the park that could possibly show the woman in the park with Detective Matters?"

"There were a couple of cameras but…"

"They weren't working at the time Bill and the woman would've been together," Janet interrupted.

"How did you know the cameras were temporarily not operating during that time span?"

The car and truck accident at the intersection on their way to the West Port High School in Ocala, Florida a few days ago flashed through her mind when the traffic intersection cameras mysteriously shut down at the time of the pickup truck ramming the rear end of their car. She told the captain about the intersection accident.

"Sort of a coincidence. Don't you think?"

"I don't believe in most coincidences. Especially this one. I believe we're dealing with the same people. I mean 'you're' dealing with."

"No. You said it right. You're sort of our crime consultant."

"I'll take that as a compliment. If I think of anything, I'll let you know. Please let me know if there are any changes in Detective Matters' condition."

"I sure will. Good night."

"Good night. Again, thanks for calling."

Janet reached over and placed the phone on the cradle. She laid back in the bed as the coolness of her pillow touched the back of her head and neck. Her thoughts focused on Bill and the cause of his coma. When she and the FMI team met for breakfast, she would bring up her ex-partner's medical condition and surrounding circumstances. *Maybe one of them, particularly Danny, who was directly involved in the missile demolishing his farmhouse, will have an idea on what to do to help solve or find a clue in the bombing and Bill's coma.*

Janet began to drift off into sleep. Her last conscious thought asked, *Was Bill getting closer to the answer of who blew up Danny Emerick's house?*

Chapter Five

Simon stood in the bathroom and adjusted his shoulder holster, then put on his dark-blue sports coat. His gray pants complemented his collegiate appearance. There was a knock on his hotel room's door. He turned, walked a few steps into the vestibule and opened the door. "Morning, Janet. Come on in. You're the first to arrive."

She walked into the room.

Simon asked, "Did you have a good night's sleep?"

Before she could answer someone was knocking on the room's door. He walked over and opened the door. Frank, Danny and Jean walked into the room. They all said their good morning greetings. Simon glanced at his watch. It was seven twenty-eight. "I love punctuality."

He walked over and stood next to Janet.

"To answer your question, Simon, I slept fair."

Small talk between Frank Danny and Jean created a murmur of voices.

In a louder voice, she continued, "I have something important to say to everyone." Everyone stopped chatting and turned their attention at Janet.

"I got a phone call early this morning around two thirty from my previous captain at the Marion County Sheriff's Office." She continued and told everybody about why he called and what was said between them.

"I'm so sorry for Bill Matters and his family," Simon said placing his hand briefly on Janet's shoulder.

The other three agents nodded, verbally acknowledging their concerns and sympathy. Simon stepped backward a couple of feet, brushing the hair hanging down off his forehead to the right. "It looks like we're still tied to our previous unsolved case in Ocala. Danny. Did you find out anything about your house being destroyed?"

"Nothing. Whoever did it covered their tracks and didn't leave any evidence. From what Frank told me on the way back from the cave today, the FBI were unable to trace the manufacturer of the missile. There weren't any identifiable markings on the pieces of the missile they found at my house. Plus, there weren't any missing military missiles at any of the government military facilities. The one thing I can say for sure, the people who did this were professionals."

Simon turned to Janet. "You said Detective Matters was in a coma. There are several causes. Traumatic head injury, stroke, brain tumor, infection, including alcohol or drug intoxication. From what you told us about Detective Matters, all these causes were ruled out...as you know, sometimes a cause is never determined."

"Even if they don't find the cause, I hope the detective comes out of his coma?"

"We all hope the same for his recovery." Simon walked over to the hotel room's desk chair and sat in front of his laptop. His screensaver displayed multicolored microscopic bacteria meandering throughout the screen. He pushed the enter key on his keyboard. A list of duties for each FMI agent was on the monitor. Earlier this morning, he'd made out the list.

He turned back around and said, "Frank, since you and Danny decided not to do a computer search of the six dead cavers or explosive distributors in around Central Pennsylvania last night, this will be your task today."

"Sorry again, boss. Danny and I got to talking about other things last night until almost midnight. We were too exhausted to do any of the computer search work we said we'd do when we left the restaurant last night."

"Like I said earlier this morning when you called me, no problem. You and Danny deserved a break away from our investigation, especially after what we all went through in the cave. Also, see if you can hack...I mean, get into any security cameras around Sullivan Park in Ocala. It would be great if we can visualize the mysterious woman Detective

Matters was supposed to meet."

"We'll see what we can do," Frank glanced at Danny.

Danny put his hands on his hips and nodded. "If there's a security camera in the area of the park, I'll find it."

"Thanks, guys."

Simon turned his chair to the left and looked up at Jean. "Jean. I'll need you to talk with the medical examiner and ask questions about the six deceased cavers. You know what kind of questions to ask the medical examiner, including gut feelings the ME didn't put into the autopsy report. You're an expert at questioning them now. Plus, drop off the newspaper clippings and envelopes for fingerprint and DNA analysis. I was going to have Frank do it, but since you'll be heading to the ME's office, you can drop off the material at the Crime Scene Lab."

"Thanks for your confidence in me regarding the medical examiner and his staff. I'm also going to check on Deputy Robinson later this morning and make sure nothing happened to her in the past twenty-four hours."

"Good idea. I'm sure you changed her deadly fate."

"My visions haven't been wrong yet."

Simon now turned his attention to Janet, who sat at the end of his bed. "I thought we would talk with the six cavers' families. There may be an adversary who wanted to do harm to one or all the cavers. Possibly each of them had a medical or even a dental history pointing toward their deaths. We know the Franklin County Sheriff's detectives talked with the families, according to Detective Spurrier. Our investigation focuses more on the medical aspect of their deaths. Now with you as part of our team, we have your detective expertise."

Simon turned around one hundred and eighty degrees in the desk chair and turned off his laptop. He then stood, facing everyone. "Let's go down to the restaurant and have breakfast."

"Best news I heard so far this morning," Frank said with a smile. "You know breakfast is the most important meal of the day."

Jean huffed. "Who are you kidding, Frank? Every meal is your most important meal of the day."

They sat at the same restaurant table where they ate dinner

yesterday evening. About forty-five minutes later, Jean stood. "Great breakfast." She reached into her purse and retrieved the car keys to her rental car, a cream-colored Ford Escape. The vehicle was delivered to the hotel's parking lot yesterday afternoon before they got back from their harrowing experience in the cave. Since the FMI division's first investigation a few months ago, rental vehicles were used by the agents. The number of vehicles was dependent how diverse their investigation turned out to be. Jean looked at Simon. "I'll call you if I learn anything from the pathologist."

"Okay. Talk to you later." As Simon glanced at Jean walking out of the restaurant, he focused his vision on the people sitting at the tables. There were about sixteen hotel residents ranging in age from about five-years-old to people in their seventies. No one glanced at Jean as she walked out of the room, and no one stared at their table. From the time they sat down to this moment, he'd periodically glanced around the room for anyone peering at them. None of the patrons appeared to pay any attention to the FMI team.

Frank set down his cup of coffee. "Danny and I are going to his van to get a few of things that'll help us in our computer search. He's got a modem satellite analytic accelerator that he invented. We'll set up our stuff in his room."

"Sounds great. I have no idea what a modem...analytic, whatever the thing is called, for you two electronic computer wizards to handle. Keep in touch. If you get any information let me know right away."

"You got it, boss. We're off to see the wizard. No. We are the wizards. At least Danny is. I'm just a computer geek." They got up from the table and left the restaurant.

Janet rolled her eyes and smirked. "Frank sure is a character, isn't he? Danny seems somewhat to be the quiet one of the two. Maybe each will complement the other, making them a dynamic pair?"

"You might be right. Since working with you the past few days, you seem to have the ability to read people for who they really are."

"I don't know. I'm a simple southern country girl."

She's not simple, but a complex southern girl, thought Simon. He respected Janet for her integrity and problem-solving ability. "That may be true. All I can say is you're a great asset to our team. After I pay the breakfast bill, we'll head out to our first family, whose daughter is, that is…was Lydia Sanchez. My questioning will focus on the medical aspect of their daughter. You can jump in any time and ask any question you feel may be relevant to the case. Pretty much what we did in Ocala with the victims' families there. Although each case the FMI team investigated was uniquely different. The only clues we have are the trace of cyanide in each of the cavers and the odor of almonds inside the cave per Frank's sensitive nose."

"You know we haven't heard anything regarding your vision of the three people with nystagmus."

"My oh my. You pronounced the word perfectly. I'm impressed."

"I utilize my smart phone's Google Search other than socializing as a lot of people do these days. Take away all forms of cellphones from people today, especially the younger generation, there will be mass depression and anxiety disorders."

"Isn't that the truth. As far as the three people I saw in my vision yesterday, no news is good news as the saying goes." Simon paid the bill. He left with Janet and headed for Lydia Sanchez's parents' house.

Simon pulled into the Sanchez's driveway and stopped behind a small compact car. Their colonial-style house sat in a subdivision in the west section of Chambersburg. They spent about thirty-five minutes with them. Their single, twenty-six-year-old daughter didn't have any medical conditions. She lived a healthy, drug-free life as a salesperson at a sporting goods store. She didn't have any enemies. She was friends with the other five cavers. There wasn't any animosity amongst them according to the mother. They left and headed for the next family.

Around noon, he and Janet walked to their car after questioning the fourth family. "No smoking guns pointing to a motive for their deaths," Janet said. "So far, all the victims were healthy with no one wanting to do harm to them. None of them consumed illicit drugs or even smoked tobacco or any other form of nicotine. We have two more families to question."

Simon started the car. "Why don't we break for lunch?"

"Lunch sounds good," Janet said as she buckled her seatbelt.

"I thought maybe we would've gotten a phone call from someone in our group. I was hoping one of them would be calling, saying they found evidence of how the cavers died or possibly a vital clue leading us to who caused their deaths. I guess it was wishful thinking."

"I was hoping for the same thing. We still have two more families to talk with. I have a feeling they're not going to add anything different than the other families this morning."

"Sorry to say, I think you're right. We'll need to complete our interviews after getting a bite to eat."

After ordering lunch, Simon called Jean. "Hi, Jean. Learn anything?"

"Nothing that we already knew. The pathologist stated to me that he never saw anything like the six deaths before. His gut feeling was they died from some type of exposure to an unknown element. There wasn't anything pointing to a cause from the autopsies. The tissue and blood analysis showed a trace of cyanide, which was insignificant to cause their deaths."

"Janet and I have two more families to talk with yet. We didn't find anything pointing to their mysterious deaths. We've stopped for lunch. I'll call Frank and Danny and see how they're doing."

"I talked with Frank a bit ago," Jean said. "They haven't found anything regarding the six cavers' deaths. Danny did find a security camera in the area of Sullivan Park in Ocala. There was a woman who appeared suspicious. Unfortunately, the camera was of poor quality, making it difficult to make out any characteristics. Danny invented a different type of image enhancer that's going to be sent to him today from Ocala. He forgot to bring the device with him to Pennsylvania. It should arrive around six o'clock tonight."

"Thanks for the information. Oh yeah. Did you check on Deputy Robinson by chance?"

"Yes. She's fine. Twenty-four hours have passed."

"Great."

"I assume you haven't heard any news about the three people in your vision yesterday afternoon?"

"No, I haven't yet. I talked with Detective Spurrier this morning between seeing the deceased cavers' families. Nothing on the cave explosion yesterday. I ask him to call me if there happened to be other cavers dying during cave explorations in Pennsylvania and Maryland. Today or in the next several days. I told the detective there could be some type of infectious organism. He said he would notify me. Of course, I couldn't tell him the real reason for wanting to know, that I had a vision yesterday of three people displaying nystagmus, and that they were probably in a cave."

"I'll be heading back to the hotel, unless there was something else you wanted me to do yet."

"No. When you get back to the hotel ask Frank or Danny to check for anyone in the past several months that died in a cave, or a healthy person or persons dying of a seizure with or without nystagmus in Pennsylvania and Maryland."

"Will do. See you and Janet back at the hotel this afternoon."

Simon and Janet ate lunch and left the restaurant about forty minutes later. He reached over and turned the vehicle's GPS on. They had downloaded the name and addresses of the families before leaving the hotel this morning

"Let's see who's the next family." Rita and Henry Rhode came across the GPS screen with their address.

Janet peered down at the sheriff's report file on a Robert Rhode. "It says he was a thirty-year-old male without any arrest or even motor vehicle offenses. He worked at Brighton Research as a chemist for the past three years. He's divorced with one child, a boy who's five years old, living with his mother in Philadelphia."

A woman in her fifties came to an elaborately scrolled wooden front door of a Victorian-styled house. A small black dog stood next to her, yapping. "Muffin. Quiet." The dog stopped barking and began wagging its short stubby tail "Can I help you folks?"

"My name is Simon Woods. This is Janet Bennett." They both showed their FMI badges. "We're agents of the Federal Medical Investigators for CDC. The reason we're here is to ask you questions about your son, Robert." A solemn expression appeared on his and Janet's face. "We are so sorry for your loss."

She stared back at them with saddened eyes. "It was a shock to me and my husband. Please come in. I'm Rita Rhode."

The three of them stood in a foyer. A crystal chandelier hung from the A-shaped ceiling. "Barbara Foster, who you talked to this morning, called me a while ago and told me about the two of you. That you'd be to our house sometime today."

They walked into the living room.

"Can I get the two of you something to drink?"

"No thank you," Simon answered, then looked at Janet, realizing he had answered for the two of them. Maybe she wanted a drink? "Sorry. Did you…"

"I'm fine," Janet interrupted.

She turned her attention toward Mrs. Rhode. "We appreciate the offer."

Simon felt like an idiot. He still hadn't gotten completely used to having another FMI agent with him during his investigations. Prior to Janet assisting him in the Whispers Before Death case in Ocala, he had worked alone in the field. She had now become his investigative partner in the field.

"I'm not sure what more I can tell you agents. The Franklin County Sheriff detective asked me many questions when he was here a few days ago."

"Our line of questioning will be a little different. We're focused on the medical aspect of deaths."

"Oh. I see."

A man walked into the living room.

"This is my husband, Henry. These are people from CDC I mentioned to you earlier this morning that Barbara mentioned on the phone to me."

"Hello." He sat down on the couch next to his wife.

They sat in the living room and talked about ten minutes. So far, no significant information unfolded. Simon, who told them he was a medical doctor, turned the page on his small notebook, glanced down at some writing, then asked, "Did your son ever talk about something that bothered him?"

"You mean physically?" Henry asked.

"Yes."

Henry cocked his head, peered down at the carpeted floor for a few seconds, then looked up and stared at Simon. "Matter of fact, Robert mentioned he was at times having problems with his vision."

"In what way and for how long?"

Henry glanced at his wife, then back to Simon. "He'd have wavy lines in one eye lasting a couple of minutes. I'd say he told us about it about a month ago. We advised him to go see an eye doctor. He never did. He said there wasn't any pain or loss of vision. The symptoms only lasted less than a minute or two. Since you're a doctor, do you know what it was?"

"It can be a few things that causes this condition. The two most common causes of wavy lines are ocular migraines and macular degeneration. From what you said, I'd lean toward ocular migraine. Since it lasted less than a couple of minutes and there wasn't any other associated symptoms or signs."

"You mean a person can have a migraine headache without a headache."

"Yes, they can. That's why they call it an ocular migraine."

Simon wondered if their son also had nystagmus. "Have you ever noticed your son's eyes flickering, oscillating back and forth?"

"No, I haven't," Henry said.

"I have seen it once," Rita answered. "It was the day before he went cave exploring with his friends. I was talking with him when he turned his head away from me then looked back at me. That's when I saw his eyes quickly moving back and forth. It lasted for several seconds then stopped. Is that part of this type of migraine?"

"It could be."

Simon knew Robert's ocular migraines and apparent nystagmus might be a manifestation of something else, something more serious that could've caused their son's mysterious death inside the cave. Maybe the other victims had ocular migraines and nystagmus, but they didn't mention it to their loved ones or parents? They might have to call the previous people they'd interviewed and ask them these two specific medical conditions. Simon turned his head to the right toward Janet and asked, "Can you think of any more questions to ask the Rhodes?"

"No. I don't have anything else to ask them."

Simon and Janet thanked the Rhode's and left. Simon backed out of the driveway and drove up the residential street. "We may have found a common link connecting our six victims. We'll need to…"

"Re-question our previous victims' families regarding if their love one had any visual disturbances?" Janet interrupted.

"We think along the same wavelength. That's what we need to do. Before we do that, let's talk with the wife of our last victim."

"I agree."

She reached to her left and set the GPS for Brittany Glover, wife of Edward Glover. The sixth victim.

It was three o'clock when they finished their questioning with Mrs. Glover. Simon walked out the apartment building with Janet. He rubbed his forehead. "I thought we were on to something with the ocular migraine and the nystagmus."

"I thought the same thing too. Unfortunately, her husband, Edward, didn't relay any signs or symptoms displayed by our last victim Robert Rhode. Although, he may have had them but never told his wife. Plus, his wife never noticed nystagmus from her husband."

"That's true," Simon agreed. "When we get back to the hotel, we'll make our calls to the other families."

~ * ~

Unbeknownst to Simon and Janet, a white SUV with a man and woman inside was parked eight vehicles away from them in the apartment complex parking lot. It was the same people who had been at the cave site yesterday wearing camouflaged clothes and riding ATVs.

Chapter Six

Janet got out of the Suburban in the hotel parking lot. She glanced around and saw Danny's burgundy van and Jean's cream-colored Ford Escape parked a few spaces down from them. On their way to the hotel, she'd periodically glanced into the front passenger sideview mirror for anyone following them. No suspicious vehicle tailed their car. If someone wanted them dead and didn't succeed in the cave-in, there was a better than fifty-percent chance they would try again. She and Simon discussed this ominous possibility while driving back to the hotel. They agreed the team would never put themselves in harm's way again by staying alert in all situations and assuming someone was watching them or planning a deadly action against them. Janet stopped before reaching the front entrance door of the hotel. She turned, peering one hundred and eighty degrees. No moving vehicle entered the parking lot.

"No one following us?" Simon asked as he also stopped, turned around and looked around the parking lot.

"No. I guess I was kinda obvious in my action. I don't see any suspicious vehicles or people…yet."

"After our discussion on the way here, I also kept looking at the sideview mirror, along with the rearview mirror. As the adage goes, it's better to be…"

"Safe than sorry," Janet interrupted, finishing his statement right on cue. "Like what we said about each other in the past, great minds think alike."

"True. On the other hand, one of us or maybe both of us can read each other's mind?"

Thank God that's not true since he would've read my sensual thoughts about him. "It's one ability I don't possess."

"Me neither. My premonition visions are enough for me to cope with. Adding mind reading would be a curse, not an asset."

Simon knocked on Frank's hotel room door. Frank let them in. Danny and Jean where inside the room.

As Simon and Janet passed Frank in the vestibule, he sniffed. "So, one of you or maybe both of you had a Ruben sandwich for lunch." He smacked his lips. "It's one of my favorite sandwiches."

Janet and Simon chuckled. Janet then said, "We both did. Can't get anything by you, especially food."

"Isn't that the truth?" Jean added from across the room. "Like I said many times, he has an endless appetite. His favorite four-letter word that begins with the letter 'f' is food."

Janet looked at Simon and rolled her eyes. He reciprocated with a grin.

Simon looked at Frank. "Did you guys find out about anyone dying in a cave or dying of a seizure the past several months in this area or northwestern Maryland?"

"No. Danny and I didn't find anything on the Internet. Only the six cave explorers."

Simon summarized his and Janet's interviews with the families of the six dead cavers and that they were going to call four of the families and asked if their love ones complained or showed signs of ocular migraines and nystagmus. Simon removed his cellphone as did Janet. "Janet and I will be making our calls. Please no loud talking until we're done."

Janet called the Sanchez family. Neither of them had any knowledge of their daughter having either medical condition. She then asked Mr. Sanchez, "Does your daughter have a computer?"

"Yes. She has a laptop. Why do you ask?"

"Can you get into it and check her search engine such as Google or Bing to see if she had looked up eye disturbances, visual problems, wavy lines or anything related to the vision in the index section under history? We're investigating the possibility your daughter and some of her caver friends may have had a visual condition prior to your daughter's death and her friends' deaths."

"Sure. I can do that."

"Call me back if you find any of these things in her computer history section." Janet had already given them her phone number this morning.

"I sure will." Mr. Sanchez hung up.

She glanced at Simon and heard him say to the person at the other end of his call, "Call me if you find anything on his computer history section. Including any reading material referring to visual problems." A short pause. "You're welcome. We're doing everything can to find the cause of your son's death." Simon looked at Janet as he dropped his hand with the phone to his side. "Anything at your end?"

"No. Mr. Sanchez will check out his daughter's computer and get back with me if he finds out anything." Janet stared down at her cellphone. "Each of us have one more call to make." She searched for the name of the next family and called. Simon raised up his phone and called the next family.

The last two calls turned out to be the same answers as the previous family members. No history or mention of visual problems. The families were to check their deceased love ones' computers for computer searches for visual conditions.

Simon put his phone away. "I hope we'll hear back from at least one of the family members."

"I sure hope so, too."

"We have one of the six cavers with nystagmus and ocular migraines. All six cavers had no history of seizures prior to the day they died in the cave. Although, I had a visual premonition of three possible cavers with nystagmus yesterday afternoon." He glanced at his watch. "Matter of fact, in about thirty minutes, twenty-four hours will have passed since I had my vision."

Janet's cellphone rang. She glanced at the caller. No name. Only a phone number was displayed. Was it one the families calling her back? They had found some information regarding visual disturbances. "Hello. This is Agent Bennett."

"Agent Bennett. I thought it was Detective Bennett?"

You gotta be kidding me. It's Rick. My Ex. "I thought I told you not to call me anymore." She glanced at everyone in the room. They were all staring at her with inquisitive expressions. "Hold on a second." She covered the phone with her hand. "It's my ex-husband." Janet hurried out of the room and into the hallway. "Why are you calling me? I have nothing to say to you."

"When did you change professions? Agent of what? The FBI or CIA?"

"First of all, it's none of your business. And second, I don't have to tell you anything."

"You don't have to be so mean. The reason I called, I thought you'd want to know my mother died this morning of a heart attack."

Janet's ire dissipated as sadness overtook her emotions. "I'm so sorry to hear that Rick." She had liked his mother. She was a jubilant and honorable woman who spoke what she was thinking. Too bad her son didn't absorb some of her traits. "Give my condolences to your father."

"I will. So...Janet, you won't tell me about your new profession?"

"I work for an investigative division of CDC. Thanks for calling and letting me know about your mom. You take care."

"Oh. That's all? I thought we..."

"Bye, Rick." Janet pushed the red phone icon on her cellphone, ending their conversation.

She knew he wanted to talk more and ask her if she wanted to meet somewhere for dinner or a drink. It seems after being divorced for two years and him calling a few times a year, he'd get the hint she didn't want to get back together with him and for him to stop calling her. Although, this call was legitimate. Janet went back into the hotel room.

"Is everything all right?" Simon asked.

"Yeah. That is, no. It was my ex-husband. His mother died today."

"Sorry to hear that. It's tough when one or both your parents die. Especially at a young age."

"True. She was in her late fifties."

"That's young today. Since most people live into their eighties."

Simon's phone rang. He answered it and listened for several seconds before his eyebrows raised; his jaw dropped in a surprised expression. He then said, "Thank you for calling me back. We'll let you know when we learn anything about your son. Take care."

Simon put his phone in his blazer pocket. "Mr. Young's son, Matthew, searched for visual wavy lines on Google. Either he had them or was checking for it for someone else. We'll probably never know."

"So far, we have two of the cavers seeing wavy lines," Janet speculated. "What are the odds of this medical condition happening in a group of six people?"

"Slim to none statistically," Simon answered. "I'd say we're dealing with a sign and not a disease. In other words, something other than the two most common causes of wavy lines being ocular migraines or macular degeneration produced this medical condition. If we add nystagmus and seizures to this scenario, we're dealing with something not in the medical archives of diseases or conditions. All we have to do is find out what it is."

"Do you see what you got yourself into, Danny?" Frank asked.

Danny rubbed his lower lip with his upper teeth, then answered, "A challenge. Something I strive for every day."

"With that kind of attitude, you'll fit in perfectly with us," Simon said. "Let's put our heads together and try to figure out where we go from here. My suggestion is to check out each of the victims place of work and see if we can uncover a clue or clues that'll lead us to a cause of their deaths or at least someone at their place of employment wanting them dead."

"That's the most logical next step in our investigation of the six cavers' deaths," Janet said. "The forensic evidence is nil so far. Unless some hard evidence shows up, we're at a plateau in our search for the truth."

Jean, who was sitting at the end of the bed, stood and said, "If it's okay with you, Simon, I'll take Frank with me and check out three of the cavers' employers. You and Janet can check the other three employers. Danny is waiting for his image enhancer to check out the woman in Ocala."

Simon smirked. "You may be not as talkative as others in our group. But when you do speak, your words are usually profound and to the point. All the victims worked the day shift at their jobs." He glanced at his watch. "It's almost four-thirty. Most of their coworkers will be getting off from work soon. Some of them will be enjoying a Sunday off with family or friends. We'll need to talk with them, but not until tomorrow morning. I'd say we call it a day. Except for Danny."

He turned toward Danny. "Call me when you get your image enhancer. I want to see if you'll able to get a good image of the woman's face."

"Sure will," agreed Danny.

"I'd like to see how it works too," Janet said.

"Me too," added Jean.

"That leaves Frank," Simon said turning toward him. "I'm sure you'd already planned to be here anyway. Am I right?"

"Wouldn't miss it for anything."

Simon added, "Why don't we all go down to the restaurant and have an early supper before the image enhancer arrives?"

"Best news I heard all day," Frank answered with a pronounced grin.

While the group walked to the hotel restaurant, Janet thought about the first time she had met Simon in person at the restaurant in Ocala. She thought he was on the fringe of being a nerd but that dissipated as their conversations progressed that first day in her role as a liaison for the Marion County Sheriff's Office. She then saw Simon's persona reflecting a level-headed, professor-type man in control of himself. Of course, along with his good looks and intelligence. The sound of Simon's cellphone ringing brought her back to the present as they walked into the restaurant.

"Hello, Agent Woods." Silence for several seconds as he lowered his eyebrows and listened intently to the person at the other end. "Can you hold. I'll need to write this down." Everyone sat down at their usual round restaurant table. Simon removed his notebook then a pen from his blazer. He glanced at everyone at the table, placed his hand over the phone and announced, "Someone found the three people in my vision yesterday…dead in a cave." He put the phone to his ear. "Tell me again where they found the three cavers' bodies." He began writing down the direction and location of the cave.

Janet glanced at her watch. They had almost four hours of daylight left in the day since it was early May in Pennsylvania. Besides, it didn't matter what time of day or what month of the year it was since there wasn't any daylight inside a cave other than near the entrance. She remembered Frank saying, "*It's always a moonless night inside a cave.*"

"Thanks, Steward," Simon said. "We'll meet at the cave in about thirty to forty minutes." He put his phone back inside his blazer. "The three cavers in my dream were found dead by a brother of one of the cavers about an hour ago. A sheriff deputy is there now at the cave. CSU is on their way to the scene. Detective Spurrier left a moment ago. According to Steward, the deputy at the cave said the three men appeared as if they were sleeping, No signs of trauma to their bodies."

"It's the same physical description as the six victims found six days ago," Janet said. "What will be different now is that we'll be able to observe the bodies at the crime scene. This time we'll have someone stationed at the entrance to the cave. We're still not sure if all of us were the targets in the bombing at the cave or one person was the target such as Detective Spurrier. The rest of us would've became collateral damage."

Simon turned his attention toward Frank. "We'll need you present in case there's the odor of almonds inside the cave near our three victims."

He turned his head to his left. "Jean, we'll need you there too for the obvious reason."

"I know. My supernatural ability of seeing yellow glows of people with impending doom hovering over one or all of us."

"Yes."

Simon looked at Danny, who sat next to Jean. "Danny. I need you here to receive your image enhancer and try to clear up the woman's fuzzy image in the security camera disc. Once that's done, use the facial recognition computer program to identify the woman. Also, you'll need to be here if we need you to check out something on the computer."

"I'm here to serve our unit."

"We're not like a military unit, Danny," Frank said as he raised his eyebrows, then grinned. "Our commander, that is our boss, won't put you on KP duty or put you in the brig if you don't follow his orders. He'll put you in front of a firing squad."

Simon grunted. "Frank, can you be serious for a moment? You don't want to scare away our newest recruit."

Danny smiled. "I know Frank is kidding. I have no problem following your orders."

"You sit here and have dinner. The four of us will pick something up at a drive-through burger place on the way to the cave. We'll take one vehicle, the Suburban." Simon glanced at Frank, Jean then Janet. "You guys ready?"

"Aye, aye, Captain," Frank said with a stately tone.

Simon shook his head. "Frank. I don't know what I'm going to do with you. And please don't reply."

The four of them left the hotel's restaurant. Simon got in the driver seat with Janet in the front passenger seat. Frank and Jean sat in the back seat. After picking up hamburgers, fries and drinks at a drive-through restaurant, they headed for the cave. The cave was in the opposite direction from the first cave they explored yesterday.

This cave wasn't on the normal public sightseeing country registrar according to Frank, who checked it out on his smartphone after they left the hotel. They set the vehicle's GPS to a ranger's station near the site of the cave. A ranger would be waiting for them to take them to the cave of the three deceased cavers.

The sun was setting to the rear of their vehicle as he drove. No need for sunglasses as the sun's piercing glare avoided them. The mountain range lay ahead of them.

About thirty minutes elapsed when the GPS's female voice synthesizer announced, "You have arrived at your destination."

Janet saw a tall medium-build man standing outside the ranger's office building. The building was more like a medium-sized wooden cabin. The man appeared to be in his early thirties and was wearing a light gray brimmed hat and shirt along with dark gray pants. Simon pulled up next to the ranger's pickup truck.

The ranger walked over to their Suburban. Simon rolled down his window and said, "I'm Agent Woods."

"Glad to meet you. I'm Ranger Smith. If you follow me, I'll take you and your party to the cave site."

"Thanks." Simon then rolled his window back up.

They followed the ranger along a meandering, one-lane dirt road. Pine trees and a variety of deciduous trees intermingled together creating a dense wall of trees encompassing the trail-like road. Soon up ahead, Janet saw several vehicles parked to the right and left of the road. A CSU and Franklin County Medical Examiner's van were among two sheriff vehicles and an unmarked sedan, *probably Detective Spurrier's car,* thought Janet. She was impressed by the rapid response time of the various departments. Simon parked behind the dark blue four-door sedan. The ranger turned around and waved to Simon as he passed by, heading back up the dirt road. They all got out of the Suburban. To their right, about ten feet away, a footpath led into the woods. A sheriff deputy stood at its entrance and asked, "Agent Woods?"

"Yes, I'm Agent Woods."

"Detective Spurrier asked me to escort you and your team to the cave site."

"Thanks, deputy."

The FMI team followed the deputy along the narrow trail through the dense forest at the foot of the mountain. Janet glanced into the shaded woods periodically, not for nature's creatures, but for the human kind of animal. She had the sensation that human eyes were observing them from the darkened abyss of the forest.

Chapter Seven

The towering trees around them along the footpath ended as they walked into a clearing about hundred feet wide by fifty feet deep. An opening to a cave into the mountain appeared straight in front of them. The opening was about ten feet wide by seven feet high. A burly sheriff deputy stood guard to the entrance of the cave. Simon pursed his lips as he lowered his eyebrows.

No one's going to set an explosive charge at the opening to this cave, thought Simon. Unless someone set a timed explosive device inside the cave, he and his FMI agents should be safe from any catastrophic event while they were inside the cave.

Detective Spurrier walked out of the cave wearing a particulate respirator mask covering his mouth and nose. He waved at them as he removed his mask.

Simon had called the detective on their way to the ranger's office and advised him to have everyone entering the cave wear a protective mask, gloves, and a protective body suit. The mask would block any possible airborne spores or organisms. Spurrier told Simon that he'd let CSU personnel and sheriff deputies know of the precaution.

"Hey, Steward."

"Hi Simon, and everyone else. The scene in the cave with the three deceased people appears the same as the six cavers found dead in the other cave last weekend. No apparent evidence of trauma to any of the victims. They're lying next to each other as if they decided to take a nap. The medical examiner's staff and the Crime Scene Investigators are doing their assessments and investigations. You'll see the deceased cavers in a few minutes."

Frank handed Simon, Janet and Jean their protective masks. He carried them in a backpack, along with several other items, including an air analysis machine that would check for deadly toxic gases, which would also take an air sample for analysis in a lab.

Frank hadn't brought the analyzer with him when they investigated the other cave yesterday. He removed the air analysis machine. It was about the size of a nine-hundred-page paperback book.

"Let's see if the cave's air contains any toxic substance," Frank said, turning it on as they walked into the cave.

An artificial light source coming from battery-powered lanterns about every twenty feet on a limestone floor lit up a cave the height and length of a high school gymnasium.

As they reached the back of the cave, voices could be heard coming from a crevice to their right. The crevice was half the height of the cave and about five feet wide. Detective Spurrier led them into the narrow nature-made corridor.

The voices became louder as they trekked about fifty feet into the crevice before it widened to about twenty feet. In front of them, Simon saw a group of five people. Three were looking around in different locations, and one was taking a sample of water from a small pond about six feet in diameter in the far-left corner of the chamber. Two men kneeled around three bodies lying on the floor to their right. Spurrier walked ahead of Simon and his team. Simon stopped, turned around, raised his eyebrows and said to Jean, "Anything?"

"Everyone's okay."

He turned toward Frank. "Anything on the air analysis machine?"

"No. The air is normal." Frank removed his protective mask and sniffed. He held it for a few seconds, then let it out. "There's a slight odor of almonds along with a variety of other odors such as aftershave lotion, cologne, perfumes and deodorants. Also...the odor of urine."

He put his mask back on.

Simon sighed. "We're likely dealing with the same type of death with these three cavers as the other six cavers. Including the likelihood they had seizures. The medical examiner will probably find a trace of cyanide in their blood."

"You're right, boss. I wonder if any of them bit their tongue or urinated on themselves?"

"We'll ask the CSU investigator." He turned toward Janet. "What about you? Feel anything before we entered the cave, including this widened crevice?"

"I didn't have any ominous feelings before we walked into the cave or before the crevice widened."

Frank said, pointing up at the ceiling to their left about fifty feet away, "Bats." He then peered down at the floor below the bats. "Bat droppings. Guano. I haven't gotten any reports on the guano from the other cave yet. I'll ask the forensic people to get a sample of this bat guano for analysis."

"I'll go with you," Jean said.

Simon and Janet walked over to the three victims on the floor. Steward was talking with the medical examiner's assistant, Carl Belmont, and a CSU investigator, John Thomas. Both were wearing light jackets with their department name on the back of each jacket. Steward introduced them to Simon and Janet.

Simon glanced down at the three cavers. Two males appeared to be in their early thirties and a female in her late twenties.

He asked, "I was wondering if you checked inside their mouths?"

"I did check inside their mouths," John Thomas answered. "All three of them had bitten their tongues. They also urinated on themselves. I'm not a doctor but I'd say they all had seizures."

Simon nodded. "Your assessment and conclusion are right regarding they had the signs of seizures. All that needs to be done now is try to find out what caused them to have these convulsions." Simon put blue latex examining gloves on. "Will it be all right if I check the bodies?"

"You sure can, Simon," Steward answered. "Since you're a medical doctor representing CDC."

Simon easily opened the mouth on all three victims indicating rigor mortis hadn't started or rigor mortis had completed its normal duration of time. He saw clotted blood on all three victims' tongues.

"As you know, rigor mortis begins within two to six hours of death, starting with the eyelids, neck and jaw, then working its way down the body, A body can stay in this rigid state for twenty-four to eighty-four hours until the muscles relax. This will depend on environmental temperature. A cave's temperature such as the one we're standing in is in the mid-fifties Fahrenheit. Which would be considered cool. Did you take victims' temperatures?"

"Yes, Doctor Woods. I used a rectal thermometer on each victim," Carl, the medical examiner's assistant answered. "All three bodies were eighty-two degrees Fahrenheit. Meaning they all died about the same time."

"I agree." Simon checked the abdomen on the three dead cavers. The skin appeared normal with a mild distention of the abdomen. He stood and faced Janet. "You know why I checked their bellies?"

"Yes. Since none of the victims were embalmed or had speedy cremations, the body putrefies. The first sign of putrefaction is a greenish skin discoloration appearing on the right lower abdominal area about the second or third day after death."

"Very good. So, when do you think the cavers succumbed to their death with what we know about their body condition and appearance?"

"I'd say they died between twenty-four to thirty-six hours ago. The three cavers likely had seizures."

Simon turned to Steward. "You agree?"

"We do. The three of us already discussed the likely time of death, along with the deceased probably had seizures. It's good to have two separate assessments, yours and ours. We both came up with the same conclusions."

"I assume you've checked all their pockets for drugs either illicit or prescription?" Janet asked, peering down at the bodies.

"Yes, we did. No drugs or drug paraphernalia."

It was the same scenario as the other cavers who were found dead six days ago, thought Simon. *How many more people are going to die before an answer is found?*

Simon glanced over at Frank and Jean standing next to a female CSU investigator. The investigator was putting bat guano inside a plastic container.

"I'll be right back, Steward."

He and Janet walked over to where Frank and Jean were standing. "Frank smelled the odor of almonds in both caves, indicating the possible present of cyanide. We believe the blood and tissue analysis on these three victims will also show a trace of cyanide for whatever reason."

"I agree," Janet replied.

"If all three victims inhaled hydrogen cyanide it would've been detected by Frank using the air analysis machine inside the cave. Besides, when Frank removed his protective mask, if cyanide gas was present, he would've inhaled the toxic cyanide gas and died in less than a minute." Simon glanced around the chamber, looking for some clue, something out of the ordinary. "There was something else going on inside the two caves, something causing the death of nine cavers."

"We'll find out what caused these deaths," Janet said as they stopped a few feet in front of Frank, Jean and the CSU woman. "We have a lot of smart people around us."

"Thanks for the compliment," Frank said, pushing his shoulders back as he raised his head, smiling in a gloating gesture.

"How do you know Janet's referring to you?" Jean asked. "You may be the exception to her comment."

"Oh…oh, I thought…"

Janet smirked. "You're included, Frank. There's no exceptions."

Simon glanced down at the name plate attached to the front of the CSU woman's jacket, K. Lasky. "Ms. Lasky, did you find anything unusual?"

"No. There wasn't anything out of the ordinary. We found bat guano which is common in caves. We obtained samples of it. Over there," she pointed to her left at a small pond, "we took water samples."

Simon glanced down at his watch. It was almost seven-thirty. He walked back toward Steward pinching his lower lip between his thumb and index finger, thinking about what they needed to do next in this investigation.

As we did with the first six cavers, we'll interview family members trying to find if someone had a vendetta against their love one. For sure there's a common link between the nine cavers' deaths. There weren't any genetic anomalies or physical aberrations in the first six victims according to the autopsy report. The toxicology report was negative, not showing any type of poisoning or deadly chemicals in their blood or body tissues. More than likely, these three cavers will have the same autopsy, blood and tissue results.

Simon stopped a couple of feet from the three deceased cavers. He said to Steward, "I believe your CSU team and the county medical examiner's office handled everything surrounding these deaths according to forensic protocol."

"Thanks. We appreciate your comment."

"It's now a matter of waiting for the medical examiner's report on these three deaths. Since we don't have a diagnosis of what caused the deaths of these nine victims and that they all died suspiciously inside caves, I'd recommend we close all public caves in central Pennsylvania until further notice. I think we should also notify the northern part of Maryland to our south. As far as the other caves not registered in the state's public site-seeing caves, we'll need to notify the TV and radio stations to broadcast a warning to the public not to venture inside any cave in central Pennsylvania due to a possible health hazard."

"I agree," Steward acknowledged. "I'll have my department and the state ranger's stations post warning signs at cave entrances, along with covering the cave entrance with "danger do not enter" tape. As for the other caves, we'll notify the property owners of our warning. We'll also notify the news media stations."

"Thanks, Steward. I hope we can avoid any more mysterious deaths inside caves. We will continue coordinating our investigation with yours. I believe, as do my colleagues, the answer to these deaths must be inside these caves. Something is causing these cavers to have deadly seizures."

"I heard somewhere if you draw blood and test for prolactin hormone levels, you can determine if someone had a seizure," stated Steward.

"Very true," Simon said. "But the blood has to be drawn within twenty minutes of a suspected convulsion. It would be fruitless in all these cavers since they weren't discovered for at least twenty-four hours."

"Hum. I guess I was half right regarding the prolactin level. Can a person die from a seizure?"

"Usually not. Our victims fall under 'sudden unexplained death in epilepsy,' or SUDEP. There are various theories but none of them are conclusive enough. People with grand mal seizures, where a person shakes all over, bites their tongue, and sometimes urinates or defecates are at higher risk for SUDEP. Another medical condition is a prolonged convulsion for more than five minutes, or status epilepticus, one convulsive episode after another without immediate treatment. Both run the risk of death. Since no one witnessed them, we're speculating. From all the physical evidence we do have, I'm sure all the cavers fall within one of these types of seizures."

"That's what I'm facing with the explosion at the other cave. No witnesses. No security cameras in the area of the cave. So far, no specific identifying pieces of the explosive to follow up on."

"We're both running into dead ends in our investigations. I'm sure you already know this regarding solving a crime…sometimes all you need is an insignificant clue that'll lead you to the who, what and why of a crime or suspicious death."

"How true that is, Simon."

"We'll be moving the bodies now," said Carl Belmont. He and John Thomas had encapsulated the bodies in plastic shrouds.

Steward turned around, facing Carl and John. "Okay."

"We're all done here too," CSU Investigator Lasky said, as she and the other two CSU investigators walked up to them.

Frank and Jean walked over to Janet and stood next to her. "Don't you think we're seeing a continuation of the same scenario of the six deaths at the other cave?" Frank suggested. "Only difference, no explosion at the entrance to this cave trapping us inside."

"That's why I have a deputy outside at the cave's opening," Detective Spurrier said, as he moved a few steps to his right, allowing two CSU investigators enough room to pass by him as they carried a body bag containing the second victim toward the entrance to the cave.

Spurrier looked at CSU Investigator Lasky, who was bending

down over the last victim. "I'll help you carry the third victim out."

"Thanks, Detective." Lasky and Steward picked up the third body bag by holding onto looped straps at either end of the bag. The cave's uneven rock floor was too uneven to wheel a gurney through.

"By the way, we'll pick up all the lanterns as we walk out of the cave," Simon suggested to Spurrier.

"Thanks. That would be appreciated."

Simon walked over to the far end of the chamber and picked up a lantern. He looked up at the bats, then turned around and proclaimed, "The bats will be happy we're leaving their domain."

"I'm sure they are," Janet said.

Frank grabbed two more LED lanterns. "I'd say our work in solving these deaths has just begun."

"That's a fact you guys," Janet said.

Frank led the way for Simon, Jean and Janet out of the crevice chamber into the cave.

Janet picked up a lantern at the entrance to the crevice. After they'd trekked about ten yards inside the cave, the uneven rock floor began to shake.

"My God, what's happening? Another cave-in?" Jean shouted.

"No," Frank answered calmly. The quivering floor stopped. "It's probably a tremor. Tremors, believe it or not, are not uncommon along the Appalachian Mountains. Most people don't feel them unless they're inside a cave or cavern. The seismic events with a magnitude of less than two won't usually be felt on the surface. Although, there have been earthquakes with magnitudes around five point one in Central Pennsylvania in the past with numerous aftershocks or tremors. For your information, the Appalachian Mountain Range is among the oldest mountains on Earth. They were born of powerful upheavals within the terrestrial crust and formed by the recurrent action of water upon the surface."

Simon still couldn't believe the vast amount of knowledge Frank possessed. He was a regular walking encyclopedia. He looked around the cave. No cracks in the floor or ceiling. "Let's move along. I'll feel better when we're outside."

Twilight greeted them when they walked into the evening air. An early evening dark blue sky hung over their heads, not the tenuous rock ceiling of the cave. In front of the four FMI investigators about twenty feet away were the three deceased cavers secured to gurneys.

Simon's cellphone rang. He stopped and glanced at the caller's name: Danny Emerick. "Hi, Danny. We're leaving the cave site. What's up?"

"I got the identity of this female walking into Sullivan Park in Ocala around the time Detective Matters was to meet with a woman. You're not going to believe who this woman works for."

One name crossed Simon's mind. "The Circle?"

"Yep. You're right. The woman's name is Donna Tessler. She's listed as a security consultant for The Circle."

"You'll need to call Marion County Sheriff's Office Major Crime Unit and talk with Captain Robins about what you found. I'm sure he'll have a lot of questions to ask Donna Tessler once he or one of the sheriff detectives locates where she lives."

"I already checked where she lives. I have her address. I'll also pass this information to the captain."

"Great job, Danny. We should be back at the hotel in about thirty minutes. Talk to you then."

Simon turned to Janet, who was standing a couple feet away from him. "Danny found the identity of the woman who was to meet Bill Matters at Sullivan Park to discuss the bombing of Danny Emerick's house. She's a security consultant for The Circle. Coincidental huh?"

"Remember. I don't believe in coincidence, especially in that scenario. Like what we said before leaving Ocala, we probably haven't heard the last of The Circle."

"You're right."

Less than twenty yards in front of them, Detective Spurrier, the county medical examiner's assistant and CSU personnel pushing three gurneys entered the trail through the woods. Simon and his team walked toward the trail. Once Simon and his team got to the road, they handed the lanterns to the appropriate owners. Simon walked over to Steward and thanked him.

"I'm sure you and your agents felt the tremor inside the cave."

"Yeah. We did."

"A three-point-two earthquake occurred in Shippensburg, Pennsylvania about thirty minutes ago. You and your agents felt an aftershock inside the cave."

"We wondered what was going on."

Simon didn't tell him what Frank had commented inside the cave about earthquakes in Pennsylvania.

~ * ~

About a hundred yards up the road and about a foot outside the densely spaced trees, a man and a woman dressed in camouflage clothes were peering through binoculars at the FMI agents, CSU team, county medical examiner assistant, sheriff deputies and Detective Spurrier.

Chapter Eight

The sun was below the forest's tree line, creating a dimly lit landscape. Janet sat in the passenger seat of their black Suburban SUV as Simon began turning around. They were the last vehicle to leave. When their SUV was perpendicular to the dirt road, she saw something about a hundred yards up the road to the left and a few feet from the edge of the forest. Her first thought visualized deer. Janet knew deer came out at twilight and in the early morning hours. Maybe it was another creature of Mother Nature's family? Whatever she saw stood perfectly still.

Their vehicle turned a hundred and eighty degrees, heading back to the hotel. Janet thought about her previous partner, Bill Matters, lying in a coma at the hospital in Ocala and the woman named Donna Tessler, who may be responsible for Bill's medical state.

About ten minutes into the ride, Janet said, "Adding Danny to the FMI team has surely paid off in the last twenty-four hours. First, he rescued us ingeniously with his inventions and now this evening, he identified the woman who may have something to do with Bill's coma. I pray the detectives in Ocala can talk with this woman. If you remember, we wanted to talk with Caleb Johnson, who, it turned out, was an alias for Alex Mendelson, but he disappeared, vanished from Ocala before we could speak with him."

"I hope this woman will be found. We need to think positive."

Janet was normally an optimist. Since being involved in two different investigations with the FMI team, optimism took a backseat in solving the investigations. Evilness surrounded both investigations. Being an optimist, she still believed good would overcome evil. "Like I said earlier, we have a lot of smart people on our team."

"We do. Plus, all of us have ESP/supernatural abilities, excluding Danny. Of course, he adds his ingenious mind for inventions and wizardry of computers, which is an added asset to our team. What do you think, Frank?"

No answer.

Janet turned around and peered into the back seat. Both Frank and Jean were asleep. She chuckled to herself. It was like driving back home with your kids after a long day of fun and frolic. The rhythmic movement of the vehicle rocked them to sleep. Even though she never had kids, she had heard this scenario many times from other people over the years. She turned back around and looked at Simon. "They're both taking a nap."

"I don't blame them. It's been a long, trying day. I'd probably be napping right along with them if I wasn't driving."

Simon turned right onto a four-lane blacktop road and headed south toward Chambersburg.

A minute later, a white van also turned right from the gravel road onto the highway, heading south. It was difficult to see inside the vehicle due to the fading light of evening.

Simon pulled into the hotel parking lot and announced in a loud but not yelling voice, "We're home. Frank. Jean."

The two sleeping agents opened their eyes. "Sorry. I must've dozed off for a moment," Frank said.

"Me too," Jean added.

Janet's cellphone rang. She glanced down at the LED screen. "It's Captain Robins. I'll put him on speaker phone."

Simon heard anxiousness in her voice. "Great." He too was anxious to hear what the captain had to say. Were they going to get closure in the Whispers Before Death case in Ocala?

"Hi. Captain Robins, I have you on speaker phone so Agent Woods and our other agents can hear what you have to say."

"That's good." A short pause. "I personally went with Detective Anderson to the home of Donna Tessler. Matter of fact, we're standing in the living room of her house. She apparently committed suicide. At least that's what it looks like. We found her sitting in a lounge chair, dead. She'd probably been dead for less than a couple of hours, since rigor mortis hadn't set in yet. An opened and empty vial of oxycodone lay in her lap. She died watching TV. As soon as we get the toxicology report and autopsy report on her or any other pertinent information, I'll call you. We'll also be calling her employer, The Circle. Sorry to be the bearer of bad news. We still may find why she was at Sullivan Park after a thorough search of her house. If she's connected to Detective Matters coma state. Still a lot of unanswered questions."

"Thank you very much for calling, Captain Robins." She put her phone back in her belt holder.

Simon removed the keys for the ignition then said, "Why don't we go to Danny's room and discuss what Captain Robins told us. I'm sure Danny will want to hear all this."

They all agreed. As they walked through the front entrance to the hotel a white van pulled into the parking lot and parked several spaces down from FMI's SUV.

~ * ~

Frank was the last person to walk into Danny's room. Simon told Danny about the conversation with Captain Robins.

"I tried to get into The Circle's computer frame," Danny said. "I could only get into their human resource department with limited information available. Their computer system has firewalls I've never encountered before. So far, impossible to penetrate."

"I agree with Danny," Frank interjected. "I tried also to get into their computer system when we were in Ocala. I couldn't break through their security firewalls either."

He turned to Simon. "Can we believe Donna Tessler took her own life?"

Simon was skeptical about everything related to The Circle. He believed what he was told in Detroit, that they wanted world control of governments and its people. "Not sure."

"Knowing the Marion County Sheriff's Office," Janet said, "and the county medical examiner's office, they'll expedite the autopsy results. We should know something tomorrow morning about Donna

Tessler's suicide. All we need is confirmation, proof through an email, a text, a written journal by the deceased, that she had something to do with Bill's coma. We need to know if The Circle was directly involved with what happened to Bill and possibly their security consultant's death."

Simon was sure of one thing: their quest for answers wouldn't be discouraged or dampened by setbacks. "We'll continue our diligence until the truth is uncovered."

"Amen, boss," Frank said.

"We all need a good night's sleep," Simon said. "We'll meet in the restaurant around eight tomorrow morning."

They left Danny's room and walked into the hallway. Everyone said their good nights and headed to their respective rooms. Except Janet, who said to Simon, "Would you like to go to the lounge for a nightcap?"

"Sure. Sounds good."

Frank and Jean, who stopped in front of their rooms, which were across the hall from each other. They looked up the hallway toward Simon and Janet, then turned facing each other. Frank raised his eyebrows and smirked. Jean nodded and smiled.

As they were about to walk into the lounge, Janet stopped. Simon saw an expression of concern on her face, similar to before they walked into the parking structure in Greek Town when they were in Detroit. "Are you feeling something?"

"Yes. Although it's neither a good nor bad vibe. I can't explain it."

"Do you want to forget about getting a drink and go back to our rooms?"

"No. I'm not going to let a feeling interrupt our purpose in coming here."

There were about twelve patrons in the lounge. They found a table to the right against the wall. Simon ordered their drinks, then brought them back to their table. He peered around the room for any familiar faces or anyone looking suspicious. No, in both cases. What was a suspicious person supposed to look like? Two to five people sat at tables. No one sat alone. His gaze fell upon Janet's eyes as he approached the table. He smiled as a warm wave washed over him. Janet reciprocated with a warm smile. She had an ardent effect on him. And he sure enjoyed her attention toward him.

"See anyone suspicious?"

"Was I that obvious?"

"To me, but probably not to anyone else in the room. I already scanned the room and didn't find anyone I'd take a second look at."

"Are you referring to a perp, a suspect? Or were you referring to good-looking guys?"

Janet smirked as she raised her eyebrows. "Maybe all three. I am single and available."

Simon swallowed hard without taking a drink from his bottle of beer. *This woman is great at comebacks. I'd bet she was on a debate team in high school or college.* "Were you ever on a debate team?"

She frowned. "I was. Why would you want to know that?"

"Because, since I've known you, which has been a few days, you're great at quick comebacks."

"I'll take that as a compliment. I think?"

"Yes. It was meant as a compliment. It's one of things I admire about you." *Actually...it's what I love about you.*

"Thank you, Simon. That was sweet of you."

~ * ~

Across the room sat a man and a woman in their early thirties, periodically glancing at them. It was the same two people at the cave sites and in the hotel's parking lot the past two days. Janet's sudden unexplained feeling she experienced before walking into the lounge must've generated from this mysterious couple.

~ * ~

Simon and Janet sat and drank for about forty minutes. "It was nice sitting talking with you. We may not have solved any world problems, but there's always tomorrow."

"That's one thing I noticed about us when we're together, alone, without other FMI agents with us. We never seem to have a moment where we have nothing to say. It's a perpetual conversation. I like that."

Simon sighed. "So, do I. You really…"

The vision of a man and a woman lying on a bare floor flashed across his mind. Both were having seizures. Their bodies and limbs were shaking violently. Their eyes were rolled back. The vision abruptly disappeared. He shook his head. "I just had a vision."

"I thought so. What did you see?"

He described the vision to Janet. "I'd say the two people had grand mal seizures."

"Can you describe the surroundings? You said they were lying on a bare floor. What kind of bare floor?"

He thought a moment. "Planking. Wood planking like you see in an old house. The planking had to be at least ten to twelve inches wide."

"What were they wearing?"

"He was wearing a light-blue, buttoned-down shirt. The name Emmett was embroidered on the left upper front of the shirt. He wore tan pants. He was clean shaven with long brown hair reaching the top of his shoulders. The petite woman who was lying next to him about a foot or two away was about the same age as him. Both were in their early fifties. She was wearing green overalls. She had dark-brown hair."

"Great information and detail. Although, no way to know where they are or will be in the next twenty-four hours. Two things for certain, they weren't lying inside a cave and they had grand mal seizures. I'd say the nine cavers' seizures were likely this type of seizure. Wouldn't you say so?"

"Yes. A high probability they all had grand mal seizures. The big question is what caused all these people to have them at nearly the same time? Logic tells me that they were exposed to a substance with rapid absorption. Otherwise the victims would've been found at different areas in the cave. My recent vision, two people lying side-by-side would confirm my assumption of rapid absorption of a deadly toxic substance."

Janet began to stand. "Again, we're faced with another medical mystery. Hopefully we'll find some answers tomorrow."

Simon also stood. "A good night's sleep and our minds and

bodies should be ready for another day in the life of an FMI agent."

He pushed his chair, then Janet's back under the table. They walked out of the lounge and down the hallway toward their rooms.

The covert couple in the lounge sat at their table and continued drinking.

Janet said, "Something strange happened when we were leaving the lounge."

"What was that?"

"I got that unusual feeling, again. It's not the normal feeling of something impending, like danger. This feeling is different. Not sure what it means."

"Maybe your premonition feelings are evolving to something else?"

"I guess that's possible," Janet answered. She stopped in front of her door and removed a keycard from her jacket. "Thanks for the drink."

"My pleasure. Talk to you in the morning."

He thought about giving her a platonic good night kiss. *Whatever that means,* he thought. Maybe under some situations a nonromantic kiss on the cheek might be proper, but not between two healthy, young adults with hormones primed for more than a platonic relationship. He walked to his room's entrance door, removed his keycard, then glanced at Janet's door. She was already inside her room. He sure liked Janet's company. After a long sigh, he opened his door.

Simon rolled to his left side as he laid in bed and opened his eyes. Morning sunlight was sneaking around the edges of the drawn window curtain. The clock on the nightstand read seven fifteen a.m.

He had set the alarm for seven-twenty. He reached over, turned off the alarm, then turned on a nightstand lamp. He rolled to his right onto his back and stared up at a stucco ceiling. The vision he had in the lounge last night of the unknown man and woman having seizures crossed his mind. He replayed the convulsive incident. Like most of his premonition visions, he felt helpless knowing someone or a group of people were about to face a lifechanging event or death.

Simon got up, showered, then dressed. He walked into the restaurant a few minutes before eight. The entire FMI team were already sitting at the round table in the far-right corner of the room.

He walked up to the table and sat next to Janet. "I guess everyone must be hungry. Being here before eight o'clock."

"I can't speak for everybody, but I missed our sit-down supper last night," Frank answered. "I didn't want to miss breakfast."

Simon raised his eyebrows and smirked. "Anyway. I'm glad you're all here. We probably will have another busy day ahead of us. Did Janet tell you about the vision I had last night?"

"Yes," answered Jean.

Frank and Danny nodded, acknowledging her answer.

"I hope we'll find out about this man and woman today. After breakfast, we're going to interview the families of yesterday's three dead cavers. We'll work in pairs. Janet and I will be one pair. Jean and Frank the second pair. You know what questions to ask them. After talking with the family, call us to see where we are in our interview. Whoever is done first will talk with the third victim's family. After that we'll visit the place of employment of all nine victims." Simon turned to Danny. "Danny. You'll be assigned searching the Internet and tapping into the first six cavers' employers, then the three cavers' employers from yesterday. Find out as much as you can about the employers. Also search for any connection with The Circle, such as a subsidiary."

The waitress walked up to the table and received everyone's breakfast order. It was almost nine o'clock when they left the restaurant. Simon asked Janet to drive. He wanted to call Detective Spurrier about informing him of any couple deaths today. Simon dialed the detective's number. "Hi, Steward. My team and I were discussing the deaths of the nine cavers and we wanted to expand our search regarding suspicious deaths other than inside caves. Can you let me know of undetermined, nonviolent couple deaths in Franklin and surrounding counties, including northern Maryland? Also, let me know if there's any mention of anyone or all of them having seizures."

"Sure. Be glad to help, Simon. So, you think there might be other deaths with the same presentation as the nine cavers?"

"We're only speculating, Steward."

"Okay. You and your team might to correct in your speculation. Seems feasible. Talk to you later." Their conversation ended.

The SUV's GPS told Janet to turn right onto a black-topped four-lane highway. "So, Detective Spurrier didn't question your request?"

"No. He seemed convinced it was a good idea."

Simon felt helpless in this recent vision. He didn't have any specific clues to steer them to where these two people will die. Like he told Janet and others in the past, his premonition visions were both a Godsend and a curse. It was amazing he didn't have high blood pressure due to the stress his visions created.

"Turn left at the next traffic light," commanded the female GPS voice.

The light was green including a green arrow for Janet as she put her left directional signal on. She slowed to make the turn but stopped in the left turn lane before entering the intersection.

"Why are you stopping?" Simon asked.

Janet didn't answer. Traffic to her left and right sped through the traffic light. Vehicles behind and in front of her also sped through the intersection. Two to three-ton vehicles can't occupy the same space. A simple law of physics. Squealing tires, then metal and plastic colliding against each other. Two cars crashed, then three, then four, then six. A catastrophic collision of metal and plastic erupted beneath the traffic light. Steam from damaged radiators created an ominous cloud over the heap of metal, plastic and glass. "I had a premonition feeling to stop and not enter the intersection."

"If you hadn't stopped, we would've been sideswiped and probably injured or even killed."

"The traffic light must've malfunctioned, causing a green light to be displayed in all directions. It's the most logical explanation for the multiple car accident."

Janet moved their SUV to the left side of the street, away from the intersection. They got out and hurried to the crash site, assisting the injured. The odor of gasoline permeated the area, increasing the anxiety of victims and first responders. Any second, the gasoline could create a fireball, burning anyone near it. "We must get everyone away from their vehicles before an explosion engulfs the area."

"I agree." Simon turned to bystanders and non-accident people getting out of their cars and walking toward the intersection. He shouted, "We must get everyone out of their vehicles, if we can."

He and Janet hurried from one car to another, assessing the occupants' injury status, medically triaging the car victims. At least six bystanders assisted in extracting people from their vehicles after Simon determined who could be moved. Miraculously, no one was unconscious, pinned inside their vehicles or critically injured. Within eight minutes, all ten car accident victims, were sitting, lying or standing at the side of the road. A massive explosion shook the ground as a car became engulfed in flames. Simon wiped the sweat from his forehead as a chill overwhelmed him. A young woman with her three to four-year-old daughter would've burned alive if he and Janet hadn't pulled them from their car.

The fire department, paramedics and the Chambersburg police department arrived at the scene. In less than thirty seconds, the firemen extinguished the car fire. Janet told the patrolman what caused the accident. Malfunctioning traffic light displaying a green light in all four directions. After she and Simon gave statements to the police officer, they got in their SUV and headed for their interview.

Simon sat in the driver's seat. "All I can say again is thank God you had one of your premonition feelings."

Janet pressed her lips tightly together and sighed, then said, "It definitely was a blessing. Something else happened beside the ominous feeling I normally will experience…I heard a voice in my head say, 'stop' to me. The voice I heard was me, not another person."

"Like I said earlier. Your ESP feeling may be evolving into something different."

"I've read where people who hear voices in their head are schizophrenic. Is that my situation?"

What Janet proclaimed about hearing voices in your head, auditory hallucinations, was a symptom of certain mental illnesses.

Schizophrenia being one of them. It would be highly unlikely that was what she was experiencing. No. The voice she heard was tied to her premonition feelings as an added ability. "You're not crazy. You probably added another dimension to your premonition feeling."

"That's a relief. Maybe I'll never hear my inner voice again?"

"Maybe. I guess you'll have to wait until your next premonition feeling."

Janet nodded. "Do you think it was a coincidence that we were almost involved in an intersection vehicle accident again? You know how I feel about coincidental situations."

"I remember someone saying to us recently about how troubling events seem to follow us."

The two of them worked great together as an investigative team. Since Janet first involved herself with him and the other FMI agents there had been at least five death defying incidences where the Reaper of Death stood on their doorstep.

"As we talked about before, there seems to be a force working against us, trying to impede our investigation. We saw it in Ocala and now we're seeing it here."

Janet reached into the inside pocket of her blazer and removed a folded sheet of paper. "You're right. We are. It makes me more determined to find out the answers to these deaths and who or what entity is trying to prevent us from obtaining the truth."

She unfolded the paper. The first person we're going to interview is Margaret Whitman. Her daughter, Susan, has lived with her for the past eight months since her divorce. No children."

Simon glanced at Janet, then straight ahead as another EMS passed them, rushing to the accident scene. *Maybe today will be the day we'll find answers to these deaths?*

Chapter Nine

Simon knocked on the front door of a rambling ranch in a subdivision of ranches and colonial-styled homes. The odor of lilac blooms scented the air. "I love the odor of lilac flowers."

"I do too. Did you know that purple lilacs symbolize the first emotions of love, while white lilacs represent youthful innocence?"

Simon turned to his left and saw purple lilac bushes. A flushing feeling gently slapped his face. *Was she trying to tell me something*? He cleared his throat. "No, I didn't."

Before any further conversation between them, the front door opened. A middle-aged woman with redness in the whites of her eyes, likely from crying, thought Simon, stood in the doorway and asked, "Can I help you?"

"My name is Simon Woods, and this is Janet Bennett. We're agents from the Federal Medical Investigators of CDC." They showed their badges. "We're so sorry for the loss of your daughter. We like to ask you some questions about your daughter. If that would be okay with you?"

"Do you know what caused her death and her two friends? The sheriff deputies didn't have any answers yesterday when they came to our house."

"No, ma'am. At least not yet. We're investigating their deaths."

"Please come in." She stepped aside.

They walked into the living room and sat. Simon and Janet sat on a Queen Anne couch with elaborate scrolled end tables with Tiffany lamps on top of them, complementing the rooms décor. "You have a lovely home, Mrs. Whitman," Janet said, as she looked around the room.

"Thank you. My husband would be here, but he had to go to the airport and pick...pick up my sister and her husband." Her voice began to crack as she stared down at the floor.

Simon forced a stealthy deep breath, hoping no one noticed. He felt a tear forming in the corner of his eyes. "We need to know if your daughter had any medical conditions?"

"No. She had a yearly checkup with her family doctor about a month ago. Everything was normal."

Janet asked, "Did she have any enemies you know of?"

"Oh, no. Everyone loved her. She was a giver, not a taker."

Simon peered at a photograph of Susan standing with her parents in front of a building. He leaned forward to get a better look. The name on the building was Brighton Research. *Robert Rhode, one the six victims of the first cave deaths worked there.*

Simon leaned back and asked, "Where did your daughter work?"

"Brighton Research. Why do you ask?"

"There was another person that died while caving several days ago. He also worked at that company. Did she know a Robert Rhode?"

"No. Not to my knowledge. At least, she never mentioned his name."

Simon wasn't sure if there was any significance in them working for the same company. "Had your daughter mentioned anything about her vision?"

"Matter of fact, a few days ago she told me that she was going to make an appointment with an eye doctor because periodically she saw wavy lines. They lasted a minute or two, then went away. She thought maybe it was eye strain. She'd been watching a lot of TV programs lately on her tablet."

No. She probably was having ocular migraines, thought Simon. He already knew she had nystagmus, since in his visual premonition two days ago, he saw Susan and her two companions displaying the horizontal oscillations of their eyes. That confirmed two cavers with wavy lines, possibly ocular migraines or some other medical condition. "You're right about watching movies and TV programs on a tablet or laptop for long periods; it can cause some eye conditions." He turned and glanced at Janet. "Do you have any other questions for Mrs. Whitman?"

"No." She put her pen and notebook into the front pocket of her blazer. She stood as did Simon.

"Again, we're very sorry for your loss. We or the sheriff's office will contact you as soon as a cause of your daughter's death is known."

"Thank you. I'd appreciate that, Agent Woods." She got up from her chair and led them to the front door.

Simon removed a business card from his wallet and handed it to Mrs. Whitman. "If you have any questions or remember something about your daughter you may think is important, please call me."

She glanced down at the business card. "I will, Agent Woods. Or should I say Dr. Woods?"

"Either one is fine. I hope we'll have some news soon about the death of your daughter." He noticed her lower lips began to quiver.

They walked out of the house. Janet raised her head and forced a deep whiff through her nose. "I love that smell."

The pleasant aroma of lilacs dampened Simon's saddened spirit, creating a sentimental feeling. "I do too."

When they were a few feet from their car in the driveway, he said, "I'll never get used to talking with a grieving parent or loved one. It's one aspect of this job I could do without."

"I feel the same way. It's an emotional time and one of my most difficult situations as a sheriff detective. And that hasn't changed since being an FMI agent."

They got into the car. "I'll call Frank and let'em know we're done." He pushed the speed dial on his cellphone. "Hi, Frank. We're done with our interview."

"We're almost done here. Nothing significant to report."

"Janet and I will interview the third caver's family. So, I want you and Jean to start interviews with the victims' place of work. By the way, did your victim work for Brighton Research?"

"No. He worked for a roofing company."

"You have half the list of the first six cavers' employers. Keep in touch if something relevant turns up. Otherwise, we'll meet you and Jean back at the hotel."

"Sounds like a plan. And I'm sticking to it."

Simon placed his hand on his forehead and grinned. "Talk to you later."

He started the SUV and backed out of the driveway onto the street. "We'll next interview the family of the third caver from yesterday."

Janet leaned back in her bucket seat. "I put the address into the GPS. We're about twenty minutes away. When you talked with Frank and asked him if the deceased caver worked for Brighton Research, I assume he didn't work there."

"No. The guy was a roofer."

Simon and Janet talked with the spouse of the third caver. The caver's wife didn't have anything relevant to their investigation. Her husband didn't complain of any eye problems or was there a history of seizure disorder. The man died leaving a wife with two small children. Simon told the wife everything was being done to determine the cause of her husband's death. Of course, Simon knew there wasn't any guarantee FMI would discover a cause of these mysterious deaths of nine cavers. Possibly there would be two more people added to the list. They got back to the SUV and drove away, heading northwest to Brighton Research.

"Since two of the nine cavers worked at the same place, I'd figure we'd start there. What do you think?"

"Like I've said before, you think like a law enforcement detective."

"Thanks." Simon turned onto a main highway. "Maybe we should call Danny and see if he's already researched them. It would be nice to have a detailed background of them before we get there. Especially if Brighton Research is connected to The Circle. Since I'm driving, can you call him?"

"Of course." Janet dialed Danny's number, putting the call on speaker phone. "Hi, Danny. I'm in the SUV with Simon. I have you on speaker. Have you by chance checked out Brighton Research?"

"No. I haven't. I'll get on it right away. To update what I've done so far, I've checked four of the nine victims' employers. None of the four employers are connected to The Circle. Why'd you want me to checkout this particular company?"

"Two of the victims worked for Brighton Research. Robert Rhode in the group of six cavers and Susan Whitman in the group of three cave explorers. It probably means nothing, but we thought we'd check Brighton Research first. We're about thirty minutes away from the company."

"I'll get right on it and call you back as soon as I find something relevant to the case."

"Talk to you then." Janet put her phone back in her belt holster.

She looked at Simon. "Maybe Brighton Research will lead to something in our investigation of the cavers' deaths?"

"Wouldn't that be great?" Simon saw a state trooper parked without warning lights flashing about a quarter of a mile ahead of them on the right side of the road. He glanced at the speedometer, then a posted speed sign next to the road to his right. Both were forty-five miles per hour. *No speeding ticket for me.* In his sixteen years of driving, he had never got a moving violation ticket. "What I'd like to know is what product they're making or what kind of research they're doing."

"We'll soon find out."

Simon glanced down at their GPS. They were now seven minutes and three point two miles from their destination. When they started from Mrs. Whitman's house, the area was heavily populated with people and houses. Now their surroundings consisted of more trees and fewer houses as they trekked toward the Brighton Research facility.

Janet's cellphone rang. She looked at the LED screen, then Simon. "It's Danny. I'll put him on speaker again."

"Perfect timing."

"Hi, Danny. What did you find out?"

"Very interesting. First, Brighton Research is a subsidiary of a Chinese conglomerate. Second, I couldn't find any connection to The Circle for either one. Brighton does research on cleaning products. The company was started twenty years ago by two men, then was bought out by Yang Corporation six months ago for one-hundred-and-fifty million dollars."

The GPS announced, "Turn left up ahead onto Brighton Road."

Simon pressed on the brake, slowing down the SUV. "Anything else we should know about this company?"

"About five months ago, permits were issued by the Franklin County Building Department for an addition to the existing building. The blueprint described a clean room, an isolation room and a reverse isolation room. That's all I have right now."

"You did a great job."

He looked at Janet. "Anything you want to ask him?"

"No." She peered at her phone. "Thanks, Danny. We'll talk to you later. Bye."

Simon stopped and turned left onto Brighton Road. They were in desolate forested area without any houses or businesses immediately around them. About a hundred yards up ahead to their right in a large clearing stood a four-story building. "It looks like we've…"

"You've arrived at your destination on the right," interrupted the GPS voice.

Simon chuckled. "She took the words right out of my mouth."

"What did you think about what Danny said about this company? Plus, what is a reverse isolation room? I think I know what an isolation room is for."

"I know what it is in a hospital. Isolation room is where a person is put due to them having a pathogen capable of doing harm to others, like tuberculosis. The room's environment has a negative pressure preventing a pathogen from escaping the isolation room. A reverse isolation room is when there is positive pressure in the room. Filtered, clean air is brought into the room and allowed to vent out of the room to the surrounding corridors. Visitors must wear protective garb masks, paper gowns, shoe coverings and latex gloves to protect the patient. The visitors might pass on a virus or bacteria to the patient."

Simon turned right onto a driveway about three hundred feet long before it stopped at a security gate and gate house. A ten-foot fence encompassed the four-story building. "Reverse isolation can also mean the extraction and purification of a chemical substance of unknown structure from a natural source. It can also mean the physiological separation of a part, as by tissue culture or by interposition of inert material."

"You just left me out in left field without a glove. I have no idea what you said on those last two things."

"Sorry. I guess I got carried away. What's important to know is they are or will be working with chemical substances or organisms that are dangerous to the workers at the company."

Janet peered to her right then left. "I'd say they're expanding their research on cleaning compounds to something else. The guardhouse and fence appeared to have been recently constructed."

"It sure does look new, doesn't it?" Simon stopped at the closed front gate of Brighton Research and rolled down his window.

A security guard, holstering a gun on his waist belt walked up to Simon. "Hi, folks. What can I do for you?"

"We're Federal Medical Investigators from the CDC. We're here to talk with someone regarding two of your employees." He and Janet showed their badges.

"Wait here, please." He turned around, walked a few feet into the gatehouse and called someone from a wall phone. He then hung up the phone. The gate slowly moved horizontally to the right. The guard walked back to Simon. "Please pull your car straight ahead to visitor's parking. Go to the front door of the building. A security guard will meet you there and take you to human resources."

"Thank you." Simon rolled up his window.

"This is like trying to get into the Pentagon. I can't believe their research company is for development of cleaning products. Unless the cleaning products are for the International Space Station."

"The good news is they're letting us in to talk with someone from human resources. I first thought after seeing their security level we'd have to come back another day after setting up a scheduled appointment. Like you said, it's like trying to get into the Pentagon."

They parked the Suburban and walked to the entrance door. A security guard in his late twenties met Simon and Janet inside the entrance door. They passed through a metal detector, leaving their cellphones, coins, and any metal item in separate plastic containers. A white marble lobby floor about thirty feet wide by thirty feet deep and a twenty-foot ceiling with a glass chandelier hanging down created a majestic scene. Next to a security desk to their immediate right sat a white and tan marble-like three-person bench. "Please have a seat on the bench. Someone will be here to talk with the two of you." The security guard then sat behind his desk.

Simon looked to his right across the lobby at an elevator door. To the left and right of the elevator were closed doors, most likely leading to hallways. What seemed strange to him was there weren't any wall hangings or a directory for the different departments. A person would be lost unless they knew where to go in this building. The door to their left opened and a woman dressed in a dark-gray pant suit walked into the lobby toward them.

"I'm Darlene Shaw from human resources. I understand you need information about two of our employees?"

Simon and Janet stood. "Yes, Ms. Shaw. I'm Agent Simon Woods and this is Agent Janet Bennett. We're investigating the deaths of Robert Rhode and Susan Whitman." The resource woman didn't flinch or show any reaction of surprise or sorrow.

"We talked with a sheriff detective on the phone about Mr. Rhode's death in a cave almost a week ago. I understand Ms. Whitman died two days ago in a cave. A family member called us this morning about her tragic death. Please come to my office where I can answer any question you may have about them."

Before they left the lobby, the young man at the desk gave Simon and Janet clip-on visitor nametags. The hallway was brightly lit by ceiling neon light fixtures. Several rooms on the left and right led into the long hallway. Black room numbers with the letter A in front of the numerals were attached to the right of the door on hospital-white walls. Simon expected the hustle and bustle of people walking and conversing up and down the corridor. Not present. Only the soles of their shoes striking onto the white tiled floor could be heard. Again, no wall hangings on the hallway walls. They stopped and walked into room A-12.

A few feet in front of them stood a counter running about three quarters the width of a twelve-foot wide room. A computer sat on the counter to the left. A large, black metal cabinet with closed doors stood against the entire back wall. *Likely the personnel files of Brighton Research employees,* thought Simon. A light tan wooden desk with a swivel chair sat in front of the cabinets. Two straight-back cushioned chairs were to the right and left of the desk.

"Please have a seat," Ms. Shaw said, pointing to the two chairs.

Simon peered at the desk in front of him. A computer, a landline phone and two manila envelopes sat on top of the desk. Nothing else caught his eye. Again, no wall hangings, pictures, prints or a clock. "This may be an unusual question," Simon said. "Why isn't there any pictures, prints, wall hangings in the lobby, hallway or in your room?"

Sitting in her chair, facing them, her eyes glanced down at the floor, avoiding eye contact. A momentary pause. "You're…you're very observant. It's for security reasons, why the walls are void of objects. Since Yang Corporation took over the company, they initiated this new mandate. If an outside intruder gets through security, they will have a difficult time to find a person or department within our building, even if they have a general idea of their target."

"Oh. I see." *There's got to be more to this lame answer.*

Janet asked, "Can you tell us if there were any complaints or harassments against another employee documented by either Mr. Rhode or Ms. Whitman?"

She turned toward her desk and scanned through both Manilla files. "There isn't anything like that in their files. They were doing exceptional work for the company. No disciplinary actions against either of them."

"What exactly did Rhode and Whitman do for the company?"

"Robert Rhode was a chemist and worked in our product analysis department. As for Susan Whitman, she was a biochemist and worked in our research development department."

Janet leaned back in her chair and glanced at Simon. "Do you have any questions."

Simon gazed at the open files and saw a red infinity symbol and two lightning bolts against a white background inside a blue thick-lined circle on a letter head in Robert Rhode's file. "Did he work with any dangerous compounds?"

"All I can tell you is we've never had anyone get ill from the products we research. OSHA inspects our facility at least twice a year without any violations."

Simon stood, as did Janet. "I appreciate your time."

Ms. Shaw got up from her chair and closed the files. "I'm glad to help. I'll walk you back to the lobby."

"I don't think you have to. I'm sure we can find our way back."

"Sorry. I must escort you back to the lobby. Company policy."

Simon and Janet left the building then got into their SUV. Janet strapped her seat built, then said, "What do you...?"

Simon put his index finger to his lips in a gesture of saying, Be quiet. Don't say anything. He opened the console compartment next to him and removed a small rectangular apparatus that Danny gave them at the hotel. It was a bug detector device. He turned it on and moved it in front of the dashboard and under his and Janet's bucket seats. He stared at the LED screen. "No electronic listening devices in the vehicle."

"You think maybe someone from Brighton Research planted one in here?'

"Possibly. I didn't want to take a chance. There's something about this research facility that bothers me. Not sure what it is. It's just a feeling." He turned the ignition on, backed up and left the gated compound. "I saw a symbol or logo in Robert Rhode's folder that caught my interest."

"What was it?"

"A blue circle with a red infinity symbol in the center. Not sure what it represents. It's a circle. My first thought was directed at the clandestine organization The Circle. I'm going to call Danny and have him check it out on the computer."

"I'll call him since you're driving."

"Thanks." Simon turned right at the next road.

Janet called Danny and gave him the description of the logo. "Thanks Danny. Talk to you later."

"We'll soon find out if my hunch means something or nothing."

~ * ~

A white van without windows along the paneled side passed them and stopped at Brighton Road. The van with a couple in their thirties turned left.

Chapter Ten

Janet checked the list for the next employer and put the address in the vehicle's GPS. She peered at the Time of Arrival, then the Suburban's dashboard clock. "We're twenty-six minutes from our next employer, Shippensburg's Sporting Goods. It's where Henry Davis worked as a salesman. After him, we'll have Steve Nutting, a satellite TV service representative in Chambersburg. That'll finish the three cave explorers who died yesterday." She rotated her head, stretching the muscles in her neck as she raised her shoulders. She heard and felt a nonpainful click in the back of her neck.

Simon glanced at Janet. "Looks like you need a shoulder and neck massage."

"Know someone who's good at it?"

She stared a Simon's hands holding the steering wheel. She knew they were soft, non-calloused hands, probably capable of caressing tightened muscles, like her neck and shoulder muscles. Her face felt as if a heat lamp passed across it. *Janet, this isn't the time for these thoughts. Get ahold of yourself.*

The corner of Simon's closed lips raised. He then said, "Matter of fact I do. I charge by the minute."

They both laughed.

The lateral aspect of Janet's abdominal muscles spasmed from her burst of laughter. She leaned forward pressing against her side to relieve the spasm. Tears of laughter rolled down her cheeks. She now leaned back in her seat, rubbing the tears from her face with the back of her hands. "I've said this before. I love this job. Being an agent of FMI, there's suspense, adventure, hidden danger, death defying traumatic events and laughter. Plus, we get to solve medical mysteries."

"I have to agree, there aren't too many dull moments."

~ * ~

Their interview with the two employers was unrewarding. Both victims were liked by their employers and fellow employees with no blemishing marks in their personnel files. There wasn't any change in their work performance or complaints of any medical issues the past few weeks. Simon and Janet got into their vehicle in the parking lot of the satellite company.

Janet picked up the sheet with names of the cavers' employers. "I wonder how Frank and Jean are doing? I'll give 'em a call."

"Good idea." Simon turned the vehicle on along with the air conditioning. Inside the vehicle, the temperature had to be in the nineties from the relentless rays of the sun.

"Hi, Frank. How you guys doing?"

"We completed four employers. One more to go. So far, there hasn't been anything out of the ordinary. No smoking guns. Only water pistols. Any leads at your end?"

"Maybe. We think Brighton Research isn't telling us the complete truth about two of the victims, Rhode and Whitman."

"Why do you think that?"

"We believe there hiding something, something relevant to the deaths of the cavers. It's like The Circle, suspicion but no hard evidence to prosecute."

"Jean and I are a few blocks away from the last employer on our list. We'll call you when we're done. Talk to you then. Bye."

"Bye." She glanced out the side window at a billboard with a guy standing with his hands on the handle of two revolvers secured inside a leather scrolled western two-gun belt holster. Beside the image it read, "Need a private investigator? Call Sam Lawless. 717-555-3290." Janet chuckled.

"What's so funny?"

She told him about the billboard. "It sounds like this guy will get the job done one way or another. Maybe we should hire him?"

"You seem to handle situations and your Glock just fine. The flower shop comes to mind. We don't need anyone else."

Janet looked at the dashboard clock. It was eleven fifteen. A coffee sounded good right now. "Why don't we find a restaurant and get a cup of coffee?"

"I was thinking about that before you mentioned it. Sure. Sounds good."

He pulled out of the parking lot, heading for the nearest restaurant. A few minutes later, Aunt Betty's Diner came into view on the right. "This looks like a quaint little place."

The silver-colored metal diner building was in the shape of a railroad car. They walked inside. Booths were along the front and side walls with windows taking up the upper half of the walls. A counter with stool-like swivel chairs stood nearly the full length of the room. They sat at a front booth and ordered coffee and a sweet roll. She gazed around the room. "This place is like the diners from the nineteen-fifties."

"I wouldn't know." Simon shrugged his shoulders and frowned. "I wasn't born until the nineteen-eighties."

Janet reached over and tapped his forearm. "Of course, you weren't. I wasn't either. Although, I've seen enough movies depicting the nineteen fifties and sixties. They even had a TV series about a diner."

She saw a grin evolve from Simon's serious expression. She'd been joshed by him.

"Mel's Diner comes to mind."

His cellphone rang. He glanced at the caller name. "It's Detective Spurrier." Simon turned toward the window. "Hi, Steward."

He listened to the detective while furrowing his forehead. He then turned toward Janet and peered into her eyes. "When do you think the couple died?" A short pause. "You think they both had a seizure?" He listened for less than a half a minute, then removed a small notebook from his jacket and a pen from his shirt pocket. "I'll write down the address." He wrote the address down. "We'll meet you there."

From what she heard Simon say, the man and woman were found dead with evidence of seizures. "I assume it's another seizure death in a cave."

"Yes and no." He sipped his coffee. "Yes. It appears they had seizures. But not in a cave. They were found in the hallway of their home this morning by one of their kids who stopped by the house when his parents didn't answer their phone. Steward examined the couple and noticed they had bitten their tongues and urinated on themselves. No signs of trauma."

"Same as the nine cave victims."

Janet pushed a small dish containing a half-eaten pastry to the end of the table. Gulped down two swigs of coffee, then said, "I'm ready."

Simon called Frank and gave him the address of the house. "We'll see you and Jean there when you get done."

Janet called Danny and told him about the husband and wife. "Do a computer search on them and get as much information as you can about them, including their medical history. Call us back when you finish the search."

"I'll get right on it. Talk to you soon. Bye."

Simon parked at a curb two houses down from the victim's house. The medical examiner's van was parked in the driveway. Detective Spurrier's car and two sheriff deputy cars were parked on the street in front of the house.

Both sides of the street contained two-story houses that appeared to have been built in the early twentieth century. *Most of the houses are well-maintained considering their age,* thought Janet.

They walked into the living room through an opened front door. The odor of an air freshener permeated throughout the living room. She glanced down on an end table and saw an automatic dispensing air freshener. "I wonder if the people living here were trying to cover an offensive odor?"

Simon looked around the living room. "Could be. Frank would be the one to determine that."

Straight ahead about twenty feet stood Steward and the medical examiner assistant, Carl Belmont, who was at the cave yesterday. Two bodies lay on the floor in front of them. Janet walked in front of Simon as they entered the five-foot wide hallway. "Hi, Steward. Hi, Carl."

Simon now stood next to Janet. He looked at Steward. "Anything new since I talked with you on the phone?"

"Yes. We figured the time of death was between ten o'clock last night and one a.m. this morning. That would be between twelve and fifteen hours ago. We…that is Carl's, assessment was based on the stage of rigor mortis was approaching its final stage, low core body temperature and the skin condition of mottling hadn't started yet. Plus adding their son said the family talked with their parents late yesterday afternoon and at that time everything was fine with them."

Janet wanted to say, *Simon's premonition vision of the husband and wife having seizures last night confirmed Carl's estimate of their approximate time of death.* Of course, she couldn't divulge FMI's ESP abilities. "This puts a different perspective into our investigation, gentleman. The place of these mysterious deaths isn't exclusively caves."

Simon rubbed his chin as peered down at the deceased couple. "We can't quarantine an entire county. There must be a common link to all these deaths."

Spurrier brushed down on his mustache with the pads of his index and middle finger, then said, "Between CSU, the medical examiner's office, our department and the FMI you'd think we'd be able find an answer to these deaths."

Janet's cellphone rang. The LED screen displayed Danny's name. She stepped back a few steps, turned to the right and stared down at the hallway baseboard. "Hey, Danny. What did you find out?"

"Emmett and Loraine Tillman had been married for thirty years. Both were in good health with no chronic diseases. No history of epilepsy. The Tillmans were two days into a one-week vacation. He worked as a plumber and she worked as a manager in a dental office. No criminal record, not even a motor vehicle moving ticket or parking violations. Their one-hundred-and-seventy-thousand-dollar home had no mortgage. Paid off three years ago. I checked to see if they, their daughter or son were somehow connected to the nine cave explorers. If they ever touched base with The Circle or Brighton Research. Nothing came up. I have quite a bit more information on them, but I don't think it would be relevant to their deaths."

"You did an exceptional and thorough search. I'll pass the information on to Simon. Thanks Danny."

"That's why they pay me the big bucks." He snickered. "All kidding aside, you're welcome."

"I'm getting used to joking remarks from you guys. Don't stop doing it." She looked up at Simon, who was talking with Steward. "Talk to you later." She stepped forward and stood next to Simon.

Simon turned and faced Janet. "What did Danny have to say?"

Janet stood about three feet away from Simon as she turned toward him. "Nothing important to our investigation."

She then told Simon what Danny found out about the deceased couple. She left out the part about The Circle even though Detective Spurrier knew about the organization's involvement in their Ocala investigation.

"I agree. This information is irrelevant."

"FMI works fast," Steward said. "We haven't had a chance to look into the Tillmans' history."

"We'll be glad to pass on this information to you, if you like?" *Of course, without mentioning The Circle*, Janet said to herself.

"Sure. That'll be great."

Footsteps approached the approximately twenty-foot long, glossy hardwood hallway floor. Everyone looked toward the sound of thumping footsteps. Frank and Jean walked up to them. Frank had a distinct lumbering gait. Jean made short, dainty steps. *Quite a contrast of gaits*, thought Janet.

"Hi, everyone," Frank said.

He reached up and began scratching the back of his head and frowned.

"Hey, guys," Simon said. "Glad you got here so soon.

"There goes our theory that the deaths only occur in caves," Frank said looking down at the bodies. He then squinted, raised his head toward the ceiling and sniffed. "Guano. Almonds. It's the same odors I smelled at the two caves."

Janet glanced up. "Is there an attic in this house?"

"Not sure," Steward answered. "We haven't checked the upstairs yet. Just this level of the house and the basement."

"So, maybe there's bats in the attic?" Frank questioned. "Or is it bats in the belfry? No. This house doesn't have a bell tower. Did you know the phrase bats in the belfry came from the late nineteenth century and meant a person was crazy or eccentric? It's also the name of a plant with bell-shaped blue-purple flowers."

"Where do you come up with this information?" Steward asked.

Jean looked up at Frank and answered, "We think he has an encyclopedia computer chip in his brain."

Frank grunted. "Don't let out my secret."

"Can you guys be serious for a moment?" Simon interjected. "Let check to see if there's an attic."

Carl said with a puzzling expression, "Does Agent Frank really have a computer chip in his brain?"

"One thing you have to learn about our team," Janet said, "we do a lot of kidding around. This was one of them."

The FMI team and Detective Spurrier got to the second floor. A hallway ran the full length of the upper level. They encountered a bathroom and two bedrooms to the right. Their footsteps created a cadence on the hardwood flooring. At the end of the hallway, the wall to the left stopped as the wall to the right continued another eight feet. A bedroom door was to their left. Behind them, to their left an opened door stood leading up to the attic. On the floor a few feet from the doorway were three large plastic containers with black marker writing on the lids. Old dishes. Pots and pans. VHS tapes, and VHS recorder.

Janet bent down and wiped her hand across the top of the boxes. There wasn't any dust residue. "The Tillmans must've been packing things into these containers to take up to the attic for storage."

"Good assumption," Steward agreed.

Frank walked over to the attic doorway and rubbed his nose. "The strong odor of guano is coming from the attic." He looked at Simon. "Since we don't have lab results from the bat guano yet, it would be wise to wear a particulate protective mask. Don't you think?"

"I agree," Simon answered.

Frank nodded as he removed keys from his pocket. "I have all of our masks in my car. I'll run and get them."

"Can you ask Carl if he has an extra mask?" Steward asked.

"Sure."

A few minutes later, Frank returned with the protective masks. Simon reached out to his left to a light switch on the left side of the doorframe and flipped it on, lighting up the stairway and attic. Each of them wore their masks, as they ascended the stairs to the attic.

A V-shaped ceiling about six and a half feet high in the center and about five feet high at the side walls ran the length of the house. Janet saw a large air vent with missing horizontal slats at the far end wall of the attic. A lightbulb hung about every twenty feet from the approximately sixty-foot-long ceiling except for the last twenty feet near the air vent. The last twenty feet was dimly lit from the outside light coming through the vent. A wooden floor covered the entire attic. Numerous plastic storage containers with lids lay scattered on the floor. The temperature was in the eighties. Even through their masks, a musty odor enveloped the hot and humid air.

Frank sniffed in different directions of the attic, then declared, "I believe the flying creatures are in that direction." He pointed toward the air vent at the far end of the attic. "It's where the smell seems to be strongest." He sighed, wiped the sweat from his forehead. "I guess I'll…I'll go check the odor out."

Janet realized Frank wasn't fond of bats, maybe even had a fear of them. He hid his uneasiness with bats while in the two caves. The attic is a more confined area with no place to run if the bats decided to swoop down from their perch. "I'll lead the way," Janet insisted. She looked up. "Make sure you all walk in the center of the attic, otherwise you'll bump your head on the ceiling joists."

"Yes, mother," Simon replied in a childlike voice.

"Sorry. I guess my statement did sound like a mother talking to her kids. Anyway. Be careful." *I'll probably be an overprotective mother if I have kids.* Janet removed an LED penlight from her blazer, then slowly shuffled along the wooden floor, shining the beam of light to the left and right along the ceiling joists, waiting for the glowing eyes of bats staring back at her. When she was about twenty feet from the wall vent, she shone the light above her at a light fixture with a broken off light bulb. *Someone must've sheared the bulb off with their head.* She shone the light in front of her feet. The glass of a broken lightbulb lay on the floor. "Careful, there's glass from a lightbulb on the floor." She stepped around the glass, continuing the search for the bats. She stopped. "Quiet, everyone. I hear something." A soft rustling noise emanated to her right between two joists a few feet ahead of her. She slid her feet forward as her heart rate increased and her breathing became deeper. The beam of light moved down to the space between two joists until it met eight small piercing eyes staring back at her. "I found them."

Simon, who stood behind Janet also had a penlight. He directed the brilliant narrow beam of light onto the floor below the area of the bats. "There's the bat poop. We'll need to get a sample of it."

"I have a specimen bag," Jean said. "I'll be easy for me to get since I'm the short one of our group." She walked over and scooped the bat guano into the bag.

Janet shone her light on the gaping area around the broken vent. "The bats obviously came and went through this gap. I'm assuming Emmett Tillman or someone else had struck the lightbulb recently or in the past with something breaking it. They might not have known bats were living in their attic, since there aren't any boxes or junk on the floor in this end of the attic. When we go back downstairs, I'll ask their son."

Jean zipped up the plastic bag. "Maybe we should capture one of the bats and have it analyzed for any diseases or contaminates?"

"You know, that sounds like a great idea, "Simon answered. "I wouldn't want any of us bitten. We know bats can carry rabies and other harmful viruses and organisms. Plus, we haven't determined if the bats are the cause of these deaths. We should wait until the lab results of the bat guano are in before deciding to capture and analyze the bats. If we decide to grab a bat, we'll have professionals capture one or more of them."

Janet agreed with Simon to play on the side of precaution. They left the small colony of bats, closed the attic door, removed their protective masks and gave them to Frank. They then went back downstairs. Mr. and Mrs. Tillman were gone from the hallway. The medical examiner's assistant already transported them to his van. Jean gave the guano sample to a CSU investigator as he was leaving. Afterward, she and Frank left and headed back to the hotel.

Janet, Simon and Steward went into the kitchen to talk with the Tillmans' son. The son appeared to be in his late twenties. He sat at the kitchen table talking on his cellphone. Janet stood in front of him.

He peered up at her. "Do you need to talk with me?"

She could see redness throughout the whites of his eyes, likely from crying. "Yes. I'll only take a moment."

He told the person on the phone that he had to go and hung up.

Janet sat down at the table, as did Simon and Steward. "I'm sorry for loss of your parents. I'm Agent Bennett and this is Agent Woods. We're from a branch of CDC investigating your parents' deaths along with Detective Spurrier."

"CDC? They investigate diseases. Did my parents die from a disease?"

"We don't know yet. What I want to know is did your parents ever complain of visual problems, headaches or any other physical ailments in the past few weeks?"

"No." He then stared down at the table, furling his eyebrows. "Wait a minute. Two days ago, my Mom did mention something about they may have to see an eye doctor. She didn't say what the problem was."

"Any history of seizures or epilepsy?"

"No. My parents are in good health."

"My last question. Did your parents ever mention they had bats in the attic?"

"Bats? No. Oh, my God. They started cleaning out the attic two days ago. Do you think the bats caused their deaths?"

"We're not sure."

She leaned back, glanced over the grieving son's right shoulder at a wall hanging sign. The sign read, "Kitchen Help Wanted." *Mrs. Tillman had a sense of humor*. "So, don't go into the attic. We should have some answers soon."

Janet, Simon and Steward walked out of the house and stood next to Detective Spurrier's car. The medical examiner's and CSU van were gone.

Janet felt frustrated not having any definitive cause of death for the Tillmans or the nine cavers. "How many more people are going to die before the cause is found?"

"I gave the situation with the bats more thought," Simon said. "If the bats are somehow directly or indirectly involved with these deaths, we should capture the bats in the attic and have them autopsied. Plus have the opening in the attic's air vent fixed so no other bats can get inside."

Janet and Steward both agreed. They went back into the house and talked with the Tillmans' son. He also believed it was a good idea to get rid of the bats.

Detective Spurrier called an exterminator company. They agreed to come out right away. Steward then called CSU and told them about the bats. They would send an investigator to the house to take the bats for analysis at the CSU lab. He then asked them, "Any information back on the bat guano? I'll wait."

He turned to Simon. "They'd completed the analysis on the first cave's bat guano specimen. He went to get the report."

"Great, maybe we'll finally get an answer to the deaths of the cave explorers." The three of them walked out of the house and stood on the front porch.

"I'll put my phone on speaker," Steward suggested, as he pushed the speaker icon.

A moment later, a male voice stated from Steward's phone, "I now have the lab results in front of me."

Chapter Eleven

"Please read the lab report. I have two agents here with me from Federal Medical Investigators, a division of CDC. One of them is a medical doctor. I'm sure Dr. Woods will understand any medical terminology used in the laboratory report."

"Let's see. Analysis of bat guano. The bat is an insectivore since insect remains were found in the guano. The sample has ten percent nitrogen, three percent phosphorus, and one percent potash. No *Histoplasma capsulatum* fungus or spores. Bat mites present." A pause, then, "Interesting. There's a trace of cyanide."

"Is that unusual?" Simon asked.

"Yes. As you probably already know, different types of cyanide can be found in water, soil, fruits and vegetation. I've never heard of cyanide being in bat guano. It would be helpful if we could get a bat to analyze for the presents of cyanide, besides checking for rabies and other harmful pathogens."

"We're in the process of capturing the bats in their attic roost. We'll be sending them to you today."

"Great. I'll let our supervisor know. The other bat guano from the second cave should be done early tomorrow morning."

"We appreciate the results," Steward said. "Talk to you soon. Bye." He returned the cellphone to his pocket.

Simon wasn't surprised cyanide was found in the bat droppings, since Frank had smelled the odor of almonds in the two caves and the attic. There was also a trace of cyanide in the nine victims, not enough to kill a person. More than likely the medical examiner would find traces of cyanide in the Tillmans' lab results. "The central theme of these deaths seems to be cyanide, seizures, visual disturbances and the presence of bats. The suspicious activity of Brighton Research may or may not have anything to do with these mysterious deaths. As for the deliberate explosion at the first cave, I believe whoever the perp was wanted our investigation stopped. There maybe was a vendetta against one of us or all of us for something not related to the cave explorers' deaths."

Janet grinned as she put her hands on her hips. "I'd say you summarized our investigation perfectly."

"I'll second that," Steward added, glancing down at Janet. "I need to be present when the pest control guys get here. You and Simon can leave if you want to. I'll let the exterminators and CSU know they'll have to wear protective masks against any floating particles in the attic."

"That'll be great, Steward." There wasn't anything he and Janet could do at the house anyway. "Thanks."

He looked at Janet. "Did you want to stay?"

"No. Not at all." She reached out and briefly touched Steward's forearm. "Detective Spurrier is quite capable of handling the logistics."

Steward chuckled, as he glanced down at his forearm. "Thanks for your confidence in me."

Simon noticed her hand on Steward's forearm. A sudden sinking feeling overwhelmed his stomach as a surge of heat flashed on his face. *My God. Why did I react like a jealous husband or lover? I'm neither of those.* "We'll talk to you later, Steward. Thanks again."

"I'll call you as soon as I get information from the CSU lab on the bats."

"Appreciate it."

Detective Spurrier went back into the house. Simon and Janet went to their car and got in. "I was thinking about your summation on the porch about everything that's happened in the past few days." She glanced at the house as Simon pulled away from the curb and headed back to the hotel. "The presence of cyanide is the key to unlock the cause of these mysterious deaths. When we get back to the hotel, we should all put our heads together and figure out its role in all these deaths."

"Good idea. The cyanide is definitely connected to these deaths." Simon approached a traffic light intersection. The light was green for him, but he slowed down anyway and quickly looked to his left then right. The cars had stopped for their red light. He wasn't going to assume anymore regarding the right of way at traffic light intersections.

"I've been noticing you've been slowing down at intersections when you had the right of way. I don't blame you after what we've been through lately."

"It's better to be safe than sorry...or dead."

~ * ~

Simon knocked on Danny's hotel room door.

Frank opened the door. "Hey. Enter the room of D.C.W."

Simon frowned. "D.C.W. What's that?"

"The initials stand for Danny's Computer Wizardry. D.C.W is his new hashtag name on the computer web sites."

"What's your hashtag?" Janet asked as she and Simon walked into the room.

"Glowworm. Don't ask me how I came up with that hashtag name."

Jean was standing by the coffeemaker, pouring herself a cup of coffee. Danny sat at the desk staring at the computer monitor, as his fingers rapidly glided over the keyboard. Two large, cardboard soda containers, hamburger wrappings and empty French fry containers sat on the square lunch table by the window. Simon told everyone about their decision to capture the bats and have them analyzed by the CSU lab. He looked at his watch. It was almost three-thirty.

"Janet suggested on the way back to the hotel that we need to pool all our ideas, thoughts and theories on the eleven deaths. We're missing something or we need a new angle about these deaths."

Danny turned around in his swivel chair. "I've been researching about cyanide in its many forms and uses."

"So, what did you find out?" Simon asked as he stepped backward and sat at the end of the queen-size bed.

Jean and Janet sat down on chairs at the lunch table. Frank stood to the right of Simon with his arms crossed in front of him.

"There are five types of cyanide used in daily life. Pest control, mining, industry and interstellar. The fifth use of cyanide I found amazing is its use in the medical field as a compound to increase blood pressure, and cyanide's use in vascular research as a vasodilator. Also, cyanide can be found in vitamin B12 to control blood cells. I'll print out all five types if you want to read about the other four uses of cyanide. What probably astonished me more than anything else about cyanide was its natural prevalence in nature and all the different manmade use of this potentially dangerous compound."

"I never realized we were dealing with such a common compound," Janet stated. "Cyanide isn't a needle in a haystack but the haystack itself."

"The good news about my research is only sodium cyanide and hydrogen cyanide have the bitter almond-like scent that Frank smelled in the caves and the attic. Sodium cyanide is soluble in water and has an affinity with metals. Mostly used for mining industry, especially gold mining. When sodium cyanide reacts with an acid, it'll form hydrogen cyanide which makes sodium cyanide salt, a highly toxic compound, which can be used as a chemical weapon. Hydrogen cyanide is often used to kill rabbits, rodents, and some predators. Hydrogen cyanide can be used to fumigate buildings and ships. This form of cyanide will obstruct the respiratory system by decreasing oxygen consumption."

Simon knew of the medical use of cyanide and some of its other uses, but not to the extent researched by Danny. "You did thorough research, narrowing our investigation to those two types of cyanide. All we have to do now is find out how one of these two cyanides got into the caves and attic."

Janet reached down and scratched the side of her right thigh, then said, "I'd say the bats are culprits who brought the cyanide to their roosts. When CSU does necropsies on the bats, it should confirm this assumption."

Everyone agreed with Janet's theory. Danny appeared puzzled. "Necropsies are done by veterinarians, not pathologists."

"True," Simon said. "Most medical examiner offices have veterinarians on call for CSU facilities to perform necropsies on animals."

"During my years as a detective, animals can be a key factor in a murder or death investigation," Janet said. "They can even do DNA on animals and plants to determine if they were part of a crime scene."

Frank uncrossed his arms. "Plants and animals both contain DNA, which resembles a double helix or described as a twisted latter. Their DNA molecules are made from the same four chemical building blocks as in humans called nucleotides. That's my last educational lesson for the day."

Danny rubbed his lower lip with his upper teeth. "I love these science lessons."

Simon held back a chuckle. He then cleared his throat. "I'm proud how everyone is contributing information to these deaths. At the rate we're going, I believe we'll have an answer to how these victims died and who's responsible."

Simon knew he didn't want to be overconfident about solving these deaths, but a little positive pep talk would build team morale.

"I sure hope so," Frank said as he wiped the palms of his hands down his face. "I'm tired of looking at bat shit."

"Aren't we all," Jean added.

Simon's cellphone rang. He looked at the caller ID. It was Phillip Pearson, medical examiner for Wayne County in Michigan. He got up from the end of the bed and walked to the other end of the room by the front door. "Phillip. What do I have the pleasure of this call for?"

"Hi, Simon. Just touching base with you. I really enjoyed your visit here in Detroit. I was going through some of my old records when you were here doing your pathology rotation with me. I forgot about the time I had you make the 'Y' incision during an autopsy and you went too deep cutting the distended bowel. Feces exploded from the opening, covering us with the foulest odor known to man."

"I remember the event now. I think we both unconsciously suppressed the incident when we were together and reminiscing about my rotation with you at the restaurant in Detroit."

"I'm sure that's probably what it was." A momentary pause. "How are you doing on your newest investigation?"

Simon couldn't say much to him over the phone for at least two reasons. Someone could be listening and recording their conversation, be it the people or group responsible for the seizure deaths and/or the explosion at the cave. The second possible reason, The Circle was listening in on their conversation. He wasn't going to mention on the phone to Phillip what they found or speculated.

"We're in Pennsylvania investigating some deaths. Can't give you any more information since it's an ongoing case."

"Hum. A real medical mystery. Like I said when you were here in Detroit, I envy your position with FMI. You take care."

"It was good hearing from you again. Thanks for the call. Have a great day."

Simon put his phone away, turned around and joined everyone at the other end of the room. During his call with Phillip, he knew all the FMI agents' eyes were on him without a word spoken between them as they listened to his conversation. They were now talking to each other, as if he had stepped out of the room and returned. In a higher than normal voice, he orated, "I suppose you'd want to know why Dr. Pearson called me?"

Everyone stopped talking and looked at him. Each of them displayed a grin. Janet answered, "Yes. He was part of our investigation in the Whispers Before Death Case. We thought maybe he had some new information regarding the case."

"No. It was a social call."

He wasn't going to tell them what Phillip stated about the incident with the flying feces. Some things in the past need to stay there.

"How's he doing?" Janet asked.

"Fine." Simon walked over and stood next to Danny. "Did you by chance check out the blue circle with a red infinity symbol and two lightning bolts in the center?"

"Dang. Sorry. I completely forgot. I got distracted by another project, then you called regarding the Tillmans." He looked at Janet. "I guess I'll no longer get the big bucks."

Simon frowned. "Not sure what you meant by your last statement."

"It's something between Janet and me." He turned around to his computer and began typing. In less than a minute, Danny asked, "Is this what you saw?"

Simon stared at the monitor, as did everyone else. They formed a half circle behind Danny. "That's it. That's exactly what I saw in Robert Rhode's personnel file at Brighton Research." The monitor displayed a red infinity symbol and two lightning bolts against a white background inside a blue thick-lined circle. The initials E.O.Z. was below the infinity symbol. Underneath the symbol it read, *The logo represents the Eternal Order of Zeus. According to Greek mythology, Zeus is the Olympian god of the sky and the thunder. He's the king of all other gods of Mount Olympus and men. E.O.Z. is an organization dedicated to the preservation of world tranquility. Founded in two thousand and fifteen by Adam Fletcher, an entrepreneur from Camp Hill, Pennsylvania. Membership by invitation. No other information available.*

"Why would this be in his personnel file?"

"I can guess," Danny answered. "Today's employers search the social media for derogatory posts, offensive comments and deplorable organizations. I'll check the social media sites for any comments regarding Fletcher's organization."

Danny did his wizardry as his fingers flashed over the keyboard and the monitor blinked numerous panels of information and sites. In less than a minute, the screen displayed eight rectangular boxes. "As you can see, I don't have any chat information about the Eternal Order of Zeus. It's as if it doesn't exist. A clandestine entity under the social media world. The IRS labels E.O.Z as a non-profit organization."

Simon didn't think there was any relevance of this organization to their investigation of the eleven deaths facing them. He was hoping E.O.Z. somehow was affiliated with The Circle. One more thing they could do. "I think Janet and I are going to talk with Adam Fletcher. There's a question puzzling me. Why would Robert Rhode tell Brighton Research about being a member of an apparent clandestine organization? This organization still might have some relevance to our investigation. Otherwise, it'll be another dead end in our search for the truth regarding the mysterious deaths and the cave explosion." Simon touched Danny's shoulder. "Is there a phone number and address for E.O.Z. and Adam Fletcher?"

"Let's see if there is." Several seconds passed as his fingers sped over the keyboard. "There it is. I'll print it out or I can transfer the information to your iPhone."

"Do both." A moment later, Simon removed the printout, then called Fletcher's phone number.

A man answered, "Adam Fletcher. Can I help you?"

"This is Simon Woods from CDC. We're investigating the death of one of your members, Robert Rhode. We'd like to talk with you."

A short pause. "What do you what to know about Robert Rhode?" His question sounded defensive to Simon.

"We'd like to talk with you in person. It's not our policy to interview a person over the phone. A lot of our medical questioning infringes upon the HIPPA law of patient confidentiality."

"I don't want us to get into trouble," Fletcher said.

Simon knew the statement wasn't necessarily accurate regarding what he wanted to discuss with Adam Fletcher. Since he seemed reluctant to talk with them, introducing this tactic under these circumstances seemed necessary.

"I see. We can talk at my home in Carlisle?"

"Yes. That would be fine." Simon covered the phone with his hand and whispered to Danny, "How far away is Carlisle?" He removed his hand from the front of the phone. "Your house will be fine. We look forward in meeting you. I'll be bringing one of my agents with me, Agent Bennett."

Danny whispered, "Thirty-six minutes."

"We'll be at your house in about forty-five minutes. If that'll be all right with you, Mr. Fletcher?"

"Yes. Do you have my home address?"

"We do." Simon gave him the address.

Fletcher confirmed the address, then hung up.

Simon glanced at his watch. "It's nearing dinner time. Why don't you guys go eat? Janet and I will grab something on the way to Adam Fletcher's house."

They stopped at a fast food restaurant. While they waited in the drive-through lane, Janet put Fletcher's address into the GPS. As they got their food and were leaving the restaurant, Janet declared, "You know, Simon, this is becoming a regular thing for us, stopping at these fast food restaurants. God knows how many calories and how much saturated fats and salt we're consuming."

"You're still looking good and fat. I mean fit."

She frowned as she glanced down at her hips. "You mean I'm looking fat? You may want to find a slimmer partner instead of a fat one."

A flushing sensation overwhelmed him. "I...I didn't mean to say..."

"Simon. Just joking. I know it was just a slip of the tongue."

Damn. Why do I keep falling in her trap of words? You'd think I'd be used to it by now? He stuffed a couple of French fries into his mouth.

Janet smirked, then took a sip of her soda through a straw.

Simon merged onto I-81 and headed north to Carlisle. The traffic was light. Thirty minutes later, the GPS's made its last announcement. "You have arrived at your destination on the right." They had driven through numerous estate-type mansions on five-acre plots.

Simon turned right onto a driveway. In front of them stood a closed security gate with a communication box and security camera on the left. An eight-foot black iron fence encompassed the property. He was about to push the talk button when a man with a deep voice said through the intercom, "Agent Woods, please drive in and park in front of my house." The gate opened.

A three-story house in the Tudor style resembling a small castle stood majestically at the end of the fifty-yard concrete driveway. The driveway made a circle in front of the house with a fountain in the center. Water spurted out of the mouths of two water maidens in the middle of a manmade circular pond. Simon scanned the house and grounds. "I'd say Adam Fletcher's not doing too bad as an entrepreneur and founder of Eternal Order of Zeus."

"I'm waiting for two Doberman Pinschers to rush up to the car once we stop and a six-foot four man in gray shorts and a baseball cap walks out of the front door of the house."

Simon frowned then chuckled realizing what she meant by her descriptive scenario. She had an imagination. They stopped in front of the house. Simon got out of the car, as did Janet. He quickly looked around. "No dogs."

Janet raised her eyebrows and rolled her eyes. Simon then saw an expression of doom across her face. She said, "I have a bad feeling about what or who's behind the front door. A voice in my head told me, 'truth is a lie.'"

The front door slowly opened.

Chapter Twelve

The front door opened. A white-haired man in his early sixties, about six-foot tall of medium build stood in front of Simon and Janet. He wasn't wearing shorts and a baseball cap; instead, he sported tan slacks, a light-blue button-down shirt and oxford shoes. He was clean shaven. "I'm Adam Fletcher. Please come in."

Simon and Janet sat on a living room couch across from Fletcher, who sat in a cushioned armchair across from them. Both the couch and chair were of Victorian-style and obviously not bought in a bargain basement sale, Simon thought, as he peered around the elaborately furnished living room.

"Did you know Robert Rhode died before I talked to you on the phone earlier?"

When he told Fletcher on the phone about Robert's death, the entrepreneur didn't seem to be surprised, didn't ask how or when one his members died. He could've read about his death in the newspaper or heard about the cavers' death on TV or the radio. Even then, there wasn't any mention of how the cave explorers died. You'd think one of the first things Fletcher would've asked him on the phone earlier would've been, "Did you find out how they died?"

"Of course. It was in all the newspapers and on the local TV news stations. If CDC is involved with these deaths, you must think Robert along with his friends died from something they were exposed to, such as something they ate or drank?"

Who's doing this interview…me or Fletcher? "Like I said, Mr. Fletcher, it's still under investigation. We don't have all the answers yet."

"So, you want to know about Robert." He glanced down at the

carpeted floor, then looked into Simon's eyes. "Robert joined our organization about a year ago. He was a respected member and we're going to miss him."

Janet said, "Did he ever mention about someone in a negative manner, someone that wanted to do him harm?"

"No. Not to my knowledge."

"Did he talk about any health problems?"

"Like, did he have visual problems or seizures?"

Simon's heart rate increased. He felt every breath as the depth of his breathing increased. There never was any mention of seizures or visual disturbances with any of the cavers in the newspapers. The TV news media didn't have this information. How did Adam Fletcher know about these medical manifestations? He glanced at Janet, not sure if she realized the significance of what Fletcher said. She hadn't changed her unemotional expression. If she did realize it, she hid her emotions extremely well.

Janet scooted forward a few inches on the couch. "Yes. Did he ever mention those two things?"

"No. He never complained about any medical issues. Matter of fact, there was a meeting with all the members two days before he went cave exploring with his friends. He talked about his cave exploration experiences and how much he enjoyed it."

"Do you know anything about The Circle?"

Simon saw a slight twitch at the corner of Fletcher's right eye after Janet's question. Simon hadn't noticed any tic gestures during their entire conversation until now. Was the twitch a reaction to the name The Circle, a name the entrepreneur already knew?

Fletcher answered, "No. I never heard of The Circle. Why did you ask me if I knew this corporation?"

"It's a name that's come up in our investigation."

"Oh," Fletcher said with another right eyelid tic.

Simon got up from the couch, followed by Janet. "We appreciate your time in answering our questions."

"I'm glad I could help. We're going to miss Robert."

He escorted them to the front door.

Simon peered through the driver's side mirror at Fletcher standing at the front door. A chill engulfed him. The front gate opened when the Suburban was several yards away.

Janet grunted, then said, "Fletcher was lying. Besides that, how did he know The Circle was a corporation?"

"I agree. We didn't tell him it was a corporation. The Circle could be a fraternity, a society or an association. Plus, did you notice his tic?"

"You mean when his right eyelid twitched?"

"Yes."

"I saw the eye twitch when I mentioned The Circle to him and right after that."

"There was something else." Simon stopped for a traffic light then looked at Janet. "How did he know the cave explorers had seizures and were having eye problems? There wasn't any mention of seizures by the sheriff's department to the newspaper and TV reporters according to Detective Spurrier. As far as some of the cavers having eye problems, we discovered this information in our investigation and didn't tell anyone. So, how did Adam Fletcher know about these two things? Your premonition feeling and your inner voice telling you 'truth is a lie' depicted Fletcher's answers. He was concealing the truth in his lies."

"I know I've said this before. I think it was in Ocala during our investigation: 'there are a lot of pieces in this puzzle.' And I'm not talking about two different cases. It may be one large puzzle we're dealing with regarding all these deaths."

"I agree with your puzzle analogy. We need to find solid evidence in determining what or who's responsible for these deaths here in Pennsylvania. I really think the bat guano is the source for all these people dying. The guano seems to be the common link to these undetermined deaths. We now have a deceptive chemical company and the leader of a clandestine organization who may be involved with these unexplained deaths. As they say in numerous murder mystery novels, 'the plot thickens.' Call Frank and let him know we're on our way back to the hotel." Simon pulled onto southbound I-81.

Janet called Frank and told him what they found out during their interview with the head of the Eternal Order of Zeus. "We'll be at the hotel in about thirty minutes." A short pause, as she listened to Danny. "I'm going to put you on speakerphone, so Simon can hear what you have to say."

"Hi, you guys. I did a different type of search on Robert Rhode and Susan Whitman trying to link them together. Like if they were boyfriend and girlfriend. Anyway, I hit the jackpot. I checked their credit card uses over the past few months. It seems they were meeting at various locations such as restaurants, community parks, Hershey Park and tourist caves. At least their credit cards put them there on the same day and around the same time."

A prickling sensation electrified the hairs on his arms and the back of his neck. "So, they did associate with each other. I wonder if it was a romantic relationship or something else."

"Something else?" Danny questioned.

"We know the human resource woman at Brighton Research was hiding something about the company. Robert and Susan may have been collaborating with each other as potential whistle blowers. When we interviewed their parents, neither mentioned any relationship between Robert and Susan. It's a gut feeling I have about the two of them."

Janet said, "That's a big jump from Brighton Research changing security and décor protocol to them doing something illegal. I obviously believe in a gut feeling, but this is more in the realm of a revolutionary thought."

"May I make a suggestion?" Danny asked. "Let me pretend I'm a Franklin County Building Inspector. My reason for me being there will be to check the electrical and computer wiring from the annex to the main Brighton Research building. It'll get me into the new addition. Once inside, I'll get access to Brighton's computer mainframe. I can also try to find out if there's any illegal activity going on. What do you think about my idea?"

Simon liked Danny's proposal. It would be the first time an FMI agent would go undercover. There's always a first for everything. "I think it's a good idea. I'll have to clear it with Director Littlefield. I'll have an answer before we get back to the hotel."

Janet disconnected the call. "I like the idea. It'll be like when law enforcement goes undercover. Knowing Danny, I'm sure it'll only take him a day or two to obtain the information we'd need."

"Don't put your phone away. Can you call the director for me? Put him on speakerphone."

"Sure." Janet dialed his number.

The phone rang twice. "This is Agent Bennett. Simon wants to talk with you."

"Director Littlefield, I'm here with Janet. We have you on speakerphone. We have a proposal for you."

Simon went into detail what had transpired today during their interviews. A few minutes later, he told him about Danny's stealthy plan of going undercover.

"I like the plan," agreed the director. "It sounds like Danny Emerick was a wise decision to invite to join FMI."

"Yes, sir. He's been a tremendous asset to the team."

"Keep me informed."

~ * ~

The sun was low in the western horizon as early twilight began drawing its blanket over the mountain range and Franklin valley.

Simon and Janet walked into Danny's room. Frank and Jean were present, sitting at the kitchenette table. Danny sat in front of his laptops. The odor of pizza hung in the room. Simon glanced down to his right at the trash container overflowing with two pizza boxes. Danny turned toward them. "What's the verdict?"

"Director Littlefield agreed to your idea."

"Great. I already did the preliminary work. I'll show up tomorrow morning for an inspection. I downloaded an email and text message to the general contractor and Brighton Research regarding the inspection."

"What if Director Littlefield denied the idea?" Simon now stood in front of the desk and Danny.

"I would've notified Brighton Research the inspection had to be cancelled and would be scheduled in the near future." Danny glanced to his right at Frank. "Although, after talking with Frank, I felt his brother would accept our proposal."

"How are you going to get identification showing you're a Franklin County building inspector?"

"I'll talk with a person who has the capability to obtain false ID. It'll be in my hands before I leave for Brighton Research tomorrow morning. I'll also have a magnetic building inspector sign and a Franklin County license plate for my van."

"You…computer guys are out of my league. I'm capable of online purchasing, nothing more complicated. What happens if the contractor or Brighton find out you're not an inspector?"

"I go to Plan B."

"What's Plan B?"

Danny raised his eyebrows, distorted his lips, then said, "Still working on it. Although, I don't plan on getting caught."

Simon rubbed his forehead with the palmar surface of his right-hand fingertips while squinting in a gesture of uncertainty. His cellphone rang. The LED spelled out the word "Spurrier." "It's Steward. Hopefully, it's about the bats?" He put the phone on speakerphone. "Hi, Steward."

"Simon. The bats have been removed from the attic and taken to the CSU lab for analysis. A veterinarian will do a necropsy on them tomorrow morning. Also, the opening in the attic air vent was closed. No little flying creatures will take up residence in the attic now. How's it going with you and your team?"

Simon couldn't tell him about their suspicion about Adam Fletcher or about how one of the FMI agents was going to impersonate a county inspector to snoop around the workings of Brighton Research. "Nothing pointing toward a cause of these deaths, yet. Hopefully, the bats will give us some information."

"We need a break in this case. Talk to you tomorrow. Have a good night."

Simon put his cellphone back into his pocket. He glanced at everyone. "Let's call it a night."

"Not before we celebrate someone's birthday," Frank declared as he stared at Janet. "You probably thought we didn't know today was your birthday, Agent Janet Bennett. We thought about baking you a cake.

Since we don't have access to an oven…or the fact none of us are skilled at baking, we did the second best."

Jean walked over to a small refrigerator and removed a paper plate containing five cupcakes with a candle in the center of one of them as Frank made his announcement. "Everyone, please grab one of the cupcakes. The one with a candle is Janet's."

Janet appeared surprised as she briefly bowed her head, then said, "You guys didn't have to do this. I was hoping no one knew today was my birthday. Birthdays are just another year added on to my age."

Danny stood and handed Janet a small gift-wrapped box. "Happy birthday."

Janet removed the wrapping and lifted off the lid to the box. A smile spread across her face. "Thanks." She removed a silver FMI badge with "Agent J. Bennett" inscribed in gold lettering at the bottom.

"Now, you don't have to flash a generic FMI badge with no name on it," Frank said. He reached out and lit Janet's candle with a lighter. "We decided not to sing Happy Birthday. Although, you still have to make a wish and blow out the candle."

Janet picked up her cupcake, inhaled as much air as she could and blew out the candle. She glanced at Simon. "Great ending to another exhilarating day as an FMI agent."

"I'll eat to that," Frank said, picking up his cupcake, devouring it in two bites.

Simon stared at Janet, as she conversed with Frank, Danny and Jean. Periodically she glanced in his direction. *I wonder what she wished?"*

Jean shouted, "You have a yellow glow." Her previous expression of jubilation changed to one of doom as she stared at Janet.

The room's joyous atmosphere was replaced with shock and disbelief.

A cold wave of fear spread throughout Simon's body and mind. *My God. This can't happen.* He walked over to Janet and placed his hand on her shoulder. "I'll…we'll make sure nothing happens to you in the next twenty-four hours. I survived the yellow glow. I'm sure you will, too."

Janet peered into Simon's eyes. "I'm not afraid. We've been through some dangerous and death-defying situations since I've been with you guys. Thank God we survived every one of them. This is just another situation in our repertoire. I'll make sure I wear a bulletproof vest when I leave the hotel."

"Not knowing what exactly we'll be doing tomorrow will make it difficult to anticipate a dangerous encounter. I can have you stay in the hotel with Danny for the next twenty-four hours."

Janet put her hands on her hips and slightly leaned to the right in a defiant pose. "You didn't go into hiding when Jean saw your glow."

"True." *She's one person you don't want to intimidate.* "I'll be sure to watch your back the next twenty-four hours."

~ * ~

Janet walked over to the drapes covering her window and pulled them back. The morning sunlight burst through the sheer inside curtains, causing her to squint. Water dripped down from her hair onto her forehead. She hadn't completely blow-dried her hair after taking a shower. She turned around and removed a bulletproof vest off the back of a chair. Janet put it on, followed by her holster, then the Glock.

She finally put her blazer on. The clock on the nightstand displayed seven forty-five a.m. She had eleven hours and ten minutes before her twenty-four hours ended. She didn't die in her sleep, no one broke down her hotel room door and emptied bullets into her body. A meteorite or a small plane didn't crash into her room. No other deadly scenario occurred. The FMI team was supposed to meet in the restaurant around eight o'clock. There was a knock on her door. *It's probably Simon or one of the other agents*, she thought. She peered through the peephole. It was Simon. She opened the door.

He stood in the hallway with a stoic expression on a cleanshaven face. "Ready to go down for breakfast?"

"I am."

"I bet you had your gun ready to use on your nightstand last night."

"True. I always have my Glock with the safety off next to me when I go to bed. A single woman can never be too safe."

Simon leaned back, as he stood in the open doorway. "I know now not to suddenly wake you up from a sleeping state when I'm standing near you. I might get a bullet between my eyes."

Janet grinned. "You never know what may happen." *Of course, that would mean you had stayed the night with me.* A warm and pleasant sensation touched her skin.

The rest of the FMI team were already sitting at their table in the far corner of the restaurant. The waitress was placing two coffee carafes on the table, one for regular and the other for decaf. There were several other patrons scattered throughout the room. "I'll be back to get your orders."

~ * ~

Unbeknown to the FMI agents, a couple in their early thirties, who had been stealthily positioned at both cave sites, sat at a table about twenty feet away. Between the man and woman, sitting on the table, was a rectangular object the size of pack of cigarettes with a small, circular opening at one end pointing at FMI's table. A tiny green light glowed at the other end of the device.

~ * ~

Janet looked at Jean, who pursed her lips and nodded, confirming she still possessed the yellow glow. "The good news, I'm still here. The night reaper didn't visit me last night." Janet sat down next to Jean, and Simon sat on the other side of Janet.

No one laughed.

"We were just talking about you," Frank said, looking at Janet with a serious expression.

"Huh. No wonder my ears were ringing before walking into the restaurant." Again, no one laughed. "You guys are acting like I'm going to die today."

"We're going to make sure that doesn't happen to you. Anywhere we go today at least three of us are going to be with you until your twenty-four hours ends. I talked with Simon earlier and he thought it was a good idea."

Janet felt a tear forming in the corner of her right eye. "Thanks, you guys." She reached up and caught the tear with her finger.

She then turned to Simon. "What's on our agenda today?"

"That's what we need to discuss." He poured a cup of coffee, adding a teaspoon of sugar and a little cream. After taking a sip, he set his cup down. "We should be hearing from CSU regarding the second cave's guano this morning. I got a call late last night from Detective Spurrier regarding the bats' necropsies scheduled for nine-thirty this morning. He asked me if I'd like to be present when they cut open the bats. I agreed to be there."

He turned to Janet. "Would you like to see the autopsies?"

"Sure. I've only seen autopsies on humans, not an animal necropsy."

"Danny will check out Brighton Research this morning. You told me if you can get to one of their computers, you'll be able to get into their mainframe. Once you're in, you'd be able to download vital information and send it to the computer in your room."

"Yes. Should be a piece of cake, once I get access to one of their computers."

Simon turned his attention to Frank. "I want you to stay in the hotel room so you can receive the information on Danny's computer from him about Brighton Research."

"As for you, Jean, would you like to see a bat necropsy?"

"Sounds good to me. I've never seen one done before."

She looked at Janet and patted her forearm. "I'll also be able to see if Janet's glow goes away. Plus, I'll be able to keep an eye on her for any potential danger, along with Simon."

Janet turned, looked at Jean and touched the top of her hand. "Thanks."

A feeling of contentment and comradery toward Jean, along with the rest of the agents, sealed her commitment to the FMI team's purpose of solving challenging mysterious medical deaths.

She thought of Bill Matters, her ex-partner, lying in a coma. She hadn't heard any recent news about his condition, which could be good. Meaning he hadn't died, or that some devastating medical entity hadn't invaded his body.

They ate their breakfast. Their conversations didn't include any rehash of the last two days' events. They talked about sports, political and world news, avoiding mention of the eleven mysterious deaths.

~ * ~

The couple in the far table sat unemotional, periodically glancing at the FMI agents. The device on their table still pointed in the same direction with a green pinpoint light glowing, apparently indicating the device was on.

Chapter Thirteen

Danny pulled his van with a circular décor of Franklin County Code Enforcement on the driver side door up to the front gate of Brighton Research and stopped. He rolled down his window and said, "Good morning. Looks like we're going to have another beautiful morning." He showed the guard his official looking ID.

"I've never seen you here before," said the security guard.

"I was recently hired."

"Oh." He wrote down Danny's alias name, Justin Moore. "You're all set." He handed the I.D. back to Danny. "Do you know how to get to the construction site?"

"Yes. I drive to the left around the main building to the back where the new annex is located." Simon had told him how to get to the annex when he and Janet were here yesterday and had noticed temporary signs directing vehicles to the back of the main building to the new addition.

"You got it. Have a good day."

"You too." Danny rolled up his window and headed for the annex.

The annex was nearing completion and was scheduled to open in a month. All Danny had to do was to find a functioning computer and download what information he could and send it to his computer at the hotel. He had tried to hack into Brighton Research's mainframe from the hotel but couldn't due to an impenetrable firewall. He parked his van near the back entrance to the new building. Danny put on a hardhat, grabbed a leather-like folder and walked to the back door. A security guard stood inside the door. Danny told him who he was and showed him his ID.

"Larry, the security guard at the main gate, called me and said you'd be coming here. Do you need someone to take you around?"

"No. I know where I'm going. Thanks anyway." Danny had obtained the building's layout by hacking into the county planning commission's computer system. He carried the plans inside his folder.

"You have to leave your cellphone or any electronic communicating device such a tablet here with me before you go into the annex."

"I left those things in my van. I already knew the restrictions about communication devices."

The guard passed a metal and electronic detection wand around Danny. No alarm sounded. The odor of freshly painted white walls hung in the air as he walked up a long corridor. Danny opened the folder and glanced down at the building schematics. The computer lines from the main building should be hooked up to the annex computers. All that had to be done was to add a password to a desktop computer and he'd have a functioning pathway to Brighton Research's mainframe.

Footsteps echoed from behind him. He turned around and saw a man in his mid-fifties wearing a hardhat and dressed in casual clothing walking toward him from the direction of the back-door entrance. The man peered a Danny with a smile, then said, "Good morning. I understand you're from the code enforcement office."

"Yes I am."

"The guard at the backdoor told me you were here. I'm Jack Daniels, the general contractor. No. I'm not related to anyone in the distillery business. Most people ask me that question when I first meet them. Anyway, what do you need to inspect today?"

This puts a damper into Danny's plans. Thank God, he reviewed the building codes. "I need to check out the two isolation rooms for negative and positive pressure gradients to start."

"No problem. I'll show you where the rooms are."

"You don't have to. I know where they are."

"Suit yourself. Matter of fact, I do have something else to do. If there's any questions you have ask me, I'll be on the second floor for the next thirty minutes." They walked to the elevator up the hallway and stepped inside.

After Mr. Daniels got off on the second floor, Danny rode the elevator to the third floor. When he got off the elevator, a man stood with his back to Danny, attaching a sign to the wall that read "Authorized Personnel Only." The isolation rooms were to the right according to the schematics.

He glanced into rooms along the hallway, looking for a computer. None were seen. "Why aren't there any computers?" Danny whispered.

In front of him about halfway up the hallway an opened security door stood with a key panel to the right on the wall. *In a month, you'll need an access code to open the door and enter. Simon and Janet were right about the Brighton Research facility. The security level reflected the security level of a military or government building holding highly classified data. Why would a company that specializes in cleaning products want this much security? Simon was right, there's something else going on besides producing and analyzing cleaning products.*

Danny walked through the doorway. A nursing-type station with a counter was to his left. Across from the station stood two isolation rooms. A silent eeriness surrounded him as he stood between the isolation rooms and the nursing station. He was alone. He walked around the counter to another hallway to the left, then through an archway leading into the nursing station. A computer sat on a lower counter to his right. "Please be on," he whispered.

He sat on a swivel chair, then reached over and turned on the computer tower and monitor. The monitor lit up displaying the name Brighton Research. He was in their computer system. His fingers raced across the keyboard, periodically standing up, leaning forward and looking to his right down the hallway from anyone entering the isolation area. He was still alone. The monitor now displayed a series of numbers, words and symbols. "I'm in the mainframe."

Danny opened his folder, removed several papers, and pulled back the bottom covering, revealing a small LED screen and a keyboard. The reason the security guard's wand hadn't gone off was because Danny had invented a covering for his folder capable of deflecting any beams from a metal and electronic scanner. He removed a USB thumb drive from a molded area at the bottom of the folder and plugged the drive into the computer tower. He began downloading the data from the desktop computer and Brighton Research mainframe.

The sound of voices interrupted his concentration. Danny quickly got up from his chair, leaned forward over the top counter and peered down the hallway. It was the general contractor talking with the guy across from the elevator. He sat back down and stared at the horizontal icon on the bottom of the monitor's screen telling him the remaining percentage for completion of the download. The blue horizontal line displayed eighty-two percent completion. The sound of voices seemed to be getting closer. Perspiration appeared on Danny's forehead. How was he going to explain the reason he had turned on Brighton Research's computer? He didn't have a reasonable explanation. Should he remove the thumb drive now before it completed the download? He reached out pinching the thumb drive between his thumb and index finger, ready to remove it at the last moment. His breathing increased as beads of sweat now cascaded down from his forehead onto his cheeks.

"I wonder where the guy from the code enforcement office is?" Mr. Daniels questioned the worker next to him as they walked through the doorway of the security door. They were about thirty feet away from the nursing station.

Danny glanced down at the monitor. Ninety-seven percent glared back at him. The clucking sound of the general contractor's leather-soled shoes momentarily stopped.

"What was his name…oh yeah. Mr. Moore."

The moving horizontal line from right to left stopped. One hundred percent appeared. Danny quickly removed the thumb drive, then turned off the computer and monitor. He placed the thumb drive into the folder, stood and walked out of the nursing station wiping the sweat from his forehead and face with his hand. "I'm here," Danny said, as he walked around the corner of the nursing station and faced the two men, who now stood in front of the isolation rooms, across from the nursing station. He stopped a few feet away from them.

"Did you find the isolation rooms up to code?" Mr. Daniels asked.

"Yes. They comply to state standards."

"Is there anything else you need to inspect?"

"No. That should do it." He was home free, getting away with his stealthy charade.

"Good. I want to show you something and get your expert opinion on a possible change to the original building plans. I don't want to spend the time writing up added changes if the change wouldn't pass code. What I'm talking about is on the second floor. I'll take you there and show you."

"Sure. Glad to." Could he concoct a feasible answer that would be close to the building code?

Danny and Jack Daniels got off the elevator onto the second floor. They walked down a long hallway with research laboratory "clean rooms" to the left and right with glassed-in front walls. Hospital-white walls, white ceilings with florescent lighting along with white tiled floors and white counter tops in different positions highlighted the future research rooms. The rooms needed to be void of contaminates from outside the rooms in order to analyze, test or create an agent, specimen or entity.

Danny had studied the schematics and knew the clean rooms were here. The thumb drive he had hidden in his folder might hold the answer to the rooms' ultimate purpose. They stopped. Daniels opened a solid door to his left and they walked into an eight by eight cubical room. The general contractor next opened another solid door in front of them and walked into a ten by ten square room. Metal lockers lined the wall straight ahead and to their right.

Daniels looked up at the ceiling, then said, "As you probably know, this is the changing room for personnel before entering the decontamination room. The vice president of Brighton Research suggested to me that they'd like an intercom on this wall." He placed his hand on the wall to his left next to the solid white metal door leading into the next room. "What do think? Are there any code restrictions for installing the intercom on this wall, the wall between the changing room and the decontamination room?"

Danny didn't change his stoic expression as he looked up the ceiling then the wall. He had no idea if the intercom could be placed on the wall mentioned, and he didn't want to create any suspicion in the mind of the contractor. "I'd say there shouldn't be any problem installing the intercom on this wall."

Knowing the bureaucracy of government, Danny figured it would take at least a week or two before the planning commission got back with Daniels regarding the proposed changes. He and the FMI team should be long gone by then.

"Great. I'll write the proposed changes and submit the changes to Franklin County Planning Commission."

A man in his late twenties entered the changing room and said, "You're needed at the utility room."

"It was nice meeting you," Danny said as he reached out and shook hands with Daniels.

Danny got into his van, leaned back against his seat and sighed. He then whispered, "Can't believe I actually did it."

He started the van, drove around the building, and headed toward the main gate. The gate opened. The security guard waved for him to stop when he got through the gate. He came around to the driver side window.

Danny's heart felt like it had surged to the back of his throat. Did they find out he wasn't from the code enforcement office and want an explanation? Would the county sheriff department's patrol car soon be pulling up to arrest him? Danny rolled down his window.

"There's something sticking out at the bottom of your front passenger side door."

Danny removed his seatbelt, scooted over to the passenger seat, opened the door and looked down at the floor. The sleeve of a shirt was partially hanging outside the bottom of the door. The sleeve must have got stuck there when Frank got out of the van and closed the door yesterday. He pulled the sleeve back into the van and threw the shirt on the passenger seat. Danny thanked the security guard and drove away.

Danny dialed Simon on his cellphone to let him know the good news.

~ * ~

Simon's cellphone rang. He looked at the caller's name. "It's

Danny."

Janet and Jean stood next to him in the animal necropsy room. Detective Spurrier had left about an hour ago but supposed to return any minute. The room was almost identical to a human autopsy room except this one appeared to be about one-third the size. Dr. Stonebridge, the veterinarian, was running an hour late due to car problems.

"Hey, Danny. I have you on speakerphone. Did everything go all right?"

"Yes. I got into Brighton's computer mainframe and downloaded data on a thumb drive. I couldn't send the data to Frank on my mini-laptop due to being interrupted by the general contractor. Anyway, I just left the facility. On my way back to the hotel. I'm anxious to see what I downloaded. How did the necropsy go on the bats?"

Simon told him what had happen to Dr. Stonebridge. "The three of us will be here a while. I'll call and let you and Frank know when we're done here. Talk to you then."

He put his phone away. The pathologist's assistant, Jacob Pollock, walked into the room carrying a tray of instruments. When they were told the veterinarian would be an hour late, the three of them were taken to the CSU lab at the other end of the building and given a tour of the facility by Jacob. The analysis of the bat guano in the second cave was the same as the first cave's results: traces of cyanide in the bat guano. No other deadly pathogens or substances found in the guano.

Detective Spurrier walked into the necropsy room. "I saw Dr. Stonebridge and he'll be here in a few minutes. How did you like our CSU facility?"

"Very impressed," Janet answered. "I'd say if someone committed a crime in Franklin County, the CSU criminalist only needs trace evidence to identify the perp. The technology they utilize is at the top of the chart in forensic science."

A short-statured man in his late fifties walked into the necropsy room wearing blue scrubs and a surgical cap. "Sorry to keep everyone waiting."

Everyone replied with either no problem, that's okay or we understand.

Detective Spurrier said, "Jacob gave them a tour of the CSU facility."

"Great."

He looked across the room toward his assistant. "Jacob. I'm ready for our first bat."

His assistant brought over a small plexiglass container containing a bat and set it down at the end of a long metal necropsy table in the middle of the room. "Did you turn on your recorder?"

"No. Thanks for reminding me."

He reached down and turned on a recorder the size of a cellphone attached to a waist belt. He said the day's date, then, "This is Dr. Stanley Stonebridge doing a necropsy on bat One-A. Case number 447. STOP."

The recorder paused upon this command. He turned his attention to his spectators. "We put each of the six bats into one of these containers yesterday evening when Detective Spurrier brought them in. As you see there's a circular opening covered with a metal screen door at the side which allow air to flow inside and for us to easily reach inside and grab the bat or whatever other small creature scheduled for a necropsy."

The bat huddled into the far corner as Jacob, wearing protective gloves, opened the screen door, reached in and grabbed the bat where it was huddled in the far corner of the container. The bat didn't make a sound as he removed it from the cage. He brought the bat to the center of the table. The table was about six feet long with two small openings two feet from each end to allow fluid and blood to drain through into a reservoir in the center of the table.

Stanley slipped on blue latex surgical gloves, then stepped up onto a two-foot square metal lift about nine to ten inches high. A surgical movable light hung over the necropsy table. He reached up and directed the light at the bat held by Jacob. Stonebridge then picked up a syringe. "CONTINUE. I'm injecting the bat with potassium chloride. STOP."

"This will stop the bat's heart. It won't suffer at all." In less than ten seconds, Jacob released his grip on the bat and laid the deceased creature on the exam table.

Janet leaned forward from across the table, peering down at the bat. "Since a bat is a mammal, it'll have organs like humans. Right?"

"Yes," Stanley answered as he put eyeglasses on with a circular protruding telescope-like attachment on each lens. "As you can guess, examining such a tiny creature as this one, I must use loupes to be able to see what I'm doing during my dissection."

"Including small surgical instruments," Jacob said, handing Stonebridge a scalpel with a small narrow blade. The metal tray next to him contained numerous instruments.

Simon stared down at the veterinarian's small hands, which went along with his five-foot three-inch stature. He could visualize Stanley doing orthopedic surgery on small animals' joints like dogs and cats. His small hands would make it easier to work inside joints and abdominal cavities. When Simon did a two-month rotation in surgery during medical school, he didn't like being awoken in the middle of the night to assist an acute abdomen such as an appendix ready to burst. His medical forte was diagnosis followed by treatment through medicine and therapy, not the surgeon's motto of "if in doubt, cut it out."

Stonebridge handed the unused scalpel back to his assistant. "Let's measure the wingspan before I do my dissection."

He grabbed the metal tape measure from Jacob and extended the metal band across the bat's wings from tip to tip. He then laid the bat on a small scale at the end of the table. "CONTINUE. Wingspan is fourteen inches. Weight is thirteen ounces. STOP."

He reached out with his right hand toward Jacob, who placed the scalpel handle onto the palmar surface of Stonebridge's hand.

"How do you determine if a bat has rabies?" Jean asked.

"The test of choice for detecting rabies in animals is the direct immunofluorescent antibody, or the IFA test. You need a sample of the mammal's brain tissue."

Simon stared down at the bat lying on its back, exposing the abdomen and chest. The torso excluding the head probably measured eight inches by four inches. Stonebridge made a "Y" incision as same as a medical examiner would do on a human. Two tiny lungs were exposed at the top and the organs of the abdominal cavity exposed at the tail of the 'Y' incision.

He meticulously removed the organs, handing them to Jacob. He then said, "CONTINUE. Made a 'Y' incision exposing lungs and abdominal cavities. Removed all the organs. All organs appeared normal through loupes. STOP."

He then made an incision at the base of the bat's neck, decapitating the head and handing it to Jacob, who put head inside a plastic bag and sealed the bag immediately. "CONTINUE. Decapitated the bat including the neck and placed them into a plastic bag and sealed the bag. STOP."

He removed his gloves, placing them on the metal exam table. He removed his loops and handed them to Jacob. Removing his face mask, he looked at his audience across the table. "The brain, spinal cord, salivary glands, and saliva of the animal may contain the rabies virus. We're not suspecting rabies, but under the circumstances, the medical examiner doesn't have a diagnosis on the people who died in the caves and the couple in their home, so it's best to check for all possibilities. So, any questions about the necropsy?"

Simon glanced down at the remains of the dissected bat. "It seems if these bats have anything to do with all these unexplained deaths, the answer will come from the microscopic analysis of the blood, fluid, tissue or brain."

"Correct, Agent Woods. The bat didn't have any gross anatomical deformities. And I'll suspect the remaining bats' necropsies will have the same results as the first one. We'll have the results of the bats' analyses hopefully by tomorrow and at the latest, in two days."

"Thank you for allowing us to witness the necropsy of the bat."

Everyone thanked Dr. Stonebridge and Jacob. Simon glanced at his watch as they walked out of Franklin County Medical Examiner's Office facility. Seven more hours left on Janet's yellow halo perilous predicament. "Seventeen hours has elapsed. I thought bringing her to the necropsy would change Janet's twenty-four-hour deadly fate?"

"It didn't," Jean answered. "Since she still has the yellow glow. We haven't changed her fate. Meaning the point in time of a deadly incident is still in front of us."

They got into their SUV. Simon drove out of the parking lot, checking twice both ways before turning right onto a busy highway.

"We'll go back to the hotel and have lunch at their restaurant."

He didn't want Janet to be exposed to a potential accident in an unfamiliar eating establishment. He slowed down at traffic light intersections, making sure no one was running a red light. A nervous chuckle came from him.

"What's so funny?" Janet peered at Simon with a puzzled expression.

"It's nothing funny. It's more a nervous laugh. I was thinking how much we're looking out for you, making sure nothing bad happens to you. If anything happens it'll probably be a one in a billion odds something falls from an airplane landing on top of you. We'll never see it coming."

Janet smirked, then chuckled. "You know. You're probably right. We better listen for planes flying near us in the next seven hours. If we do, duck."

Simon and Jean laughed.

As they headed for the hotel, thunderclouds could be seen up ahead with periodic flashes of lightning. They got to the hotel parking lot without any traffic incident and parked the SUV across from the front entrance of the hotel.

"We made it before the rain started," Simon announced as they got out of the Suburban.

The three of them walked side by side with Janet in the middle. About halfway across the parking lot, Janet stopped. "I forgot my notebook on the console. I'll be right back."

The sound of a jet engine roared from the sky above them. The three FMI agents looked up, then at each other. Panic spread across their faces. Simon shouted, "Run." They rushed toward the front entrance canopy with their shoulders hunched forward in anticipation of a foreign object crashing down on them.

Chapter Fourteen

Simon stopped under the entrance canopy, as did Janet and Jean. Nothing had fallen from the sky. "At least nothing fell from a plane, injuring Janet or all of us."

A brilliant flash of light followed by a crackling sound caused the ground beneath them to momentarily shake. Janet grabbed Simon's forearm. The three of them turned around and stared at their Suburban. Lying on top of their vehicle and crushing the roof from the rear to over the windshield and extending six feet beyond the hood was half of a fallen tree smoldering. A lightning bolt had struck a large oak tree behind the Suburban, splitting the trunk of the tree in half. The largest half had crushed the top of their SUV. The diameter of the tree was nearly the width of their vehicle. Simon's mind quickly figured Janet would've been leaning over the front passenger seat and picking up her notebook when the tree would've come crashing down on her, likely crushing her to death.

"You're definitely a clairvoyant," Janet said, rubbing the back of her neck. "Was it a coincidence that you happened to mention something falling from the sky earlier? We were all thinking an object would be from an airplane, not a falling tree. Either way, thank you for saving my life."

"Amen to that," Jean added as she turned her attention to Janet. "Oh, my God. Your yellow glow is gone."

Two employees from the front desk rushed through the front door. "What happened?" The three FMI agents stepped aside, allowing the hotel's staff a full view of the fallen tree lying across their vehicle. "Was anyone hurt?" Asked the middle-aged, female employee.

"No. No one was injured. Only our Suburban appears to have been damaged."

The other employee bowed his head and made the sign of the cross with his index finger, then said, "Thank the Lord. Everyone is safe."

Simon sighed, then glanced down at Janet. *Vehicles can be replaced...not Janet.* "I'll have to call the car rental company."

Janet reached over and gently squeezed Simon's hand. "Thanks to you, it's not EMS."

Simon called the rental company. They would be sending an insurance adjuster out to assess the damage and work on getting Simon another vehicle. The three of them went into the hotel. He knocked on Danny's door. A moment later, the door opened. Frank greeted them as they walked into the room.

Jean told Frank and Danny what happened in the hotel's parking lot. Simon had changed Janet's deadly fate.

Frank threw his arms up and said, "Holy, crap. You did a great job, boss. Saving Janet from impending doom."

"You did the same thing with changing the bus people's schedule and saving their lives and preventing serious injuries."

Simon walked over toward Danny, who was sitting in front of his computers. "It goes to show, we all work together for a common goal: either for one of our investigations or for the welfare of each other."

Danny looked up at Simon. "I've been sitting here for about ten minutes and still haven't found any incriminating data against Brighton Research. Either they're a squeaky-clean company or know how to hide secrets. Not sure yet which one it is. It looks like I'll be here awhile."

Simon stared at the monitors and saw conversation memos, policies and other information. "Did the annex appear to be following the building plans?"

"Yes. No deviations from what I saw. Although there wasn't any equipment or apparatuses in the research labs yet. I haven't come across any orders for furnishings or equipment. It'll have to be in here somewhere since everything in today's world goes through computers."

"We're going to the hotel's restaurant for lunch. You can leave this and come to lunch with us."

"No. I'll stay here and order room service. Once I start something, I'd like to stick with it until I'm finished."

"Huh. You remind me of someone else I know."

Simon glanced over Danny's head to the right and toward Frank, who raised his right hand as if he was in school responding to a teacher's statement.

"I know who you're talking about." He put his hand down and sniffed the air. "He has a nose for solving mysteries."

"You're quite astute, young man. I suppose you'll want to stay with Danny?"

"Yes, boss."

Simon turned his attention toward Janet and Jean. "You guys ready to go down to the restaurant?"

They both nodded.

The waitress wrote down their orders and left. The room's tables and booths were three-quarters filled with guests.

Janet told Simon and Jean before they entered the restaurant, she had a premonition feeling of uneasiness. Something wasn't quite right.

Simon gazed around the room for familiar faces, which didn't mean anything since they were hotel guests and belonged there. He didn't notice anyone staring at them when they walked into the room or when they were ordering their lunch from the waitress. The conversations in the room intermixed with one another, making it difficult to hear any one table of people. "Not sure why you got your ominous feeling. I assume you didn't hear a voice in your head since you didn't mention it?"

"No. Just the feeling."

~ * ~

Unbeknown to Simon and his agents, the mysterious couple who had been observing them since they arrived in Pennsylvania sat at the same table as this morning with an electronic device pointed at FMI's table.

~ * ~

Halfway through their lunch, Janet's cellphone rang. She glanced at the caller ID, then said, "It's Captain Robins. Hopefully, he has good news about Detective Matters."

She looked down at the table. "Hi, Captain." Janet listened without an expression of sorrow or elation, apparently listening attentively to what was being said to her by the captain. Less than a minute later, a smile spread across her face. "Great news. I appreciate you calling me and letting me know." She then set the phone down on the table next to her plate.

"Good news about Bill?" Jean asked.

"Yes." Tears appeared at the corner of Janet's eyes. "He came out of his coma about two hours ago. There doesn't appear to be any brain damage. He's talking."

"Do they know what caused the coma?" Simon asked, as he set down his half-filled cup of coffee.

"Yes and no. Yes, they know Detective Matters was exposed to an airborne substance blown into his face by the woman according to Bill. He was shocked about the woman supposedly committing suicide. No, they haven't isolated the substance in his body yet. The doctors will be checking his nose and lungs for any residue left by the unknown powdery substance. Captain Robbins stated to me that they're dealing with a regular cloak and dagger, James Bond type case. The doctors said because he had a severely deviated nasal septum causing narrow nasal passageways, this likely prevented Bill from breathing in the full dose of the airborne substance."

The waitress walked up to their table. "Anyone like a warm-up on their coffee?" No one wanted a warm-up.

Simon reached inside his sports coat and pulled out his wallet. "Can we have...?"

The waitress handed him the bill. "Here you are. I'll take it when you're ready." She turned and began walking away from the table.

"You can take the bill now." Simon removed a credit card from his wallet and handed the plastic card with the bill to the waitress.

The three of them shared the tip, laying several dollar bills on the table. After the waitress returned, they went back to Danny's room.

~ * ~

The mysterious couple sitting across the room from where the FMI team had sat turned off their device and left the restaurant.

~ * ~

Frank let Simon and the two ladies into the room. Danny sat in front his computers. "Perfect timing," the computer wizard announced.

There were empty dishes on a two food trays on the small café table at the end of the room near the window. "I copied and pasted all the pertinent information in one area. I printed out everything, giving us a hard copy." He handed Simon, Janet and Jean each a copy.

The room went silent as they read Danny's handout.

Simon read, *Once the annex is completed, our facility will be at a Level Four Security. Level Four—All personnel working in the annex and all visitors will leave all their electronic devices at the screening portal, including cellphones, watches, recorders, tablets, laptops, cameras or any device with the capability of audio/visual performance. No rings or any type of jewelry will be worn while inside the annex.*

Simon continued reading. There was a protocol for exposure to hazardous material. A decontamination procedure. It never mentioned what type of material could cause harm to a person. Another section he read talked about the use of the two isolation rooms. The next paragraph his eyes focused on the word cyanide. "They'll be using an cyanide compound."

"Yes, but not...will be," Danny replied. "They're using cyanide now. Further down the page it talks about cyanide. Brighton Research is buying cyanide from China, the chief producer of cyanide in the world."

"So...Yang Corporation, a Chinese conglomerate who purchased Brighton Research, is buying cyanide from China," Simon said swiping away the hair hanging down onto his forehead and eyebrows. "Something doesn't seem right here. Not sure what."

Janet. "So, what is Brighton Research doing with their cyanide?"

Frank looked at Danny. "I'll let you tell them, partner."

Danny rubbed his lower lip with his upper teeth, then said, "They're experimenting on using a new derivative of cyanide in a cleaning product that supposedly will kill bacteria and mold on various surfaces such as wood, plastic, veneer, porcelain and stainless steel. I checked with the Pennsylvania Environmental Protection Department and Board of Regulations for a cyanide permit. A cyanide permit was registered for Brighton Research under the Yang Corporation five months ago. It was the same time they began building the annex."

Simon turned his attention away from Danny, staring down at the floor as suspicious thoughts flashed across his mind. He lifted his head and peered toward the two computers, not at anyone in the room. "I can see two of the cavers working at Brighton Research having traces of cyanide in their bodies, but it doesn't explain the other cavers, and probably the Tillmans, having traces of cyanide in their bodies. We're missing something here."

"As you know," Janet said, "I don't really believe in coincidences. We have eleven deceased people. All of them had traces of cyanide in their bodies, and they were all found near bat colonies. Now adding the fact Brighton Research recently began experimenting with cyanide seems suspicious, not coincidental. Another thing, why would the Yang Corporation build two hospital-type isolation rooms? One possibility comes to mind: the potentially dangerous effects of their new cyanide derivative. I agree, we're missing something here."

"Why would they have such a high security level for a company developing and researching cleaning products?" Frank asked. "Like Danny said to me earlier, Brighton Research's facility is more like a high-level government building holding national security secrets."

Simon walked over and sat at the end of the queen-size bed, next to Janet. "Danny, since I didn't read the entire five-page handout yet, what other pertinent information did you discover?"

"Robert Rhode and Susan Whitman may have found out Brighton Research was doing something illegal regarding their use of cyanide. If you turn to page four of my handout about halfway down the page, you'll see a memo sent from the chief operating officer to the president of Yang Corporation."

Simon turned to page four as did Janet and Jean. Jean was sitting at the café table. Simon read, ...*Robert Rhode, chemist, was found with our new formula for cyanide on an analysis printout as he was being searched at our security check point. He said he must've accidentally left it in his lab coat. He also had been seen on several occasions sitting with Susan Whitman, biochemist, in the lunchroom over the past few weeks. They both belong to cave explorer groups. I'll be looking into any conspiracy against our facility...*

"I wish the memo had stated the chemical formula of the cyanide compound. We'd know what category to put their cyanide into."

Janet stood, holding Danny's printout. "Looking at this information from a criminal point of view, the memo is interesting but not a smoking gun pointing to anything illegal against Brighton Research. Even though Rhode and Whitman were found dead within one week after the posted date of the memo, there isn't any incriminating evidence toward the chief operating officer."

"Danny," Simon said. "Did you find the chemical formula of the cyanide compound they're working with?"

"No. No mention of the chemicals added to their new compound, only what type of cyanide they bought from the Chinese company. It's an inorganic cyanide. The other chemicals they combine with this cyanide will determine what their final product or compound becomes. All I found was what they called their final product, TAC-42. Not sure what the letters stand for other than the 'C'...which likely stands for cyanide."

Simon sat back down at the end of the bed. "It sounds like their research on this cyanide compound is done by sections. In other words, most of the researchers handle their particular phase of development and not the entire process from stage one to the final stage and the product TAC-42."

"Since we don't know the chemical composition of this new product," Jean said, "we'll need to access the existing labs in Brighton Research's main building."

Simon knew Jean was correct in her suggestion. How could they walk into the facility without arousing any suspicion? Could they return Danny in his previous inspector role for the county? What excuse could they use to inspect their existing labs?

"Jean might be right in what she said. We need to inspect their research labs in the main building. Does anyone have a suggestion on how we could do this?"

"I think I know how," Danny answered as he sat in his desk chair facing Simon. "I now have the password to get into Brighton's computers from my computers. Since two of their employees, Rhode and Whitman, died recently, I'm sure they haven't been replaced yet. Give me a minute and I'll check right now."

Danny turned around and began typing on his keyboard. In less than a minute, he said, "Here it is. Neither position has been filled. I can hack into their human resource department's computer and access the right paperwork and application for each of the vacant positions. I'll also send a fictious memo to the department supervisors at Brighton telling them their vacant positions have been filled and the person will be starting tomorrow morning. All we'll need is two of us to fill the two positions."

Simon could think of two people who could fill the opened positions. All they'd need would be a day on the job. "Frank, how's your chemistry knowledge? Jean, how's your biology knowledge?"

Frank raised his eyebrows. "I know H two O is water."

"You know more than that," Jean said. "Stop kidding around. You have a computer science degree with a minor in chemistry."

"True. I rarely use my chemistry knowledge, or my chemistry set I got for Christmas."

Jean frowned. "Can't you ever be serious?"

She then flipped the pages on Danny's handout, closing the five-page handout, and laying the sheets on the café table. "I took several biology courses and a few courses in chemistry in college for my physical therapist degree and a few years later for my nursing degree program. I think I can get by for a day as a biochemist."

Danny said, "I'll plant the proper credentials and completed applications for the vacant positions into the human resource department computer personnel files. I'll then send a memo to security with Frank and Jean's alias names and their new positions for Brighton Research. Before anyone finds out the truth, they should be out of the facility and back here at the hotel. I'll set it all up for them starting tomorrow morning. I'll have their proper Brighton Research IDs this evening."

"Frank was right when he called you a computer wizard," Janet said.

Simon's cellphone rang. The caller ID number was unfamiliar. "Hello."

"This is Jim Higbee of Action Auto Rental. I talked to you earlier about the accident on the Suburban. We were able to find another black Suburban. I'll have the vehicle delivered when we pick up the other one. The vehicle should be there in about three to four hours."

"Thanks, Mr. Higbee." Simon put his phone away. "I'll have another vehicle later this afternoon. There's something we can do while Danny's doing his computer magic. I'd like to talk with the people from Shippensburg University's Geology Department. They're supposed to be investigating the second cave this afternoon. When I talked with Detective Spurrier yesterday, he said the geology group decided not to explore the first cave, since the cave might be unstable." He turned to Jean. "We'll use your vehicle to get there."

Jean nodded. "Sure." She handed him the keys.

"Don't you want to go?"

"No. If it's all right with you? I'll stay here. I've seen enough caves."

"No problem." Simon glanced at Frank and Janet. "Anyone else want to stay here at the hotel?"

"I'll stay here and help Danny," Frank answered.

Janet stood. "I'll go with you."

Simon sat in the driver seat of the Ford Escape while Janet sat in the passenger seat. He drove out of the parking lot and made a right turn onto the busy highway, heading for the second cave. Several seconds later, the white paneled van with the mysterious couple followed them.

Chapter Fifteen

Simon followed the meandering gravel road surrounded by densely spaced deciduous and evergreen trees. Up ahead along the side of the road were parked three vehicles: a car, an SUV and a pickup truck with a cap. He recognized the car. It was Detective Spurrier's vehicle. Simon parked behind the detective's car. After several minutes of zigzagging between the trees and brush, they came upon the familiar opened area. In front of them the entrance to the cave led into the mountain. They brought out their protective masks and put them on before walking into the cave. Yesterday's preliminary air quality test inside the cave didn't register any common harmful gases or contaminated air. Franklin County's CSU crime lab hadn't completed their analysis of the air. More than likely there wouldn't be any significant findings, but Simon knew it was better to be safe than sorry. He and Janet slowly walked forward into the cave. There were lanterns strategically placed about every twenty feet lighting up the cave. Voices were heard further inside the cave.

Detective Spurrier came into view along with a man in his sixties wearing a baseball-type cap with a miner's lamp attached to the cap. Behind them were three young people in their early to mid-twenties. They also wore caps and miner lamps. The female student carried an assortment of cameras while the two males carried a variety of instruments. All three wore backpacks.

"Simon. Janet," Steward said. "I was about to call you and let you know Dr. DeGraff and his geology associates completed their investigation of the cave."

Simon noticed none of them were wearing particulate protective mask. "None of you are wearing protective masks."

Steward sighed. "Sorry. I was going to call you, but something came up and it completely slipped through my mind afterward. The lab didn't find anything out of the ordinary in the cave's air quality analysis."

"I'm glad and not glad about the air results," Simon declared. "I was hoping they'd find something in the air pointing to the cavers' deaths."

Steward then introduced Simon and Janet to DeGraff and his associates.

The professor, who wore eyeglasses, had a full, well-trimmed white beard and mustache, said, "I never heard of CDC's Federal Medical Investigators."

"Probably not, since our division only came into service a few months ago," Simon explained. He then quickly changed the subject, not wanting any in-depth explanation of FMI. "Dr. DeGraff, did you find anything unusual inside the cave?"

He shook his head in a negative gesture. "No. The cave is typical of all the caves in this area, natural calcareous sandstone. This cavern is within the triangle of the Laurel, Lincoln and Indian Echo Caverns. It's a small cavern compared to the Laurel Cavern, which contains over three miles of passages."

"Something caused the death of the three cavers two days ago."

A smirk appeared on DeGraff's face. "No King Tut Curse caused the cavers' death." He chuckled along with his associates.

Janet grinned, then said, "As you know, ever since King Tutankhamun's tomb was discovered in Egypt's Valley of the Kings in 1922 by Howard Carter, stories circulated that those who dared violate the boy king's final resting place faced a terrible curse, including death. Of course, the story was made up by Carter to prevent anyone from entering his newly discovered finding of King Tut's tomb."

DeGraff and his associates' jubilant demeaner quickly changed to one of surprise. "My, my. You're absolutely correct in your statement."

"I'm sort of a student of Egyptian history. There are many unanswered questions regarding the advanced mathematical and engineering knowledge of the ancient Egypt hierarchy during the era of the pyramids. During that time of history, the rest of the world only possessed primitive thinking and knowledge. I guess that's why I went into an investigative profession. First as a detective, then as an agent for FMI."

Simon was impressed by his colleague's knowledge of Egyptian history and proud of her at the same time. What other surprises would Janet reveal to him and the FMI team? No revelations by the professor or his team regarding the cave's role in the death of the three cavers. "It was nice meeting you, Dr. DeGraff, and your associates."

They all walked together out of the cave and back to their vehicles. Simon and Janet stood with Steward. The professor along with his team got into their vehicles and drove away.

"So, Simon. Have you and your agents learned anything knew about the cavers' and the Tillmans' deaths?"

He couldn't tell Steward their suspicions regarding Brighton Research and Adam Fletcher of E.O.Z. without any concrete evidence to back it up. "No. Still don't have any good leads to the cause of the mysterious deaths. I assume you don't have any suspects in the cave-in?"

"Unfortunately, we don't. It's an unsolved mystery of why someone would want us trapped in the cave or killed in the explosion." He removed his car key from his pants pocket. "Oh, yeah. There's something else. CSU lab identified pieces to a remote control mixed into debris near the entrance to the cave. They said the explosion was likely set off by a radio transmitter in the immediate vicinity of the cave or from a drone."

The events surrounding the cavers' deaths are becoming more bizarre, Simon thought as he glanced at Janet, who displayed a puzzled expression with a furrowed forehead. "I'm not surprised by anything in these cave deaths. We'll let you know if we find anything in our investigation."

"Of course, I'll do the same," he huffed. "That's if I remember to tell you."

"Don't worry about it. We both have a lot on our plates with these deaths."

Simon and Janet got into their vehicle and he made a U-turn across the gravel road. Spurrier was about ten yards ahead of them. About a hundred yards behind them a white van appeared, heading in the same direction as the two FMI agents and Detective Spurrier.

Janet shivered as she removed her seat belt, turned her body about ninety degrees and gazed into the back seat. "I had one of my premonition feelings with my inner voice saying, 'behind you.' There's nothing in the back seat or cargo area." She turned back around and put her seat belt back on.

"Maybe 'behind you' meant someone following behind us?" Simon peered into the sideview mirror. "I don't see any vehicles behind us."

Janet peered into her sideview mirror. "I don't see anyone, either. I'm not sure why I experienced this premonition without something happening. This has never occurred before."

"I'll have Frank or Danny check the vehicle for any electronic surveillance devices when we get back to the hotel. We didn't see any vehicle tailing us. If there was a vehicle behind us, the vehicle must've turned onto a side road. This leaves the most feasible explanation…this vehicle is bugged."

Simon pulled into the hotel's parking lot. The sound of a chainsaw filled the air. In front of them, four men were standing around their demolished Suburban. One man was cutting through the fallen tree while two men waited to remove part of the tree from the vehicle's crushed roof. A flatbed truck was parked several yards beyond the fallen tree. The back end of the truck faced them. Across the parking lot, in a parking space near the front entrance of the hotel sat a black Suburban. A man in his mid-thirties stood in front of the vehicle holding a folder. Simon pulled up next to their new rental Suburban.

He and Janet walked up to the man. "Are you from the car rental company?"

"Yes. I'm Jim Higbee. You must be Simon Woods?"

"Yes. I am."

"Thank the Lord no one was in the car when the tree fell on top of it."

147

Simon glanced at Janet and winked. She reciprocated with a wink. "We were lucky. That's for sure." He then signed some papers and handed them back to the rental agent. "It didn't take long for you to have a crew out here to remove the tree."

"The tree company we contacted already had a crew in the area and were finishing up a tree trimming job. I guess it was a lucky day for you and for us."

Simon exchanged car keys with Higbee for the damaged Suburban and the new one. "I appreciate your quick turnover of the SUVs."

"Thanks. It's nice to get positive comments about our company." He put the keys into an envelope. "You have a nice day."

Simon and Janet headed for Danny's room.

~ * ~

Janet knocked on Danny's door. Simon went to his room to get something. She stood waiting for someone to open the door. Janet hoped the computer wizard had completed his task of allowing Frank and Jean to spy on Brighton Research tomorrow. Like with Danny impersonating a county inspector to gain excess to Brighton Research's computer mainframe in the annex, FMI's next stealthy plan would hopefully give them the information needed to determine if the so-called research company was responsible for the eleven mysterious deaths. The door opened. Jean stood there with a smile on her face.

"Hi, Janet." She leaned to her right and peered around Janet. "Where's Simon?"

"He had to get something from his room."

She stepped into the room and saw Frank sitting next to Danny at the computers. They appeared engrossed, staring at the computer screens.

Jean said, "Learn anything new about the cave or the cavers' deaths from the university's geology department?"

"No. Other than Detective Spurrier received the report from the CSU lab regarding the air samples inside the cave. They were all normal, nothing that could've caused the demise of the cave explorers."

"Frank uncovered some facts about other people at Brighton Research dying mysteriously the past several months. The importance of Frank and I impersonating new employees at the research company tomorrow has been elevated to a more essential purpose."

"Frank can tell you," she said as she and Janet walked up to him.

Frank turned around in his chair. "We now definitely need to get into Brighton Research because…"

A knocking sound came from the room's entrance door, interrupting Frank. "It must be Simon," Jean said as she hurried across the room to open the door.

When he stepped into the room, she told Simon what had transpired the past few minutes regarding new information Frank discovered about the research company.

"So, Frank, what did you find out about the people who had died?" Simon said as he stood a few feet away from the two computer geeks.

"Since Danny accessed Brighton's computer mainframe, I decided to examine the personnel records. Lo and behold starting six months ago there have been three employees who died under suspicious circumstances within a six-week period. One was a janitor, another worked in the research lab, and the third one in shipping and receiving. About one month after the last employee died, the plans for an annex were approved by the Franklin County Planning and Building Department. What was odd about these deaths, all three employees died in car accidents after leaving work according to their personnel files. I was about to check to see if there were autopsies done on them."

Janet caressed her lower lip between her thumb and index finger as she looked down at the floor. She then said, "That's too much of a coincidence. All three dying in an identical scenario…car accident. It'll be interesting to know if autopsies were done."

"I'll get right on it." Frank turned around and began his computer magic.

Of course, Janet knew he'd have to hack into the medical examiner's office computer for the three car accident victims' autopsy reports. When she worked for the Marion County Sheriff Major Crime

Unit as a detective, they didn't hack into anyone's computers for information unless they had a court order from a judge. Plus, they needed to prove to the judge there was justifiable cause. FMI worked under different local, state and federal judicial rules when it came to the safety and welfare of American citizens. In other words, there weren't any restrictive rules for the FMI agents. She sat down at the end of the bed next to Jean.

Danny got up from his chair, went to the room's small refrigerator and retrieved a soda. As he was walking back to his computer, Janet asked, "Danny, how's it going with Brighton Research's two new employees?"

"I'm all done with them. I'm waiting for their IDs to arrive. Should be getting them in the next few hours. The two employees starting in their new position tomorrow morning are Charles Papas," he pointed toward Frank, "and Lucy Bradshaw," redirecting his outstretched arm toward Jean.

"I picked my name out," Jean said, raising her chin upward with shoulders moving back in a proud gesture. "I've always liked the name Lucy. As for Bradshaw, the name has a distinguished and professional connotation. Don't you think?"

"Yes. The name suites you exceptionally well," Janet answered, reaching to her left and patting Jean's forearm.

Simon, who sat at the café table, stared down at his cellphone, then looked up. "Listen up everyone. I received a text message from Director Littlefield."

Frank stopped what he was doing and turned toward Simon, as did everyone else.

"I'll read what he said: *'You and your team must wrap up your investigation in the next three days. If unable to solve deaths, pass on all information to Detective Spurrier and the Franklin County Sheriff's Office.'* End of text. All we have so far are speculations and suspicions regarding the perpetrators. No forensic evidence pointing to a cause of these deaths."

"We may find the answers tomorrow when Frank and Jean get into Brighton Research," Janet said with assurance in her statement.

"Three days should be enough time to solve these deaths."

"I love your optimistic attitude," Simon interjected. "Let's hope your prediction comes true."

"I got the autopsy reports," Frank said. "I'll print them out. From what I read on their cause of death, they all died of trauma. Toxicology report on the three people didn't show any illicit drugs, prescription drugs or alcohol in their blood."

"What about cyanide?"

"The medical examiner didn't check for cyanide."

"Too bad. That would've been vital information. I guess we'll never know if they had cyanide in the body." He glanced down at his watch then stood. "Nothing more we can do until tomorrow. Let's go down for a relaxing dinner around six-thirty. Me personally, I have a lot of paperwork to do on the computer, recording everything that happened today."

Janet knew what she wanted to do for the next hour and a half. She needed to call Bill Matters in Ocala, then relax and freshen up before dinner.

Frank passed out the autopsy reports to everyone. Janet left and went back to her room. She sat at the end of her bed and dialed her ex-partner's cellphone number.

The phone rang twice. A woman answered. "Hello. This is Harriet Matters."

"Harriet, this is Janet. How's Bill doing?"

"Hi, Janet. Bill and I were talking about you. I'm in his hospital room. He's doing good. I'll hand the phone to him."

"Hey, Janet. How's your new position going?"

"Doing okay. It's sure great to hear your voice. I've been worried sick when I first heard what happened at Sullivan Park. Thank God, you're all right now."

"Thanks for your concern. It still seems like a dream...that is a nightmare. When the woman blew this powder in my face, I first thought she accidentally blew powdered makeup in my face. I heard her say, 'I'm sorry, but I had to do it. Nothing against you personally.' Before I could react, I lost consciousness. The next thing I remember was waking up in a hospital bed with a nurse standing next to me."

"Does anyone know why she tried to kill you?"

"Nope. Complete mystery. Other than the woman in the park wasn't the woman I talked to on the phone before I went to the park. It was two different voices. Captain Robins thinks, as do I, the woman on the phone had information regarding the bombing of Danny Emerick's house. They, whoever they are, may have found out she had talked with me on the phone, not knowing what was said but knew she was meeting me at the park. The phone she called me on wasn't traceable, making the event even more intriguing, a cloak and dagger scenario. The woman on the phone is probably dead."

"Holy crap, Bill. I believe you and Captain Robins may be right in your speculation."

"We're hoping the analysis of my lung test will give us a clue about who instigated the hit on me. We know the woman worked for The Circle but can't tie them to what happened to me."

"I can understand what you're saying there, Bill."

The Circle didn't leave any evidence of wrongdoing when she and the FMI team were in Ocala last week. It appeared the clandestine organization were covering their tracks in any situation they were involved in. Although so far, they weren't tied to the events here in Franklin County, other than Adam Fletcher of Eternal Order of Zeus seeming to recognize the name "The Circle." Janet knew it would be difficult to prove.

"Have they done any test on you once the doctors found out what happened to you?"

"They drew some blood and did a lung test on me, sticking a flexible tube into my lungs for a bronchial washing. Seeing if there was any powder residue in the lining of my bronchial tubes. I haven't heard any results yet."

"Hopefully, it'll answer what caused your coma?"

"I agree. I really appreciate you calling me. I'll call you when I get the results of my lung test."

"Thanks. You take care. Talk to you later."

Janet stood and placed her phone on the dresser in front of her.

She began to undress to take a shower, a shower that would relax the tension in her weary muscles.

~ * ~

Around nine o'clock, Danny received the false ID for Frank and Jean. Everyone congregated back in Danny's room to discuss tomorrow's plans. They didn't want to mention their stealthy plans in the restaurant in case someone overheard them.

"I hope tomorrow we'll be successful," Simon said. His face went blank as he stared down at the floor.

Janet knew he was having a vision. Several seconds passed. Simon blinked twice as if coming out of a trance. *The fact is, his visions are trances*, thought Janet. "Did you have a vision?"

"Yes." He inhaled deeply through his nose, then let his breath out slowly through his mouth. "I saw bats flying into an air vent opening at the pediment of a building. Then people having seizures on pews…church pews. There were hymnal books lying next to the people. I saw ten people. The ages ranged between thirty and seventy years old."

Janet thought for a moment. "Since your visions are about something to happen within the next twenty-four hours, and that the vision you had will likely take place in a church, we know bats only fly at night, and since this is Tuesday, we'll have to find a church that routinely has church functions on Wednesdays. We have a time span which ends at nine-thirty p.m. tomorrow night. I wonder how many churches there are in Franklin County?"

"I'll let you know," Danny answered, as he turned around to his computer.

Within fifteen seconds, he announced, "According to these statistics from my computer search there are one hundred and forty-four churches. I'll check to see how many have church activities inside the church on Wednesdays." A few seconds later, he said, "There are thirty-two." He turned and looked at Simon. "Do you remember the name on the hymnal books?"

"No. All I saw was the name hymnal."

Janet asked, "If you saw an outside air vent near a building's pediment in your vision, could you recognize the vent if you saw it on the church?"

"I'm sure I could," Simon answered confidently. He glanced at his watch. "It's nine-thirty. The good news, there's a full moon. Let's start checking the thirty-two churches." He stood and walked up to Danny. "Print out the name and addresses of the churches."

"I can do one better than that. I'll highlight then print out a map showing where the churches are in Franklin County, along with their physical addresses you can put into your GPS. Another thing, you're going to need a flashlight with a beam bright enough to illuminate the pediment of the churches. I have such a light in my van. I'll get it for you after doing the printout."

"Great. That'll expedite our hunt for the churches. If I can find the church, we may be able to save the lives of ten people."

I can't let Simon go by himself, Janet thought. "I'll go with you. You'll need someone to watch your back. You never know what you'll encounter on the ground walking around churches."

"I appreciate your offer."

Frank turned around after performing something on his computer. "I roughly figured out how long it'll take you to check all thirty-two churches. Sixteen hours if it takes thirty minutes to check out each church, including travel time. Hopefully, it'll be one of the first few churches you'll checkout and not the last church on the list."

Simon sighed as he gazed into Janet's eyes. "Are you up to this? We may be up all night."

Simon's endearing piercing stare sent a tingling sensation through her, exciting every inch of her body. She would be spending the night with a man she dearly cared for. She cleared her throat. "As a previous sheriff's detective, this won't be the first time I had to be up all night investigating a case." *Although, not with a man I have amorous feelings for.*

Chapter Sixteen

Simon drove to the first church on the list. Before leaving the hotel, Janet downloaded all thirty-two churches into their portable GPS device and attached the GPS to the Suburban's dashboard. Several minutes later, the female voice on the GPS announced, "You have arrived at your destination." To their right stood a church with a cross projecting out from the top of a small cupola that rested at the peak of a deeply angled roof.

They got out of the car and walked side by side to the front of the church. *The wooden sided church appears to have been built over one-hundred years ago,* thought Simon. The front of the sixty to seventy-foot tall church was lit up by security lights. He and Janet peered up at the pediment. Simon squinted. "No air vents. If there's one, it'll be behind the church."

"I agree."

Simon held a large flashlight given to him by Danny, pointing its wide LED beam several feet in front of them as they walked across a darkened blacktop parking lot to the left of the church toward the back of the A-frame structure. The full moon shone onto the church's multicolored stained-glass windows to their right, enhancing a beautiful picturesque scene. He also noticed the moon light caused her facial skin to glow like an angel from heaven. There weren't any security lights to dampen the visual aura. A cool night breeze gently blew against them. A moment later, they turned right as they reached the back end of the church and walked about sixty feet, then stopped. Simon pointed the beam of light toward the peak of the darkened church's backside and roof line. A pediment with a square air vent came into view. "It's not the round air vent I saw in my vision."

"So, one down and thirty-one to go. One thing about checking out these churches, I'm sure we're going to see a lot of quaint churches like this one."

"I guess that's one consolation we have to look forward to on a potentially tragic future event." *If we were a couple looking for a church to be married in, it would also be the ideal scenario.* "Let's check out the next church."

Two hours later, they stood at the rear of the fifth church, a stone block two-story structure. No security lights surrounded the premises. The flashlight lit up a pediment with a square air vent. Another disappointment in their search for the round air vent with a broken slat allowing bats to enter and leave at night in search of flying insects. Silence encompassed them as they stared up at the air vent.

The sound of crunching footsteps walking over fallen acorns approached them to their right. A small beam of light oscillated across the ground, then, "Sheriff's Department. Stay where you are. Don't move," commanded a male with a deep baritone voice as the beam from his flashlight lit up their faces.

"I'm Agent Woods and this is Agent Bennett from the Federal Medical Investigators. We're investigating a case, deputy. Detective Spurrier from your department can vouch for us."

"Not necessary, Agent Woods. I know who you and Agent Bennett are. We were briefed at our daily meeting about you a few days ago. If you don't mind me asking, what in God's name are you doing here this time of the night?"

How would he answer the deputy? He couldn't tell him the whole truth, about them searching for a broken round air vent he saw in a foreshadowing vision with ten parishioners lying dead on pews inside the church. "We're searching for a church with an outside air vent allowing bats to enter the church. The bats may be carrying a contagious lyssavirus." He hoped his answer satisfied the deputy's inquiry.

"Why not check for the bats in the daytime?"

"Good question." *How do I answer this question?*

Janet answered, "Bats only fly at night. We need to see if they're entering a church through an outside air vent."

"Oh. Yeah. Makes sense. I'll notify other deputies of your presence at churches tonight along with the color, make and model of your vehicle. I already wrote down your license plate number and ran the plate numbers through the system. The plate was registered to a car rental company. Which made me more suspicious before I searched for the two of you. A woman called in about two people with a flashlight milling around the church."

"Sorry," Janet said as they began walking around to the front of the church. "I should've called your department and let them know what we'd be doing."

"No harm done."

Simon drove to the next church on their list. "Thanks for answering the deputy's question. I couldn't think quick enough."

"It's what partners do for each other."

Did she mean agent partners or the other kind of partner? "I've never had a real partner. You're my first."

"Does that mean you had unreal partners before?"

"What…what do you…?"

Janet chuckled, interrupting his answer. "Just a play on words. I thought I'd lighten things up."

"I know I've said this before, but for some reason, my mind can't immediately interpret when you're pulling my leg."

"I like the way you are. Don't change."

"Should I take that as a compliment?"

"Of course. You're everything a person would want as a partner."

A warm amorous impulse wrapped around his body. "I like being your partner." He reached over and briefly touched the top of her hand that laid on top of the console. "We work good together."

Janet reciprocated with a smile, then said, "Yes, we do." She reached toward the GPS and touched the small screen on the address section for the next church. The computer voice said, "In two miles turn, left onto Franklin Road."

The clock on the dashboard read, "one-oh-two a.m."

Simon tried to focus on the investigation, but flashes of Janet's warm smile, entrancing eyes and sensuous touch crossed his mind. It wasn't the appropriate moment to express his feelings toward her, even though he would like to take her in his arms and engage in a passionate kiss. He breathed in deeply, expanding his lungs as much as he could, trying to dampen down his amorous feelings. He then breathed out slowly. "Maybe we'll luck out and the sixth church will be the one in my vision."

"Six is my lucky number."

"I thought you once told me seven was your lucky number?"

"I did. I'll change seven to six if this next church turns out to be the one in your vision."

They both laughed.

A small one-story wood-framed church sat back from the road about fifty yards. Simon drove up a blacktop driveway and parked in front of the church on a blacktopped parking lot. Security lights on poles stood on both sides of a brick walkway leading to the church. The warm glow of the lamplights illuminated the religious structures ornately scrolled front entranceway's wooden door. The church sat in a U-shaped cove surrounded by a heavy wooded terrain. The mixture of deciduous and evergreen trees stood eerily about twenty yards from the church.

The moonlit grass was high, covering their feet and ankles as they made their way to the back of the church. The sound of crickets and other noisy insects made their presence known. Simon pointed the flashlight's beam up at the pediment behind the sixth church on their list. A round air vent appeared. "It's not the air vent in my vision. Plus, there aren't any broken slats. The space between the slats are too narrow for a bat to fly through."

"Damn. When I saw the vent was round, I was ready to change my lucky number seven to..."

A rattling noise like a baby rattle in front of them near the back wall of the church interrupted her comment. Darkness surrounded them as the light from the full moon was being blocked by the church. "Don't move. A rattlesnake is close by. Point the flashlight down in front of us."

Simon shone the light onto a rattlesnake four feet away from them. The snake was coiled in a striking position. He and Janet stood frozen like statues, staring down at the snake. Beads of sweat cascaded down his forehead. His increased pulse caused his heart to thump against his chest wall, while each breath became laborious. His sweaty right hand began to shake causing the beam of light to flicker. "I'm…I'm not a big fan of snakes."

"Slowly move to your left. Do not hurry or run. If the rattlesnake stays in a coiled position, we'll be all right. We're too far away for him to strike us," Janet said calmly. "We must've infringed upon the snake's nesting site and startled it. They usually sleep at night and are more active in the early morning and evening."

When they were about eight feet away from the rattlesnake, they turned their backs to the viper and hurried away, heading toward the front of the church as Simon shone the light on the ground in front of them, hoping not to encounter another venomous creature hiding in the tall grass. They now sat in the car, unscathed by any night creature. "I guess we'll have to be more aware of our surroundings," Simon suggested as he turned the ignition key.

"Isn't that the truth." Janet then set the GPS for the next church.

"You didn't seem to be rattled…I guess that's the wrong word to use. You didn't seem to be frightened at the sight of the rattlesnake. I'm a city boy. I didn't grow up concerned about encountering poisonous snakes, only harmless garter snakes."

"Being a Florida country girl, venomous snakes and alligators were part of my upbringing. We learned how to handle and respect them."

"Great to know you have this type of forte. My forte would be to medically treat the consequences of a person who'd encountered them."

"It's one of the reasons why we work so good together. We depend on each other's strengths." She reached over touched his forearm resting on the center console.

I love this woman. "I agree in what you're saying." *When this case is completed, I'm going to tell her my feelings about her.*

They searched for the broken, round air vent on four more churches to no avail. "We're almost one-third through our list," Janet said, as she tapped the GPS screen with her finger on the eleventh church address.

The dashboard clock read "four seventeen a.m."

Thirteen minutes later, the eleventh church came into view to their left. The GPS's female voice synthesizer announced, "You have arrived at your destination." The church sat about one hundred feet from the road. A paved parking lot was to the left of the church. They were in a small town about ten miles northwest of Chambersburg. Two old-fashioned lamp posts stood about ten feet from the front of the church, lighting up the entranceway. Written on a bronze plague about three-foot square and imbedded into the brick wall to the left of a large mahogany front door was "Built 1910 A.D."

Simon gazed up at the church's pediment, which was about sixty feet from where they stood. No air vent present. "Like the other churches, the air vent is probably in the rear of the church."

"I agree."

As they walked across the moonlit parking lot, Simon directed the beam of their flashlight on the ground several feet in front of them. When they reached end of the parking lot and church and were about to turn right toward the back of the church, Janet stopped. "Why did you stop?"

"I got one of my feelings. Although, I don't hear an inner voice. Not sure if it relates to the air vent or danger awaits us behind the church. Since I didn't have this feeling on the past ten churches," she removed her Glock from the shoulder holster, "it's better to be safe than sorry."

Simon also brought out his gun, ready to use his weapon if a situation behind the church warranted its use. The grassy grounds behind the church were well-maintained with short grass and no weeds or shrubbery along the back of the building. No unwanted entities, neither human nor Mother Nature's creatures, were present. They now stood behind and in the center of the bricked religious building. The flashlight's wide beam slowly raised upward to the apex of the roof. A round air vent with a broken slat appeared. "Thank God. It's the air vent in my dream." A small-bodied creature with large wings, a bat, flew through the vent and into the church. "This is definitely the church in my vision."

"Simon. A voice in my head just said, 'Beware.' What do you

think the warning means?" Janet continued to hold onto her Glock at her side.

Simon thought a moment. "I'd say 'beware' had to do with the bat we just saw fly through the air vent and into the church."

"If what you said is true, why didn't I get the ominous feeling or hear my inner voice when we were about to enter the attic at the Tillmans' house, including the two caves?"

"Not sure. There must be a logical explanation. At least now we found the church in my vision. We'll be able to warn the minister and parishioners not to enter the church today. Like what we discussed earlier about when we found the broken air vent in my vision, we'll tell the minister that we suspect the bats in their church have rabies."

"I feel good we've changed the deadly fate of ten people's lives. Although, should I say, you changed their fate. I'm only the tagalong."

"No way. You mean more to me than a tagalong. You're my partner." He wanted to reach out and hug her. *Not now. The time will come. Be patient.*

"When we get back to our car, I'll call the minister and inform him about the bats."

"Okay. I'll put a warning notice on the front entrance and side door of the church." Frank had made official looking warning notices in case they came across a house or building needing to be closed during an investigation. Simon taped the notices on the two doors to the church. Between eight or nine o'clock this morning, they'd call the pest control and exterminating company that was used to remove the bats in the Tillmans' attic. He, Janet or Danny would take the bats to the county medical examiner's office for analysis, as Detective Spurrier did with the bats in the attic of the Tillmans' house.

Simon returned to the SUV and sat behind the driver seat. "What did the minister have to say?"

"The minister was stunned that their church may have bats infected with rabies. He wondered why I called him so early in the morning. I told him we'd been investigating a possible rabies case in the area of the church. There are a few homes in the area of the church with no commercial structures or caves in the immediate area. We did observe bats flying into his church through a broken air vent in the back of his church. The way I look at it, I wasn't completely lying to the minister. There was a lot of truth in what I told him."

"You handled the minister perfectly. How do we get the key to open the church?"

"The minister will drop the key off and put it under the rubber mat at the side door." Janet stretched out her arms and yawned. "Sorry. I'm not used to all-nighters. Even as a sheriff's detective, I tolerated middle of the night investigations but didn't like them one iota. I give the night-shift working class a lot of credit and admiration in what they do while most people are sleeping."

There weren't many vehicles on the road as they drove back to the hotel. Most people were still sleeping, cuddled up to a loved one or their pillow and covers. The pillow and covers fit Simon, Janet and the rest of FMI's agents' nighttime scenario since all of them were single and without a soul mate. Simon parked the Suburban.

A few moments later, Simon stood in the hallway with Janet. He gazed down into her brown eyes. "Thank you for coming with me."

He stepped forward, reached out and hugged Janet. She didn't resist. Matter of fact, her arms squeezed him tighter. Her fully endowed breasts pressed against his chest.

She slowly pulled away then said, "Talk to you at breakfast."

A sensuous sensation touched every nerve ending of his body. "Okay. See you at breast…Ah, breakfast." He felt a wave of heat wrap around his face, knowing his blushing face must be as red as a ripe tomato.

Janet smiled while snickering, then said, "Good night."

She removed her room keycard from her blazer, walked to her door and slid the keycard into the slot above the door handle, unlocking the door. She went inside the room.

Simon unlocked his door and walked inside. He glanced at Janet's door across the hallway as embarrassment overwhelmed him. *I can't believe I said that to her.* He closed and locked his door.

In about three hours, his nightstand clock would call out for him to get up and lead the FMI team to another day, a day that might reveal answers to the pending questions of their investigation. As he drifted off to sleep, the sight of bats flying into the church through the broken air vent filled his thoughts. Less than a minute later, silence and darkness engulfed him.

Chapter Seventeen

A piercing buzzing sound saturated Janet's darkened room, causing her to jerk awake from an early morning dream. In her dream, she was being chased by a colony of swooping bats through a forest, when suddenly the trees opened to a clearing about thirty yards across, which ended at the edge of a cliff. Beyond the cliff, a two-hundred-foot drop into a canyon awaited her demise. She awoke about ten yards away from the deadly plunge.

Janet sat up and peered to her right to see "seven-thirty" on the nightstand's clock. Her heart raced as it pounded against her chest wall. She reached over and turned off the alarm. Silence. Light was peeking beyond the edges of drawn curtains to her left. *Would I had fallen off the cliff?* Some people think if you don't awaken from falling, you might die from a heart attack. Although if you did die, you wouldn't be able to tell someone because you'd be dead. Janet didn't believe in this urban myth.

She got up, showered and dressed. It was five minutes to eight when she walked into the hallway. A memory caused her to chuckle to herself as she stared at the spot where she and Simon hugged earlier. She'd have to admit the hug felt great. He was gentle and the closeness of his body against hers stirred amorous excitement. If she hadn't been so exhausted, things might have turned out quite different. One thing for sure, the hug had excited him, by his slip of the tongue.

The sound of a door opening in front of her interrupted her thoughts. Simon stepped into the hallway. "Good morning, Simon."

"Oh. Morning." He briefly glanced down at the floor. "Quite an unusual and rewarding night. Don't you think?"

"Last night was a million dollars' worth of experience and

knowledge, but I wouldn't give a nickel to do it again."

They started walking up the hallway to the restaurant. "Of course, unless I had to do it. I'm not as young as I used to be. I need more sleep than three hours."

"I agree to the part of needing more sleep than three hours." He glanced down at the front of his blue dress shirt. "See. I forgot to button one of the buttons." He reached down and completed getting dressed. "The coffee's caffeine should help wake me up."

The restaurant was a least a third filled with guests. The FMI team sat at the same table. Janet saw a few familiar guest faces and several new ones. The normal low murmur of voices filled the room.

~ * ~

A little while before Simon and Janet arrived, the unknown, mysterious couple sat at a table across the room with their apparent listening device pointed toward the FMI team.

~ * ~

Janet stared at Frank, who wore a suit, not his usual pullover shirt and slacks. She then looked at Jean, who wore makeup, a stylish white blouse and shoes, and a pair of blue slacks. She normally wore blue jeans, a casual blouse and tennis shoes. Janet sat down, as Simon sat next to her at the table. For the past few days, the other agents always made sure she and Simon sat next to each other at the hotel's restaurant table.

"Good morning everyone," Simon said briefly looking at Jean, Frank and Danny. "We found the church in my vision. I've already contacted the minister early this morning. I will call the bat exterminating company and have them capture the bats. We'll then take them to the medical examiner's office for evaluation. Another thing, Janet had one of her forewarning premonition feelings, then a minute or two later, while standing behind the church and watching a bat fly through the broken air vent and into the church, she heard her inner voice say, 'Beware.'"

Janet added, "Like what Simon and I discussed, why didn't I get this feeling inside the two caves or the Tillmans' attic?"

The table went silent as everyone at the table appeared to think about the answer to her question. Danny then said, "There's one feasible explanation to your question. No one else, including the sheriff's deputies, CSU personnel, or the four of you died or had seizures after going into the first cave. The deputy who went into the second cave to confirm the death of three cavers was unaffected. Finally, no one other than the Tillmans died in their house. There's one logical answer to all these scenarios: the bats and/or their guano are contagious for a limited period of time. There's no way to know how long the contagion stays effective. It could be hours, days, weeks or months. We do know when this substance enters a human, the substance will kill them, then somehow dissipate into untraceable matter. The bats are immune to the substance since they don't die. Also, the substance is untraceable in the bats and the guano. The only common element found is cyanide."

Everyone agreed to Danny's conclusion.

Simon tapped his fingers on the table, then said, "If what you say is correct, which I wholeheartedly believe it is, anyone entering the church today may be exposed to the active contagion. From all the information we've obtained and from our observations the past five days, whatever the contagion is, it's likely airborne. We'll have to inform the exterminating company personnel. They'll have to wear Hazmat protection gear for airborne and skin contact protection. At least one of us will have to be at the church to take the bats and their guano to the county medical examiner for analysis. Of course, excluding Jean and Frank."

Janet put her cup of coffee down on the table. "I'll do it."

Over the past ten years, she had handled crime scene evidence on many occasions. Although, she had never handled dangerous and potentially lethal material evidence.

"Thanks. Since I've handled dangerous material before, I'll go with you. Not that you couldn't handle the bats or guano yourself. Plus, there may be many bats, needing at least two people to complete the task of taking them to the county medical examiner."

"Makes sense to me."

Janet agreed with Simon's statement. Also, they were becoming inseparable on the Deadly Seizures Case. Frank had coined their investigation's name a couple of days ago. Everyone agreed "Deadly Seizures Case" depicted their investigation of the cavers' and the Tillmans' deaths.

Danny said, "Before you and Janet got here, we discussed an emergency plan at Brighton Research in case one or both needed to get out of the building in a hurry. They'll grab their right ear and rub the ear lobe in front of a security camera. I'll be monitoring their security cameras inside and outside the facility from my computer. This way, I'll be able to keep my eye on Frank and Jean through this system. If things get dangerous for them, I'll set off the fire alarm system for the whole building, evacuating everyone outside."

"Great idea. I hope we don't have to implement this tactic."

Simon looked at Frank then Jean. "Don't take any chances that'll jeopardize your life."

They completed breakfast.

Frank and Jean stood. Frank had to rent a car since he couldn't ride to Brighton Research with Jean without drawing suspicion. They discussed at the table about Jean arriving several minutes ahead of him. Neither of them could take any electronic devices inside the facility including their cellphones. Any revelations they learned would have to be stored and etched in their memories. Brighton Research's two new employees, Charles Papas and Lucy Bradshaw, left the hotel's restaurant and headed toward their vehicles in the parking lot.

Simon stood. "Why don't we go back to Danny's room? We'll need to make phone calls to the exterminating company and the county medical examiner's office. They'll have to know about the potentially contagious bats and guano. I'll also call Detective Spurrier and let him know the situation."

Janet sat on the partially made bed and dialed the medical examiner's office number. Even though she had a few hours of sleep, her energy level was high, knowing they might be close to a resolution of the unexplained deaths. A woman at the other end of the line said, "Franklin County Medical Examiner's Office. Can I help you?"

"This is Agent Bennett from the Federal Medical Investigators of CDC. I need to talk with one of the doctors regarding a case."

"Hold please. I'll connect you with Dr. Williams."

"This is Dr. Williams."

Janet told him who she was and why she was calling. "We wanted you to know what Dr. Woods and I will be bringing you later this morning."

"Thank you. I'll get things set up for the guano analysis here for Dr. Stonebridge. As you know, the past two guano specimens were negative except for traces of cyanide."

"Yes. Although these bat droppings may contain contagious substances."

"We'll be taking all precautions, Agent Bennett."

"I'll call you when we're on our way with the bats and their droppings." Janet hung up, then dialed Detective Spurrier's cellphone number.

She stared at Simon who was still talking with the exterminator company. The phone rang twice. "Steward. This is Janet from FMI. I wanted to let you know about our investigation."

"About your investigation of bats possibly carrying the rabies virus flying into churches? I found a note on my desk when I got to work this morning from the officer you talked to last night."

"Most of that was true except for the part about the bats carrying the rabies virus. Although now we believe some of the bats may in fact be carrying a contagious substance which caused the deaths of the cavers and the Tillmans. The substance probably exists a short period before dissipating. It is our working theory. The good news is we found a church that may have the bats with this unknown substance. The exterminating company we used at the Tillmans' attic will be capturing the bats at the church this morning. Simon's talking with them right now. We will take them to the medical examiner's office. You now know as much as we do regarding the bats and their possible link to the eleven deaths."

"I appreciate the update. I'll send a sheriff deputy to the church to stand guard, preventing any unauthorized person from entering the church."

"Thank you, Steward. Good idea. We'll let you know if the medical examiner finds anything out."

Simon sat at the café table next to the window, facing in the direction of Danny, who sat in front of his computer. Janet sat at the end of the bed behind Danny. Holding his cellphone, he said to the person at the other end of their conversation, "We'll see you and your men there."

He put his cellphone away. His eyes met Janet's. "The company will be going to the church about ten o'clock this morning. They're going to block the air vent from the outside before going into the church. They know of the potential hazard they'll be facing and will be taking all precautions. Under the circumstances, the exterminating company will be charging triple the normal cost of removing the bats and the guano. I told them it wouldn't be a problem. How did your phone calls go with the medical examiner's office and Steward?"

She told him what transpired between her and the medical examiner, Dr. Williams, and Detective Spurrier. "Of course, I didn't tell either of them how we came to the assumption about the bats carrying a potentially contagious organism or substance. Neither of them asked me."

Janet stood, slid her feet a couple steps forward and looked down at the computer monitor in front of Danny. "Anything new about Brighton Research?"

"No. Not yet. A moment ago, I got into their security cameras inside and outside the facility. Jean should be arriving at the front gate in about ten minutes."

"While Simon and I are gone, if there's any problems, give us a call."

Janet glanced at Simon. He stared back at her with a frown. *My God. I'm taking over Simon's role as chief agent.* "I mean…give Simon a call."

A grin appeared on his face. He obviously realized she'd taken charge of the FMI team for a moment. Janet did the same thing when she worked as a detective for the Marion County Sheriff's Department and would unintentionally take charge over Detective Matters' senior position. Being an assertive person, at times she would forget her professional role and status.

Janet sat in the passenger seat of the Suburban, as Simon drove up the church's driveway. A Franklin County Sheriff's car was parked in the parking lot in front of the church. When they got closer to the church, Janet saw a deputy sitting in the driver seat of the patrol car. She got out of her car as they stopped and parked two car spaces away from the deputy's car. Janet recognized the deputy. "Deputy Robinson. How are you? I'm not carrying any coffee, so you should be safe."

They both chuckled.

Simon glanced down at his watch, then said, "The exterminating company should be here any minute."

The sound of a large truck's engine caused Simon and Janet to turn around. Two vehicles drove up the driveway, a red pickup truck with a cap and a red paneled van. "They're here," Janet said.

The company spent about twenty minutes to cover the outside opening in the air vent. Everyone now stood at the side door of the church. It was agreed after further discussion between the extermination company's personnel and Simon, regarding the bats possibly carrying a deadly organism or lethal substance, that the exterminators would euthanize the bats before putting them in an airtight container. The exterminators would also collect some of the bat droppings and put the guano into an airtight container. Three of the employees wore Hazmat gear, including a full facemask with a respirator, preventing any airborne particles or microscopic organisms from entering their lungs. They looked like spacemen from outer space about to encounter an alien entity and environment. A video camera was attached to the front of their upper foreheads with a head strap. Inside their van were three computer screens, one for each exterminator. In real time, Simon, Janet, and the camera man would be able to visualize what each exterminator would see in front of them. There was also an audio hookup.

"We'll go into the van," said Ralph, the computer guy, to Simon and Janet, "before they open the door to the church and go inside."

He turned to Deputy Robinson. "I suggest you go to the front of the church. You better sit in your patrol car with your air conditioning on and windows rolled up."

"Will do. Don't have to ask me twice." She turned and walked to her car in front of the church.

Ralph looked at his three comrades in their protective hazmat suits. "Give me a few minutes before entering the church. I'll let you know when I'm ready."

A rush of excitement mixed with anxiety flowed over her as if she was about to descend over a hundred-foot waterfall. Janet's ten years as a detective for the Marion County Major Crime Unit couldn't compare to the emotionally charged and hair-raising scenarios that she had faced in the past several days as an FMI agent. They hurried to the van.

Periodically her hand and Simon's touched, sending a warm, sensual feeling through her body. *What a mixture of emotions I'm feeling now.* She had to stay focused on the church and the bats. Be prepared for any unexpected situations that might arise when the exterminators entered the church.

They stood behind Ralph, who sat in a chair in the back of the van, peering at three blank monitors. Two small speakers sat between the middle monitor. He turned everything on then said, "I'm all set."

A male voice said over the speaker, "We're going into the church now."

The three monitors displayed the windowless, wooden side door from three different camera angles.

The door slowly opened.

Chapter Eighteen

The three exterminators walked into the church. Two of them carried plastic containers with lids, the third one carried a round plastic canister-shaped gadget the size of a thermos bottle with a hose connected to a wand-like sprayer. The canister contained an anesthetizing chemical that would suppress the bats' breathing almost instantly without any undo suffering. The cameras with LED lights shone at least fifty feet in front of them as they made their way to the front of the church, then behind the altar wall containing a cross. A steep staircase leading up to the church's attic or walkway came into view. Heavy breathing from the three men came through the speakers in the van. "We're heading up the stairs," said one of the men.

The man with the canister ascended the stairs first. Once he reached the top of the stairs, he stepped onto a walkway about ten feet wide and running the full length of the church. He turned around toward the air vent. The vent was about ten feet away. The other two men now stood next to him, looking around. A moment later, all three LED lights and cameras were pointed near the air vent. About eight feet from where they stood and to their right a colony of at least ten bats hung from the church's rafters. A pile of bat guano lay below the bats about two feet away from a floor air vent.

Janet leaned forward. "The floor air vent is probably how the contaminate gets into the church and to the pews."

"That would make sense," Simon agreed.

One of the monitors showed one the men removing an air sampling device from an attachment to his belt. The device was similar in shape and size to the one Frank used in the second cave.

"I'll take a sample of the air." He pushed a button, followed by a sucking noise lasting a few seconds.

The air sample would be analyzed by the CSU lab. He hooked the sampling device back on his belt.

The man with the canister walked over to the bats and sprayed them. Within seconds, the bats fell onto the plywood walkway. Except for one bat that flew by the exterminators. "Damn. One got away."

He looked at his associates, then at a cluster of motionless bats lying on the floor. "Pick up the bats on the floor. I'll get the one who got away."

His light lit up the walkway and rafters in front of him as he slowly made his way to the other end of the church. A dark-brown screeching bat flew straight at him. He pointed the spray nozzle at the flying creature and squeezed the trigger. The bat made a zigzagging movement, avoiding the anesthetizing chemical spray. The exterminator quickly turned around and saw the bat fly down through the stairwell to the lower level. "We got a problem, Ralph"

Ralph stared at the monitor, along with Simon and Janet. "We saw the bat fly through the stairwell opening."

"I'll get the little sucker."

He walked over to the other two men, "Finish up here. I'm going bat hunting."

They nodded.

"We can't let the bat get away," Simon pleaded.

"Simpson will get it. He's the best in the field of capturing creatures."

Simpson descended the stairs to the lower level, then into the sanctuary of pews. His camera with headlamp scanned the twelve-foot-high flat ceiling. Wood beams ran crosswise every ten feet of the hundred-foot-long room. The camera view moved up at the ceiling, oscillating to the right, left, then down at the pews in the same rhythmic movement. He moved slowly up the middle aisle toward the back of the church.

"Where are you, little bugger?"

A few minutes later, the camera displayed the bat sitting on top of a hanging light shade at the back of the church. "There you are, little guy."

He stopped about ten feet away from the perched bat. "Just a couple more feet and you're mine."

Simpson moved forward, quietly sliding his feet on the carpeted aisle. He reached out with the nozzle pointing straight up at the bat. His finger began squeezing the trigger. The bat dropped down and flew away before he could pull the trigger. The front door of the church opened as the bat headed to the opening and freedom. Simpson ran toward the fleeing bat.

The bat entered the doorway and flew into a net held by Ralph, who wore a protective hazmat suit and mask.

Janet and Simon cheered, as they peered at the monitor and the captured bat. Simpson sprayed the struggling bat. A few seconds later, the bat stopped moving. They placed the bat into a gallon-size plastic Ziplock bag, then walked toward the side door of the church.

The other two exterminators walked out of the side door carrying the airtight plastic containers. They placed them down on the ground, then sprayed them with a disinfectant that would kill any organism and neutralize any harmful chemical compound. They then sprayed each other, including Simpson and Ralph. Afterward, the four exterminators placed their disposable waterproof, white suits and gloves into a large biohazard plastic receptacle. Their cameras, LED lights, masks and respirators were put into another container.

Janet, Simon and Deputy Robinson stood in front of the church as the exterminators came around from the side of the church. Two of them carried a plastic container, the third carried the air analysis machine.

Janet said, "That went pretty smoothly."

"It sure did," added Simon. "Thank God."

She looked up at the cross on top of the church. *I'm sure He heard you.*

Janet then called Detective Spurrier. "Steward, we got the bats. Not knowing if the church is safe to enter yet, the church should be closed until further notice, the same as we did with the caves. Simon and I will be taking the bats, bat droppings and a sample of the air inside the church to the medical examiner's office and the CSU lab."

"Thanks for keeping me abreast of things. Let me talk with Deputy Robinson." She handed her phone to the deputy.

The plastic containers, plastic Ziplock bag and the air analysis machine were put in the back of the Suburban. Simon and Janet thanked the exterminators.

Deputy Robinson gave the phone back to Janet. "Detective Spurrier said he'll call the church's minister and let the minister know about the church being quarantined until further notice."

"Thanks, deputy."

When Simon and Janet got into the Suburban, she called Danny, putting him on speaker, "Hi, Danny. We're leaving the church and heading to the medical examiner's office. We have the bats and some of their guano. Any problems for Frank or Jean?"

"No. Not at all. They both passed through the main gate without any problems and were taken to their job sites by employees once they passed through security inside the building's front entrance. So far, so good."

"Talk to you later."

Janet put her phone away, then said, "Once this case is over, I'm going to need a short vacation to recuperate."

Simon chuckled. "That makes two of us. It has been a nonstop rollercoaster ride. Five days on a tropical beach resort would be ideal."

"I could go for a short vacation." *I bet you look great in a bathing suit.*

"I'd have to buy a bathing suit."

My God. Is he a mind reader? "I'm not sure if my bathing suit will even fit me."

"We better call Dr. Williams," Simon said, "and let him know we're on our way with the bats."

"You're right."

She called the Franklin County Medical Examiner's Office and they connected her with Jacob Pollock, the pathologist assistant. "Hi, Jacob. It's Agent Bennett. We're bringing the bats in for Dr. Stonebridge's necropsy of them."

"We have the isolation room ready. See you when you get here." Jacob disconnected their call.

It was about a thirty-minute drive to the medical examiner's office and the CSU lab building. They talked about their lives growing up from humorous moments and events to interesting things each of them did to adulthood. Simon grew up as an only child of working-class parents.

Janet came from more affluent parents who owned one of Florida's largest orange grove businesses. Of course, her brother, Michael Bennett, was a medical doctor. Her parents wanted her to follow in her brother's footsteps and become a doctor. She chose a degree in criminal justice after becoming intrigued by TV shows with women in law enforcement as a teenager. Plus, she had a maternal grandfather who had been chief of police in a small Florida city.

They entered the building of the medical examiner's office and CSU labs.

"I'll see you in a few minutes," Janet said as she headed straight ahead toward the CSU's labs carrying the air analysis machine and bat guano container.

~ * ~

Simon turned right through double doors with the name AUTOPSY ROOMS above the doors. He'd meet Janet at the lab after dropping off the bats. They concluded yesterday that all the deaths were caused from an airborne entity. Since the substance didn't kill the bats, the guano had to disperse the killer substance into the air, and hopefully the lab will be able to identify the deadly entity from the sample of air taken from the church and/or the bat guano.

As soon as he passed through the doorway, the odor of formaldehyde permeated the air. *Even without the sign above the door, a person would know they were in the medical examiners' domain*, thought Simon.

He met Jacob outside the necropsy isolation room and handed over the container with the bats. "I'll be at the CSU lab with Agent

Bennett. Please call me if you get any results."

"Sure will, Dr. Woods."

Simon hurried down the hallway toward the CSU labs on the other side of the building. Janet stood in the hallway about sixty feet away and waved to him. A warm, sensuous wave flowed over him as he peered at her. The fluorescent lighting accentuated her statuesque figure, creating thoughts of them lying on the warm, soft sand of a Caribbean beach in their bathing suits as the waves splashed against the shoreline. He sighed. "Are they going to do the air analysis right away?"

"Yes. Since the air may contain something lethal, the lab technician told me to leave the room and wait out here or in their lunchroom. I told him we'd wait in the lunchroom. By the time they get everything set up and do the analysis, it'll probably be about an hour before he'll have the results. Another technician will be starting on the bat guano soon. He'll be looking for an airborne substance or organism, also done under a protective environment."

"Sounds like they got everything under control. Dr. Stonebridge will call me if he finds anything of importance. I could go for a cup of coffee."

They walked into CSU's lunchroom, got a cup of coffee from a coffeemaker, and sat at a small round table. There were several people in the room sitting at tables, eating, drinking and conversing with fellow employees. They all had CSU logos with their names on their shirts.

"Agent Woods and Bennett, how are you doing?"

Simon saw John Thomas and K. Lasky, crime scene investigators who were at the second cave, sitting at a table next to them. "Still investigating."

"I heard there was a couple who died, like the cavers, in their house," Lasky stated, as she glanced at Janet with a grin, then back to Simon.

"Yes. Unfortunately."

"Getting close to a cause?" Thomas asked.

"That's why we're here. We're hoping for an answer from your department soon."

"Nice seeing you two again," Lasky said as she stood, along with

Thomas. They left the lunchroom.

Simon had noticed how Lasky looked at Janet with a grin in an accusatory gesture of "there's no doubt you're attracted to him." *Maybe it was when I pulled the chair out for Janet before she sat down at the table. Janet did look up at me with endearing eyes.*

"Simon."

Janet's voice interrupted his thoughts as he raised his gaze from the floor to her peering eyes. "Sorry. My mind was somewhere else."

"I can understand. There's been a lot going on recently." A smirk appeared.

Did she mean regarding their investigation or their potential blossoming relationship between each other? Simon wasn't sure which one she meant. He hoped for the latter.

They sat at the table for about fifty minutes, then Janet's cellphone rang. She glanced at the caller ID. "It's the lab." She listened for several seconds. "We'll be right there."

"Good news?"

"They isolated unusual particles in the air sample and bat guano. He'll tell us more when we get to the lab."

Simon drank down the last of his coffee, then questioned, "Particles? Like dust, pollen, mold and mold spores?"

Janet stood with her empty porcelain cup that had contained coffee, then answered, "Stan Brubaker, the CSU tech, didn't say."

He stood, walked over to a porcelain sink with Janet and placed their cups into the sink adjacent to the coffeemaker. His mind ran through a host of possible airborne particles capable of killing a human. Anthrax, ricin, radioactive fallout, deadly bacteria or viruses, or a lethal dose of cyanide gas or sodium cyanide salt. The only thing found in the dead cavers and the Tillmans were traces of cyanide, but not enough to kill them. Simon was anxious to know what airborne particle the CSU lab technicians found as they hurried down the hallway toward the lab.

They stopped in front of a closed door with a small square window in the center. Above the door it read "TRACE EVIDENCE." Simon knocked on the door.

A man in his early fifties waved for them to come in. Another man in his mid-thirties stood next to him. Janet and Simon walked inside the room. A large glassed-in rectangular booth stood behind the CSU lab technicians. A microscope sat on a table behind the glass with its two scopes sticking through the glass panel. Two round openings through the glass on either side of the microscope contained a sleeve and attached gloves, allowing the user to manipulate the focusing settings on the microscope in an isolated environment. The microscope was electronically connected to a computer, documenting anything examined under the microscope. The computer sat on a counter to Simon and Janet's right and in front of the glassed room.

Janet said to the man in his early fifties, "Hi, Stan. This is Dr. Woods."

"Please to meet you." Stan turned to the other tech. "This is Glen Lolich."

Glen nodded. "Nice meeting you."

"Glen and I found something neither of us has ever seen. He also found it in the bat guano he'd examined. We didn't find it in the other two guano specimens from the caves, which tells us whatever this thing is, it has a very short half-life, degrading at a rapid rate. We want you to look at this compound through the microscope. I abstracted the particulate compound from the air sample you gave."

Simon walked over to the microscope, stuck his hands through the sleeve and slid them into the gloves. He then gently pressed his eyes against the microscope lenses and adjusted the focus. "What in heaven's name is that?"

Chapter Nineteen

Simon peered at numerous saucer-shaped particles with moving filaments projecting out from the individual structures. The entity continued losing filaments, disappearing from the saucer-shaped compound. "I've never seen anything like this before. What is it?"

"We did a spectrochemical analysis on the particle. Our chemical assessment of the particulate composite shaped like a saucer is that it's made up of hydrogen cyanide and an unknown compound. Like I said a bit ago, the compound is decaying at an accelerated rate. I'd say in about ten hours, the unknown compound will be gone, leaving a trace of cyanide. The filaments act as tiny fins, along with the cyanide, propelling the entity through the air. We theorize when the bat excretes its guano, it falls toward the ground, causing the mysterious compound to break apart from the droppings, and the particulate floats across a cave, attic or any confined area."

Simon stepped back and said, "The eleven deaths we're investigating were likely caused after they breathed in the particulate. Prior to their deaths most, if not all of them, had a seizure, likely a grand mal type of seizure from the evidence of them urinating on themselves. The mysterious compound probably caused their seizures. We know from their medical records and from their families, none of them were being treated for epilepsy."

"You're right in your assumption about the compound causing grand mal seizures. We confirmed this theory of the mysterious compound causing visual problems, seizures and final death. We exposed this airborne compound to mice. Within thirty minutes, the mice displayed visual difficulties, bumping into the cage plexiglass, then several minutes later they had seizures, followed by death."

Simon furled his eyebrows. "So, the cyanide is an incidental finding, not the substance causing their death."

"Correct, the cyanide is a radical element binding the compound," Stan said. "Glen did a molecular analysis of the compound…its DNA so to speak. We concluded the GI track of the bat with its particular digestive enzymes may have played a part in the development of this lethal compound."

"You're saying the bats' digestive enzymes may have been the catalyst causing this compound to become deadly?"

"Yes. It's a feasible possibility," agreed Glen. "We'd need to find this compound before it entered the bat's digestive track to prove this theory. Like we said, the bats aren't affected by the mysterious compound. We estimate the guano is lethal to humans for about thirty hours before the compound becomes harmless."

"Glen, can I get a copy of your chemical analysis of the mysterious compound?" Simon asked.

"Sure. No problem," answered Glen. "Give me a minute and I'll get the report for you." He walked to the other end of the room and sat behind a computer.

Simon thought about the compound Brighton Research called TAC-42. The FMI team believed the "C" probably stood for cyanide. Could this be the unknown compound found by Glen and Stan? Can Frank find out the chemical composition of TAC-42?

Glen walked back and handed Simon a sheet of paper. "Here you go."

"Thanks." He glanced at Janet.

She hadn't said much since they walked into the room. Knowing her, he was sure she'd ask him twenty questions once they leave the CSU lab. He turned his attention to the lab techs. "I think we're done here. I appreciate everything you've done."

"We'll be anxious to know where the bats got this lethal compound," Glen said.

"As soon as we can find this deadly compound, we'll be bringing it to you guys for analysis."

He turned to Janet. "Let's see if Dr. Stonebridge found anything inside the bats." They left the lab and headed for the autopsy rooms.

"Since we didn't get a phone call from Dr. Stonebridge," Janet said, "I'm assuming the necropsy was normal."

"I'd have to agree with your assumption. Although, I think we should let him know what our theory is regarding the bat's GI enzymes. He'll need to check the bats' stomach and intestines for the mysterious compound Stan and Glen found in the guano."

"That would be wise." A concerned expression caused her to furl her eyebrows. "I hope they're taking all precautions given the potentially lethal compound that may still be inside the bats?"

"I'm sure they are."

They stopped in front of the autopsy room door at the end of the hallway where Dr. Stonebridge and Jacob were. The windowless door prevented them from seeing inside the room. A rectangular sign with red letters above the door was lit, "DO NOT ENTER."

"I'll call Jacob and let 'em know we're here." The phone rang…and rang…and rang. Then, "Can't come to the phone. Please leave a message after the beep." A pause; followed by a beep.

"Jacob. It's Dr Woods. Agent Bennett and I are standing outside the necropsy room door."

Simon glanced at his watch. Ninety minutes had passed since he dropped off the bats to Jacob. Knowing the length of time for one bat necropsy from previous bat exams, Dr. Stonebridge should be nearing the end of examining all the bats. A sinking feeling weighed in his stomach like a heavy weight. What if they accidentally inhaled the deadly cyanide/saucer-shaped compound? They might be lying on the floor, convulsing from a Grand Mal seizure--then death. Simon knocked on the door firmly.

No response from inside the room. He grabbed the doorknob and turned it, ignoring the warning sign above the door. The doorknob didn't turn. The door was locked, preventing anyone from entering the room, unless you had a key to open it. "My God. They might already be dead."

"If the room is filled with the deadly compound, it'll be foolish to enter. We'd be exposed to the compound's lethal effect."

The sound of footsteps approached them from behind. They turned around. Jacob held a manila folder with a broad smile mapped across his face. "Hi, guys. The door's locked."

Thank God, he's alive. "We were concerned we didn't hear anything back from Dr. Stonebridge's exam of the bats. Plus, we wanted to tell him about checking the intestinal track of the bats for a foreign compound the bats might have ingested."

"We checked the digestive track and didn't fine the cyanide/saucer-like compound."

"How did you know about this possible lethal compound?"

"Stan from the CSU lab called us during Stonebridge's necropsy. I checked for the cyanide/saucer-shaped compound under a microscope and didn't find it in the GI track. There was a trace of cyanide in the bat's lower intestine. Other than that, the bats were normal."

"Thanks, Jacob. And thank Dr. Stonebridge for us."

"Sure will." He turned to his left and walked up another hallway.

Simon and Janet turned around and walked up the hallway, heading to their vehicle. Neither of them said anything of significance to each other. When they got outside, he said, "We'll talk when we get into the Suburban. I'm sure you have some questions to ask me."

Janet chuckled. "Huh, Agent Woods…I guess you're getting to know my idiosyncrasies and behavior."

"It's part of my behavioral science training."

"Are you saying you've spent time at the FBI Quantico facility?"

"Matter of fact, I did a six-month training session there about a year ago, right after I accepted the position with the CDC, then FMI."

"You're a man of many surprises."

"I'll take that as a compliment."

"You should."

They sat in the Suburban. Simon turned on the air conditioning. He waited for Janet to say something regarding CSU's lab results.

Janet with a puzzled expression turned toward Simon, who sat in the driver's seat. "I've been thinking about the nystagmus the four cavers demonstrated. I know we couldn't mention it in front of Stan and Glen, since we couldn't mention your ESP ability. Robert Rhode from the first cave had this eye condition, nystagmus, a day before his death from what his mother had said. According to her, her son complained of wavy lines a month before his death, again according to his mother. Then we have Susan Whitman complaining of wavy lines, according to her mother. Robert and Susan worked for Brighton Research. Of course, we can't forget Matthew Young, one of the first six cavers who died, and who we know from his parents their son had done a computer search for 'wavy lines' relating to vision. Robert may have mentioned these symptoms to him. Possibly Matthew had the condition and looked it up for his own medical concern. We'll never know which one it was."

"What we know for sure is the two cavers who worked for Brighton Research had ocular wavy lines along with nystagmus. Is this just a coincidence?"

"Like I've said before, I don't believe in coincidental happenings. Especially this one with Brighton Research. We have no other leads on these deaths other than this research company. They seem to be our focal point regarding these deaths. Can't wait to see if Frank and Jean can find out something to link Brighton Research to these deaths."

"Why don't you give Danny a call and let 'em know we're on our way back to the hotel."

Janet called Danny, putting her phone on speaker. "We're heading back to the hotel. Anything new from Frank or Jean?"

"No. Nothing. What did you find out at the lab and the pathologist?"

"Simon will tell you. I don't speak good in medical terms or its language."

Simon recapped what took place including the results from the CSU lab on the guano and air analysis, plus the negative results of Dr. Stonebridge's necropsy of the bats. "We need to know how far away bats can fly at night. And what they eat besides insects. There has to be a source, a specific area the bats are obtaining this toxic compound."

"I'll get right on it."

Janet put her phone away. She said as Simon drove out of the parking lot and onto the four-lane road, "Danny is definitely becoming a vital asset to our team."

"I agree…and so have you."

"Compliments will get you everywhere." A smile lit up her face.

He glanced at her. *I love her smile.* "We do seem to pass compliments around. I'd have to say they're all deserving. Including the ones toward me. I'm not sure if I told you. There's no conceit in my family because…"

"I have it all," Janet interrupted. "I wouldn't call it conceit. I'd call it self-assurance."

"Did you take the behavioral course at Quantico, too?"

They both laughed.

Simon turned into their hotel's parking lot and found a space to park next to Danny's van.

~ * ~

A white van with the same mysterious couple present at the two cave sites and the hotel's restaurant turned into the hotel's parking lot and parked several spaces down from the Suburban.

~ * ~

Simon knocked on Danny's hotel room door. A moment later, Danny opened the door. A smile lit up his face. "I found out some interesting information about bats." He hurried to his computer and sat.

Simon walked across the room and stood behind Danny. Janet stood next Simon and to the right of Danny.

"What do you have?" Simon asked as he peered down at the computer screen.

The top of the screen in blocked, black, bold letters spelled out the title of an article named "FACTS ABOUT BATS."

"I'll give you a condensed review of the facts on the screen. Bats can fly between six to seven hours nonstop from their roost. Bats in one night can travel about thirty-one miles while searching for food. We know from the previous testing done on the guano the bats are insectivores…they only eat bugs. Areas where insects thrive are near bodies of water, like rivers, lake and ponds. I found out two other things not really relevant to our investigation, but I found them interesting."

"What's that?" Simon asked.

"Bats can live between ten and twenty years. Female bats bear one offspring per year."

"Like I've said before," Janet said, "between you and Frank, I'm learning more science than all the years I spent as a student from kindergarten through four years of college."

Simon refocused his thoughts on the origin of the mysterious compound. "If these bats feasted on insects possessing this deadly compound, it means they had about a fifteen to sixteen square mile area to travel. Am I right?"

"Yes. You're right," answered Danny. "I realized that earlier after finding out how far they can travel from their roost. So, I checked for bodies of water in a fifteen-mile radius of the two caves, the Tillmans' attic, and the church. I put together a topographical map where the bat colonies existed and the bodies of water."

He changed the computer monitor screen. The screen now displayed the map. "As you can see, there's a few bodies of water the bats could've reached during their night feeding."

Janet leaned toward the screen. "Where is Brighton Research facility?"

Danny's fingers sped across the keyboard. "It's right here." A red asterisk symbol fell within each of the circle's radius of each bat site colonies. "I'd say the source of the mysterious compound is from Brighton Research. As you can see, there's a small pond adjacent to the facility."

Simon stepped a couple of feet away from the computer with his head down, staring at the floor. His mind concentrating on the information from the computer screen. "We're dealing with a company using cyanide in their research and in their developing products. Whatever it is, including a new product called...called..."

"It's called TAC-42," Danny said.

"Right. Whatever TAC-42 is, it may be the compound or some other compound they use that are affecting these bats. If it is Brighton

Research, are these bats being exposed to this compound accidentally or deliberately?"

Janet turned around and sat at the end of the bed. "Again, a lot of questions without answers."

"I have a plan," Danny proclaimed. "A way to find out if Brighton Research is responsible for the bats becoming contaminated with this lethal compound."

Simon walked over and stood next to Janet. "Explain."

Danny turned his desk chair around. "I have a drone with an apparatus capable of taking samples of the air, water or soil specimens, along with an audiovisual camera. We can drive out to Brighton Research and park my van about half a mile away from their property. I will then guide the drone from inside my van to the pond adjacent to the facility and take samples of whatever we decide. Unless there are security cameras pointed at every foot of their property, we should be able to do this without being detected by security."

Simon sat down next to Janet. "Great idea. There's one problem. If we do find the lethal compound in the pond, the drone will bring the compound back to us, exposing us to its deadly effect to humans."

"No problem. The specimen container is airtight, preventing any harm to whoever comes near it or touches it."

"You sure have everything figured out. Of course, all this stems on our assumption that Brighton Research has this lethal compound."

Janet cleared her throat. "From my perspective of everything we've discovered, this research company is at the top of our list for suspects. I'd say we'd have nothing to lose and everything to gain if we're correct in our suspicions."

Simon loved her detective savvy and logic. She was right in what she said. He glanced at his watch. "It's almost two o'clock. Let's do this."

Janet stood, looking at the computers in front of him. "What about observing Frank and Jean in case something endangering them comes up unexpectedly?"

"I got it covered," Danny answered as he got up from his chair. "Besides these computers being on a cloud recorder, my van has computers. So we can observe them as I drive. You'll see what I'm talking about once you get into my van."

Janet sat in the front passenger seat. Simon sat in a bucket seat behind her. Another bucket seat was positioned behind Danny. Two nine-inch monitors recessed into the middle of the dashboard with changing inside views of Brighton Research building made it possible for Danny and Janet to observe various hallways and rooms. Behind Simon were two more computers setting on a metal shelf along the driver's side panel. A stool bolted to a carpeted floor stood in front of each computer. Suspended from the ceiling was the drone with at least a three-foot span. Cabinets ran along the passenger side panel of the van. *Danny is meticulously organized,* thought Simon as he scanned the back of the van.

Danny pulled down a one-lane dirt lane about a mile from the front entrance of Brighton Research. He stopped about fifty yards from the main black-topped road. The lane hadn't been used regularly because of grass and weeds protruding from the center of the dirt pathway.

Danny opened the back door of the van, reached around, unlatched the suspended drone and carried it outside, behind the van. He set it on a bare spot in the middle isle of the road. He then got inside the van, closed the backdoor and sat on a cushioned stool in front of a monitor. A rectangular device the size of a Kleenex box with a large toggle handle in the middle sat in front of the monitor. The monitor screen lit up, displaying the back of the van.

"We're ready for flight, Houston," Danny bellowed out. He turned to Simon, who displayed puzzlement on his face, then toward Janet with the same facial expression. "It's a silly thing I do before sending off my drone."

The monitor showed the drone rising from the ground to about ten feet above the treetops. It then slowly moved forward in the direction of Brighton Research, searching for a pond, a pond potentially harboring a lethal substance.

Chapter Twenty

The drone moved over the treetops. The camera pointed down toward the ground, covering an area of approximately two football fields side by side. Danny moved the camera's view upward to where the lens was pointed parallel to the treetops. About three quarters of a mile away, the four-story Brighton Research building came into view. A clearing about the size of a football field was adjacent to the building.

"The pond is probably in the clearing," Danny said as he moved the camera lens downward as the drone moved closer to the clearing. The perimeter fence appeared.

About a minute later, a pond came into view on the screen. "There's the pond," Danny announced.

"The water is a greenish color," Janet said, who now sat on the stool next to Danny.

"Knowing a little bit about ecology," Danny said, "I'd say this green-appearing color is a type of algae growing in the water."

Simon turned sideways in his bucket seat and leaned forward, staring at the monitor. "See if there's any type of piping leading into the pond from the direction of Brighton Research."

The drone moved downward to about ten feet above the pond before moving around the shore of the pond, searching for a conduit leading into the algae filled water. After searching the entire edge of the pond, there wasn't any evidence of a pollutant being emptied into the pond.

"I was sure we'd find a drainage pipe," Janet said disappointedly.

"It might still be there" Simon added. "A drainage pipe might be below ground level where we wouldn't be able to see it."

"Do you want me to take a sample of the water?" Danny asked.

"That's what we came here for. Let's do it," Simon answered.

Danny lowered the drone a few inches above the water. He pinched a small round toggle between his left thumb and index finger while the monitor screen showed a cylindrical probe descending from the drone and stopping about three inches into the water. "I'll collect a water sample now." He moved the toggle to the left. A few seconds later, the probe ascended back into the drone. "Sample secured."

"Can you fly the drone from the pond straight toward the Brighton Research building? I'd like to see if there's a pumping station."

"Yes. Piece of cake. We're about fifteen hundred feet away from the building. I'll have to continue flying a few feet above the treetops since security cameras might detect the drone if I fly any higher."

"You're the expert. Do what you have to do."

The drone moved upward.

"Stop," Janet said. "I saw something in the pond. It looked like bubbles."

"I'll play back the video." Several seconds later, the monitor showed a cluster of bubbles breaking through the blanket of algae in the center of the pond. "It must be coming from a drainage pipe." Danny changed the monitor back to live action. "Let's see if the drainage pipe is coming from the Brighton Research building."

The drone began to ascend again then stopped and moved forward over the treetops toward the four-story research facility. Everyone's eyes peeled on the monitor screen, as the camera lens pointed straight down to the densely tree covered terrain. The edge of the woods and the cleared property around the research building came into view. "There's the pumping station over there near the building," Danny said as he maneuvered the control stick to the drone. "There's a pipe going up the side of the building from the pump."

"Follow it," Simon said. "The pipe's going to the top of the building." The drone rose passed the second floor, the third floor, then as it reached the fourth floor a silver dome on top of the building came into view. He stood and walked over to the monitor. "What's that on top of the building?"

"It looks like there's a giant greenhouse covering the entire roof of Brighton Research," Janet answered.

The drone moved slowly over the roof. The center of the dome was open about twenty feet across. Below the opening the screen displayed a fruit garden of plants and bushes. In the center of the roof was a pond. "What does fruit gardens and ponds attract?" Simon asked.

"Insects. Mosquitos," Janet replied. "At night, the roof and algae pond adjacent to the building would be a feeding grounds for these flying creatures, along with its predators…bats."

Danny held the drone in a stationary position over the artificial oasis, then said, "Why does Brighton Research, a development company for cleaning products, need nature's garden and a water oasis on top of their building?"

"Don't know," Simon answered. "What we do know…a lot of changes have been made since Brighton Research was taken over by a Chinese conglomerate six months ago. The new owners started buying cyanide. As far as I know, cyanide isn't used in cleaning products. Too bad we already got a sample of water from the algae filled pond. I'd like a sample of water from the oasis pond."

"No problem," Danny said. "I have a backup in case the first sampler apparatus malfunctions." He lowered the drone until it was a few inches from the water. Several seconds later, the drone had a sample of the water. Red lights began flashing along with a high-pitched alarm. The oval roof began to close from the periphery toward the center. "The drone has been detected by their security system. Either by a motion detector or the drone was seen on a camera by a security guard."

Simon yelled, "Get the drone out of there."

Danny began the ascent of the drone.

The opening above the drone was getting smaller and smaller. "Faster, Danny," Janet said with a voice filled with panic.

"My drone isn't built for speed. I'm moving the drone upward as fast as I can."

The opening at the top of dome was about five feet wide. The drone's diameter was three feet as it neared the center of the dome.

"Come on…come on," Simon pleaded. The opening was less than

three feet wide. "The drone isn't going to make it through the opening."

The drone turned sideways and slipped between the narrow opening, followed by complete closure of the dome.

Everyone cheered like a group of people watching their football team score a game-winning touchdown with no seconds left of the game clock. The drone moved away from the building, heading back to the FMI team and to safety. Danny guided the drone down to the middle of the dirt road and a few feet behind the van. "I'll remove the water containers once we get back to the hotel."

Simon helped him pick up the drone. "Sounds like a safe plan to me." They put the drone into the van.

"We better hustle butt out of here before security from Brighton finds us," Danny suggested.

Janet sat in the front passenger seat, peering down at the two dashboard monitors. "I haven't seen any movement of security at the front gate. I did see two security people run down the fourth-floor hallway to a stairwell leading to the roof. I'd assume the drone only set off a motion detector."

"Good assumption," Simon agreed as he buckled his seat belt.

If the drone had been seen by a security camera, they'd already would've know the drone had gotten away, and they would've gotten into a security vehicle and searched for the drone off site. Her assumption made sense to Simon.

After they were a couple of miles away from Brighton Research, Janet stated, "I'd say we got away with taking a sample of the oasis water and the water in the other pond."

Simon nodded. "We did...we did. Great job, Danny."

"Thanks."

"Although," Janet said, "we did break a couple of laws on the way to our success. The first one was trespassing. The second, obtaining evidence without a court order or a warrant from a judge."

"True. Sometimes, in the need to find the truth in order to protect the welfare of people. Besides, we did no physical harm to anyone. I've been thinking. We'll drop off the water samples to the CSU lab before we go back to the hotel."

Danny parked the van at the Franklin County Medical Examiner's Office/CSU lab parking lot. He removed the two containers from the drone, then he and Simon carried them to the lab while Janet waited in the van. Fifteen minutes later, Danny and Simon got back into the van.

"When will they have the results on the water?" Janet asked.

"The lab will call in a couple of hours regarding the results," Simon answered.

About forty minutes later, Danny parked the van in the hotel's parking lot. The three of them then walked into the hotel.

~ * ~

The van with the mysterious couple had parked several spaces down from Danny's vehicle. The man walked over to the back door of Danny's van, pushed a button on a handheld square device. A red light changed to a green light at the end of the device. He then opened the door of the van and went inside. Less than a minute later, he came out carrying something clasped in his left hand. He removed the square device from his suitcoat, pointed the device at the backdoor of the van and pressed the same button. The green light changed to a red light. The man then met up with the woman at the front door of the hotel. They walked inside.

~ * ~

Danny sat at his desk chair and stared at the different camera views of the Brighton Research building. "There aren't any security cameras on top of the building in their Garden of Eden plot. Your assumption, Janet, about them not have security cameras up there, was correct."

Simon and Janet stood behind Danny peering down at the computer monitor screen, "Call it deductive reasoning," she said matter-of-factly.

"Isn't that Frank in the left lower square of the screen?" Simon questioned.

Danny enlarged the square for a more accurate and detailed view.

"It sure is," Danny answered. "He's scratching the top of his head which means he found out something vital in our investigation."

"Earlier you only mentioned they'll rub their ear lobe if there's an emergency and need to get leave the building right away." Janet said with furled eyebrows.

"You're right. We also had this other gesture."

"Any other gestures I should know about?" Simon asked, rubbing the right side of his cheek.

"No. Just those two."

Simon glanced at the clock in the lower right corner of the computer screen: four thirty-five p.m. "They'll be getting out of work soon. Hopefully, he has the piece of the puzzle needed to solve these deaths."

"We can hope," Janet said.

Around five fifteen, Simon's cellphone rang. He glanced at the caller ID. It was the lab technician, Glen Lolich, at the CSU lab. "Hi, Glen. I'm putting you on speaker so my colleagues can hear what you have for us."

"Okay. In the first sample marked 'green pond,' I found *Volvocales*, *Chlorococcales*, and *Myxophyceae* in the water. These are the algae causing the green water. There were also a few types of bacteria and protozoans in the water. We also found the cyanide/saucer-shaped compound. The second water sample marked 'oasis' water contained mosquito larvae and the cyanide/saucer-shaped compound. The mosquito larvae contained the unknown, mysterious compound. What was even more remarkable, the cyanide/saucer-shaped compound wasn't degrading in an accelerated half-life as what we saw in the bat guano. We exposed mice to the compound. They displayed visual problems, bumping into the plexiglass walls of their confined container. They didn't have any seizures. Nor did they suddenly keel over and die."

"Do you have an explanation for this?" Simon asked.

"I talked with Stan. After further testing, we concluded the larvae hatched into mosquitos saturated with this toxic compound, not affecting the adult mosquito. The bats eat the mosquitos and carries them back to their colony in their GI system. Somehow the bat's intestinal enzymes altered the mysterious compound's matrix, making it harmful to humans. The unknown compound has the properties of a neurotoxin. Plus, the GI enzymes caused the compound to accelerate the degrading or half-life process as the compound reached the guano state. When the bats get back to their roost, the cyanide/saucer-shaped composite breaks away from the falling guano, contaminating the air with the lethal floating mixture, which confirms our previous calculations of the poisonous guano existing for about thirty hours."

Simon stared at Janet, raising his eyebrows. "Since there wasn't a trace of the saucer-shaped compound in the human host, only a trace of cyanide, this is a perfect killing method."

"I agree."

His attention returned to Glen. "Email me your findings to our FMI email address. Thank you for everything."

"You're welcome. I'll get the report to you as soon as possible. Bye."

"What about the nystagmus followed by seizures you saw in your vision of the three cavers in the second cave deaths?" Janet asked. "I assume they and all the other victims manifested these medical conditions before they died."

"Yes. I'm sure each of our victims experienced these signs."

A knock on the room door. "It has to be Frank and Jean," Simon said as he walked over and opened the door. Frank and Jean came into the room.

Simon decided to wait and hear what they had to say before informing them about the CSU lab results. "You gave the 'scratch your head gesture' in the hallway. What did you find out?"

"Oh. I'm sorry. My head itched from the cap I was wearing in my work area." A short pause, followed by a grin. "Just kidding."

Simon rolled his eyes and rubbed his forehead. "Okay. What did you find out?"

"Brighton Research isn't what it's made out to appear, concerned about cleaning products. For the past several months, they've been developing a product called TAC-42. The new compound directs its deadly effect against menacing leaf-eating insects and its larvae before they destroy various berry bushes and fruit trees."

This new information from Frank was all making sense to Simon of why Brighton had berry bushes growing on top of the building. Mosquitos and other insects would eat the nectar from flowers and fruit, such as berries. Although mosquitos aren't harmful to flowers and fruit. Was the research company aware that their tainted mosquito larvae could potentially kill humans?

Simon told him and Jean how they obtained the two samples of water and transported the samples to the CSU lab. Simon then said, "The microscopic analysis of the water on Brighton Research building's roof pool and a pond adjacent to the building showed a strange compound resembling a saucer…"

"A saucer with tentacles?" Jean interrupted.

"Yes. Exactly. You must've seen the compound?"

"I did. I viewed the compound under a microscope at Brighton's biochemical lab today." She furled her eyebrows and nodded. "That's why I wasn't affected by the deadly compound. TAC-42 hadn't passed through a bat's GI track. Although, I might get the nystagmus and wavy lines in the future?"

"Possible. Did Brighton know of any side effects to humans or animals from their new product?"

"Yes. Some employees were having visual problems. Nystagmus and wavy lines."

"So, Frank and Jean. What you now told us about their research into their new product TAC-42 being developed for killing menacing insects attacking fruit bushes and trees confirmed CSU's lab results"

"I believe we have enough evidence to present to a judge to shut down their research on TAC-42," Janet said. "Since we can prove their new product can kill people or at least cause significant side effects to a person's vision."

"I have some other information to add to our investigation," Jean said, who walked toward them as she opened a can of soda she'd retrieved from the room's small refrigerator. "I found out from the people who worked with Susan Whitman she'd talked about reporting the company to health authorities regarding the visual side effects of TAC-

42. The company told her symptoms weren't a permanent medical condition, and the compound wasn't anything to worry about. Also, the company was working on eliminating the side effects."

Simon briefly placed his hand on top of Danny's shoulder. "Jean's inquiry reflected the memo from Brighton Research's chief operating officer to the president of Yang Corporation which Danny discovered during his computer search three days ago. They felt Susan Whitman and Robert Rhode were going to give out information to authorities regarding Brighton Research's possible illegal cyanide usage or side effects of TAC-42. Unfortunately, there's no evidence the company had anything to do with the cavers' deaths, the explosion at the first cave and the Tillmans. What we do have is forensic evidence, evidence like Janet explained, that we can use to get a court order to shut down any further development of their new product TAC-42, a neurotoxin with properties capable of causing visual disorders, and likely seizures…then death."

"I'll call Detective Spurrier and inform him what evidence we have on the Deadly Seizure Case."

"While you're talking with the detective, I'll call Director Littlefield. After we make our phone calls, we'll have to take our evidence to a federal judge. The evidence infringes on federal jurisdiction since Brighton Research is importing cyanide from a foreign country and a chemical is being used to make a dangerous compound, affecting the life of American people."

Janet dialed Detective Spurrier's number. "Hi, Steward. We got evidence pointing to the cause of caver's deaths." She told him what had taken place regarding the CSU lab results of the water and the bat guano and that Brighton Research was indirectly responsible for the deaths. "We'll be taking our evidence to a federal judge today." She held the phone and listened to what Steward was saying to her.

Simon listened to Director Littlefield, then said, "Yes. We'll be taking our evidence to a federal judge here in Chambersburg."

"I'll contact the U.S. Marshalls, making sure they're with you when the subpoena is served. I'll also let CDC know what's happening there."

"When we serve our subpoena this evening at Brighton Research, I'll make sure the dome to their roof garden is closed, preventing any bats from eating their tainted mosquitos and shut down the pump leading to the outside pond."

"That would be wise. By the way, did you find out who was responsible for the explosion at the first cave?" Littlefield asked.

"No. Detective Spurrier has been investigating the incident."

"Sounds like you have things under control there. Give me a call tomorrow."

"Sure will. Talk to you then."

Simon put his cellphone into his jacket pocket. He looked at Janet, who was still talking to the detective.

Janet said, as she peered at Simon, "Spurrier found the person responsible for the explosion at the cave."

Chapter Twenty-one

"I'm going to put you on speaker," Janet said, "so the rest of the agents can hear what you have to say about the cave explosion."

A short pause, then, "I'm indirectly responsible for the cave-in. About a year ago, I was involved in a fatal shooting of a murder suspect. It was a justified killing. I was exonerated by our Internal Affairs department and the district attorney. Apparently, the brother of the suspect felt I was guilty of killing his brother. He felt I didn't have to shoot him. To make a long story short, this guy wanted revenge and placed the explosives at the entrance of the cave. He wouldn't tell us how he knew I'd be at the cave the day of the explosion. I'm very sorry you and the rest of the FMI agents had to be involved with this deranged guy."

Janet had always thought, along with the other agents, that The Circle was responsible for the explosion. She wasn't a hundred percent convinced this guy planted the explosive for the reason Detective Spurrier said. Why did he hold off doing anything for a whole year? Why didn't he just shoot the detective instead of setting up such an elaborate scheme? "You had no control of this deranged guy. Did this guy tell you his feelings right after his brother's death last year?"

"That's what was odd. Nothing derogatory was said after the shooting until we arrested him this afternoon."

Janet was suspicious, skeptical regarding the perp's reason for the cave's explosion. It would be best to go along with Detective Spurrier's story, even though there was doubt written all over the perp's explanation. "Who knows what's in the mind of a crazed person?"

Simon shuffled a couple of steps toward Janet, then stopped. "As for the quarantined caves, you should keep them closed until we shut down Brighton Research Facility and get rid of their deadly product. Did Janet tell you about TAC-42?"

"Yes. She did. It's like something out of a horror movie."

"You know TAC-42 will remain dangerous for about thirty hours after the bats ingest the compound. By tomorrow night the bats' roosts and their guano should be void of the lethal compound."

"The church should be safe to go in tomorrow morning," Steward said. "Since the exterminators closed off the air vent opening in the back of the church this morning. Am I right?"

"You're right," Simon answered.

"I'll let the minister know."

Janet gathered the printout from the CSU lab regarding the results of the bat guano from the church containing TAC-42 after the bats had ingested it during the lethal thirty-hour period. The printout also contained the findings regarding the nonlethal TAC-42 in the water sample of the pool on the roof of Brighton Research's building and the adjacent pond. These lab results sealed FMI's conclusion of their investigation of the cavers' and the Tillmans' deaths. *If there ever was the how, who and what caused the death of eleven people, this is the concrete evidence we need,* thought Janet.

The matter of most importance now was to shut down Brighton Research's production of TAC-42. Janet breathed in deeply, then let the air out slowly as she put the printout papers into a leather satchel. She felt proud to be part of this investigation and a member of the FMI team.

Her cellphone rang. She glanced at the caller ID. It was Bill Matters. "Hi, Bill. How are you doing?"

"Doing good." A short pause. "I got the report from the lab results of my bronchial washing they did yesterday. Nothing was found that would've caused my coma. Another dead end."

"Sorry to hear that."

"How's your case going where you are?"

"We're in the final stages of closing the case." Janet gave Bill a quick synopsis of their solved Deadly Seizure Case. "I'm just glad you're safe and doing well. We'll keep in touch."

"Sure will, ex-partner. Take care."

~ * ~

A caravan of three vehicles pulled up to the front gate of Brighton Research led by Simon in their Suburban with all the FMI agents present, followed by two US Marshalls. Riding in the last vehicle were two medical staff members from the Franklin County Health Department. Simon rolled down the driver side window and showed the security guard the federal search warrant.

The guard opened the gate.

Janet, Simon, a US Marshal, and a man from the health department went to the fourth floor with a security guard. They walked up a stairwell to the roof. At the top of the stairs on the wall to the right of the closed door to the roof's greenhouse was a small square security control panel. He pushed a four-digit code on the panel. The door's locked clicked, opening the door.

"Close the dome," Simon commanded.

The security guard stepped inside the greenhouse and turned to his right. On a square concrete post was an electrical panel. He pushed a button. Curved roof panels slowly moved toward the center of the dome, closing off the greenhouse to the outside. The sun was setting in the western horizon, leaving enough light to see walking around the greenhouse.

The US Marshal stood by the door as Janet and Simon put on protective masks and latex gloves. Simon collected two samples of the water, while Janet obtained samples of the berries and their leaves. The man from the health department then sprayed the artificial pond with an oil-based liquid that would kill the mosquito larvae, preventing the larvae from developing into mosquitos. He then placed three insecticide smoke bombs with a timer at each end of the garden and one in the middle. He walked over to where the roof's open doorway where Janet, Simon, the U.S. Marshal, and the security guard stood. "When these insecticide bombs go off, it'll kill any insect inside this greenhouse."

When they were all in the stairwell, the security guard closed and locked the door. "That's it. We're secured."

The health department man removed his protective mask. "The insects will be dead within a few hours." He turned to the security guard. "Don't allow anyone in there for twenty-four hours."

"Yes, sir."

Smoke began to fill the greenhouse as they peered through the glass window in the upper part of the door.

"I wonder how the rest of the team is doing?" Janet asked Simon, as they made their way down the stairs to the fourth floor.

"Since Frank and Jean know the layout of the labs, I'm sure they have everything under control."

Frank, Jean, Danny, and the rest of the entourage were waiting in the front lobby of Brighton Research.

"Hey, Simon and Janet. Everything went smoothly. I left a copy of the subpoena on the lab director's desk. Shortly afterward, I talked with the lab director on one of the security guard's cellphone. He was surprised by the court subpoena regarding TAC-42. They had no idea the compound had evolved into a deadly compound due to the bats. The lab director promised Brighton Research will cooperate and cease any further testing of the compound. We removed all the TAC-42 in the labs. The confiscated compound will be taken to the Pennsylvania State Police Bureau of Forensic Services in Harrisburg."

"Did the director know who you were?" Janet asked.

Brighton's security guards weren't standing amongst them.

"No. I didn't tell him, either. He'll get Charles Papas and Lucy Bradshaw's resignation letters tomorrow morning via email explaining our undercover positions with FMI, a division of the CDC. Since there's video cameras running twenty-four hours a day throughout the facility, he'll know anyway who Jean and I really are."

"Everyone ready? We're done here." Janet then glanced at Simon, who frowned back at her. She grimaced. *Damn. Again, I'm acting like the chief agent.*

"Like Janet said," Simon confirmed with a grin, "we're done here."

As they walked to their vehicles, the sound of a helicopter filled the air. To their left a spotlight could be seen shining in the area of the algae pond a couple hundred yards away. Frank said, "The helicopter will be dropping oil bags which will break open on impact, spreading an oil slick on top of the pond, killing all the mosquito larvae and adult mosquitos that are hovering over the water. It should be the end of our tainted killing mosquitos."

~ * ~

Simon pulled into the hotel's parking lot and parked. They had stopped a company from developing a dangerous and deadly entity. Their investigation of the cavers' and the Tillmans' deaths was done. The Deadly Seizure Case was closed. Another unsettling situation lingered without closure. He suspected the organization called Eternal Order of Zeus was somehow affiliated with The Circle. Adam Fletcher, the founder, recruited Robert Rhode for a specific reason. A reason Simon and the FMI agents would probably never know.

Before everyone got out of the Suburban, Frank said, "Another chapter ended for the Death Agents."

Jean huffed. "You know I hate that term."

"Okay, everyone," Simon interjected. "Let's get a good night's sleep. Tomorrow morning we'll pack up our things and head out."

They entered an empty hotel lobby. The sound of music projected out from the lounge. "I love the song they're playing in the lounge," Janet said touching Simon's elbow with her elbow.

"Do you want to get a drink before retiring to our rooms?" Simon asked, looking down at her.

"Sure. Love to."

Simon felt the small hairs in the back of his neck stand out, as he sensed everyone's eyes peering at him. "Everyone's invited."

Frank, Jean, and Danny declined the offer. They turned right and headed toward their rooms, whispering comments to each other.

Simon and Janet walked into a half-filled lounge. A country song about a lady was playing on the jukebox. They sat down at a booth to their left. Janet smiled as she stared into Simon's eyes. "This is becoming a regular thing between you and me. Having a drink before going to our rooms for the night. Don't you think?"

"I look forward to it." His heart increased its beats and he could feel every breath as amorous feelings overwhelmed him. "I didn't tell anyone about what Director Littlefield had said to me earlier. I was going to wait until tomorrow morning after everyone had a good night sleep. Anyway, the team will have a week of time off starting tomorrow. The director said there aren't any mysterious deaths FMI needs to investigate. Of course, that could change." The back of his throat felt parched as he inhaled deeply. His stomach muscled tightened. He then said, "How'd you like to go to Virginia Beach with me?"

"I thought you'd never ask," she answered, reaching across the table and placing her hand on top of his.

~ * ~

Across the room, the mysterious couple that had been observing the FMI agents walked into the lounge. They peered at Simon and Janet and walked toward them.

About the Author

I graduated from Wayne State University with a secondary education degree in Unified Science and a minor in English. I then graduated from University of Detroit-Mercy with a Physician Assistant degree. Life experiences and an overactive imagination motivates my passion for writing. My favorite authors are Tess Gerritsen, Robin Cook and several Rogue Phoenix Press authors.Rogue Phoenix Press published four of my mystery/suspense novels: *Frozen Death* (2009), *Sudden Blindness* (2014), *Strange Appearance* (2016, *Strange* (2018), *Whispers Before Death-Death Agents Book One* (2019) and *The Strange Horizon- -Glimpses into the world of a dreamer*, A collage of short stories (2017). I live in Florida with my wife, Holly.

Also by G. L. Didaleusky
at
Rogue Phoenix Press

Whispers Before Death

Whispers Before Death is the first book in the series called Death Agents. Agents of the newly formed Federal Medical Investigators (FMI) investigate mysterious and unsolved medical related deaths. Each agent possesses supernatural powers, helping them solve medical mysteries throughout the United States. Their newest case takes them to Ocala, Florida where eight people throughout the city die at exactly eleven fifty-eight a.m. Each victim whispers something before suddenly dying. No one hears what they're saying. A Marion County Sheriff Detective, Janet Bennett, is recruited to assist the agents. An immediate friendship develops between F.M.I.'s chief investigator, Simon Woods, M.D. and Detective Bennett. The FMI team and Janet frantically seek out answers to these mysterious deaths before deadly evilness reaches out toward others, including them.

Prologue

The students in Ms. Maddox's eleventh-grade world history class sat at their desks looking down and reading a handout assignment. On the wall to the right of the classroom door hung a wall clock. The wall clock's large hand sat on eleven and the small hand was on twelve. In five minutes, the school bell would blare its piercing ring, ending the fourth period. One of her students, Allen Murdock, who sat in the front row, peered up at her. His eyebrows raised as far as they could, displaying the upper whites of his eyes; his mouth gaping. Fear stared back at her.

A few seconds later, Murdock's lips moved up and down, uttering a faint whisper—no one could hear but him. He then gently laid his forehead on the top of his desk.

Ms. Maddox walked over to his desk and tapped his shoulder. "Aren't you feeling good, Allen?"

He didn't answer her.

His head flopped to the right, resting the right side of his face on top of the desk. Wide-opened emerald-colored eyes appeared to gaze toward the desk next to him. Drool spilled out from the right side of his mouth. His chest ceased movement. A previously energetic teenager sat lifeless in his chair.

~ * ~

The noise threshold of the high school cafeteria, filled to near capacity, neared the decibels of a rock concert. How anyone could hear their fellow student sitting across from them at the long rectangular tables seemed impossible. With their iPads playing piercing music—and not Beethoven or other classical orchestrated renditions—these students in the future would more than likely be wearing hearing aids.

"Can you believe it?" said Cindy. "Paul asking Mary to the senior prom and not you. What a jerk. And I thought you and Paul were good friends."

"I thought we were too," said Pam, sitting across from Cindy at the crowded high school cafeteria table.

"I'm sure this is for the best. I have a feeling he would've ignored you at the prom anyway."

A lanky, pimple-faced boy walked up to Cindy from behind. "Hi, Cindy."

She turned and looked up. "Hey, Aaron. What's going on?"

"Not much."

Cindy turned back toward Pam. Her head now laid on top of crossed arms. Reaching over the table, she flicked her middle finger on top of Pam's head. She didn't flinch. "Come on girl. You can't be tired. The lunch bell's going to ring in a few minutes." She flicked her finger again.

Pam still didn't move.

She reached across the table, lifting Pam's head off her arms. Dead eyes stared back at her.

Cindy's scream silenced the noisy high school cafeteria.

Chapter One

Michael Bennett, a family practice physician, pulled his car in next to his wife's SUV in the garage of their two-story colonial house at five thirty-five p.m. A few moments later he walked into the kitchen where his wife, Crystal, stood next to the stove. Sitting at the kitchen table were his two teenage children. "Hi, everyone."

"Hi, Daddy," said Carla, his thirteen-year-old daughter.

"Hey, Dad," said Matthew, his fifteen-year-old son.

Michael walked over and kissed Crystal on the lips. "How's my best girl?"

"I'm good, honey. Please sit down. Supper is almost ready."

He raised his head and sniffed. "Supper sure smells good."

The phone rang on the kitchen counter. "Are you on call tonight?" asked Crystal.

"No. John's on call." He picked up the phone. "Hello." Michael listened to the caller at the other end of the line. "Yes, Randy Mitchell is a patient of mine." He listened to the caller. His shoulders slumped; his face became ashen. "What was the cause of his death?" Michael looked toward Crystal. "Oh, I see. No. He wasn't taking any medications, nor did he have any medical problems. Thank you for calling me."

"Who were you talking to?"

"A forensic investigator from the medical examiner's office. A patient of mine died today."

"Oh, one of your older patients?"

"No. He was sixteen years old."

"Did he die in a car accident?" Carla asked.

"No. His mother got home from shopping around three o'clock and found her son sitting in front of his bedroom computer with his head resting on the desk. He was dead."

"Holy shit!"

"Matthew, don't swear," said Crystal.

"Sorry, Mom. But two kids today died at school. One was found in the classroom sitting at his desk with his head resting on his arms. The other one, a girl, was in the cafeteria sitting at a table with friends. They said she was talking with her girlfriend then laid her head down on her arms and died. They both died around noon."

In the twenty years as a doctor, Michael couldn't remember three teenagers dying in different settings with a similar presentation, heads peacefully resting on top of their arms or desks. Were they friends who ingested something in a suicide pack? A drug screen and an autopsy would answer his speculation. His sister was a Marion County Sheriff's detective. She might know something about these deaths, or she might know if the teenagers knew each other. He'd give her a call after supper.

"What do you think these kids could've died from?" asked Crystal, taking the meatloaf out from the oven and placing it on the kitchen table onto a large hot pad.

Michael told her what he thought about the teenagers' deaths. "I'll call Janet after supper. She may know something."

During supper, no one further discussed the teenagers' deaths. One scenario of these deaths crossed Michael's mind. Some type of virus, bacteria or even a devastating fungal infection could've caused these deaths. And were these three deaths the beginning stages of a contagious biological entity? Although, there should've been warning signs such as fever, headache, pain, or neurological manifestations. Did any of these teenagers have any of those medical signs before they suddenly died? There was one problem with this scenario, it would've been impossible for these victims to die about the same time, including the Mitchell boy, who probably also died near noon today. The teenagers being part of a suicide pack was a more logical scenario to Michael.

After supper, Michael called his sister, Janet, from the bedroom, where there could be privacy from his children. His kids would blab any of the latest information about the deaths of their fellow students to their friends at school. "Hi, Janet. How are you doing?"

"Doing okay. I'm sure you're calling about all these deaths occurring a couple minutes before noon today. Am I right?"

"Yeah, you're right. You always get right to the point." He was eleven months older than Janet. They were close growing up. As the big brother, he had protected her in elementary and middle school, and up to her junior year in high school from any potential bullies. Although, his little sister could handle herself with her cocky attitude of, *If you don't like me or what I think, that's your problem.* "So, are the three teenagers' deaths related? Like a suicide pack?"

There was momentary silence. "You know I can't tell you anything over the phone even if I knew the answer. Unless I was authorized by the sheriff' department's news media liaison. But there are more deaths than the three teenagers."

"What are you talking about? More people died today?"

"Don't you listen to the news? Five others died under mysterious circumstances in Ocala today. They all died around twelve o'clock noon."

"Was this a mass suicide pack? Like a cult? How could eight people all die around the same time unless it was a premeditated act by all of them?" Michael had no other explanation.

"I can't say one way or the other."

"Can you tell me this? Have you been assigned to the investigation? I'm sure this isn't restrictive information."

"You are persistent, Big Brother." She chuckled. "Yes. I'm investigating one of these deaths. The fact is, I'm at the home of the boy who died sitting at his bedroom desk. He was homeschooled. A few minutes ago, the medical examiner left with the deceased. The ME's investigator told me she'd talked to you earlier on the phone about the boy's medical status. You told her the boy didn't have any medical problems or any indications of drug abuse."

"Yes, I did tell her these facts. I guess I'm now part of your investigation." His sister couldn't say too much on the phone about the deaths of the teenagers. They couldn't be sure who might be listening in on their conversation. This was the twenty-first century, the age of the government's stealthy listening tactics of *speak no evil* against the US government or its citizens or non-citizens. There was no assurance of privacy when talking with someone by phone or any other means of communication in the world of electronic surveillance today.

"Sort of. I'd say indirectly and superficially, Big Brother. I gotta get going. Talk to you soon. Bye."

Crystal walked into the bedroom. "What did your sister have to say about the three teenagers' deaths?"

"Nothing. Other than she's the lead detective in one of the investigations, a patient of mine, Randy Mitchell. Janet couldn't say too much on the phone since she's in the middle of the investigation at the Mitchells' house. I can't imagine what Randy's parents are feeling now." He reached over, gently grabbed Crystal's hand and kissed the back of it. "We'd be devastated if it was one of our kids."

~ * ~

Janet Bennett put her cellphone into a holder on her belt then turned to her partner, Detective Bill Matters, who stood next to Randy Mitchell's bedroom dresser writing something into a small notebook. "We need to check for any suicide note and anything related to suicide, cults, or anything pertinent to him suddenly dying."

"You're right," Bill said, as he walked over to the desk. "I'll examine his computer since it's already on."

"Good. I'll look around the room for any evidence pointing to why or how the Mitchell boy died."

Matters' five-foot, ten-inch overweight frame sat at the desk chair. "I think I need to go on a diet," he muttered as he squeezed into the desk chair. His body didn't have any room to spare. He played halfback for the Tennessee Volunteers' college football team twenty years ago. Of course, he gained about thirty pounds since the last time he carried the ball through an opening in the offensive frontline.

Janet opened all the dresser drawers, looked under the bed and between the mattress and box springs of the young Mitchell boy's room for drugs, drug paraphernalia, or a suicide note. Nothing was found. "Did you find anything, Bill?"

"Nope. Not a thing. No mention of how to kill yourself without leaving a trace of evidence or material relating to dying or suicide in the computer search engines' history files."

Janet picked up Mitchell's cellphone lying next to the computer and checked it for recent messages. "The last person he'd talked with was Derrick Olsen at 11:58 this morning. It's around the time the other teenagers died. This could be the break we've been looking for." Janet called him.

"Hey, man," said Derrick. "Why did you hang up on me?"

"This is Detective Bennett from the Marion County Sheriff's Office. Are you Derrick Olsen?"

"Yeah. Why are you on Randy's cellphone?"

Janet couldn't tell him about his friend. It would be against police procedures when dealing with a minor. "Your friend Randy can't come to the phone. Did you talk with him this morning?"

"Yeah, detective. It was around noon. We were talking, then he suddenly stopped talking. I thought maybe his mom was coming, so he hung up on me. Is he all right? Did he get into trouble?"

"I can't discuss this with you. Can you tell me if he said anything unusual before he stopped talking with you?"

"No." A short pause, "He did whisper something. But I couldn't make out what he said. Then the phone went dead."

"Thank you, young man." Janet then put the cellphone in an evidence bag. She told Bill what the victim's friend had said.

"We'll have Randy Mitchell's computer analyzed for any hidden and relevant information by our computer forensic department. Also, his phone." Bill turned off the desktop computer.

They left the bedroom, talked with the parents briefly and walked to their car parked in the street. The Crime Scene Investigation team was finishing up, gathering possible pertinent evidence, including Randy Mitchell's computer and cellphone.

Janet pulled out of the Mitchell's driveway. "I don't ever remember deaths like these before," said Detective Matters.

"Because there's never been eight deaths occurring in the same manner, at different crime scenes, and happening around the same time."

Janet parked their unmarked car in the designated area of the Marion County Sheriff's Office Major Crime Unit. She'd been a detective for twelve years, the last five years with the Major Crime Unit. In all her years in law enforcement she'd never encountered so many unexplained deaths at once. Her brother might be right about a mass suicide. The toxicology report on all these victims would answer the question of suicide. If the deaths pointed toward self-induced then the next logical step in this investigation would lead to the organization or group initiating these deaths.

Janet and Bill walked into their office, a large room accommodating eight desks with space to spare, including a large coffeemaker in the corner of the room. All the detectives of the major crime unit occupied the room. They chatted on a serious tone with one another. Their faces were solemn, not displaying any signs of jovialness. Most mornings and afternoons, at least one or two detectives joked around with one another.

She talked with the other detectives about their investigations on the deaths of their victims. Eight victims had mysteriously died. Ages ranging from fifteen to seventy-five. One had died in her car while stopped at a stop sign; three were at work; three died at home; and two died at school. There weren't any signs of trauma on any of the bodies. This was all the information the detectives had on their deaths so far.

Their boss, Captain Robins, walked into the room with two men in their thirties. The two strangers wore identical dark-grey suits. Janet didn't recognize them but assumed they were federal law enforcement, likely FBI by the stoic stature and attire. Robins gestured for them to come over.

"Detective Bennett and Matters," said the captain, "these are Special Agents Williams and Carpenter from the FBI."

Janet's assumption of whom the two unidentified men represented was right on. She had the innate ability to quickly assess a situation or person and come up with an accurate observation a good percentage of the time. They wouldn't be involved unless federal law was broken by these deaths. She nodded to each of them. "I assume some federal law statute was broken due to eight people dying at two minutes to noon today?"

"Yes. Correct," Carpenter answered. "One of the victims was in the witness protection program. And he was going to testify against a major drug dealer in New York next month."

Janet's legs felt rubbery as an arctic blast of frigid air seemed to wrap around her spine. The face of the dead fifteen-year-old sitting at his bedroom desk flashed across her mind. "Why kill seven innocent people in order to kill a person in hiding from an organized crime syndicate? It doesn't make any sense to me. Or it was a coincidence the informant was included in these mysterious deaths?"

"It may be a coincidence, detective." Agent Williams answered. "Or it may be a monstrous act by criminals or a psychopath. Either one doesn't have any empathy toward human life."

"Whatever the reason for these deaths, a criminal element was involved by all indications."

Both the agents nodded.

"But what's more intriguing with these deaths…what could've caused these people to die around the same moment in time?" Janet asked.

"Just as you and your detectives, we don't have an answer yet either."

Janet glanced away. She visualized an electronic timer of some kind inside the victims' bodies switched to the off position at 11:58 this morning.

~ * ~

Michael walked out the bedroom with his wife, Crystal. As they walked into the living room a TV news anchor stated: *It has been confirmed, eight people, including three children, had died at exactly 11:58 this morning. According to reliable sources these deaths don't appear be a suicide pack. There hasn't been any medical cause of their deaths. Sources aren't excluding this was a terrorist act….*

A cold chill streaked from the back of Michael's neck to every muscle in his face, as if he had stuck his head into an opened freezer. His first assumption regarding the deaths in Ocala was that they all died due to a suicide pack. But this assumption had now lost credibility. "From what the news reporter said we're not dealing with suicide deaths in Ocala. I'm going to call Janet back and see if she can stop by the house after she gets off work. She may know more than what was reported by the news media."

Around eight o'clock, the front doorbell rang. He suspected it had to be Janet, since her sister told him she'd be over in about two hours. During the two hours waiting for his sister, he had searched the internet for the latest information on these deaths and, if any logical theory of how everyone could have suddenly died a couple minutes before noon today. Of course, there were the usual explanations: aliens from outer space had something to do with these deaths. Or all these victims had taken capsules at exactly 11:58 in the morning. Each of the victims had been brainwashed and programmed to take the capsules at the same time. There weren't any medically feasible explanations for their deaths, so far. Of course, an autopsy would be done to determine a cause of the mysterious deaths. Toxicology would determine if any substances were ingested.

"Hi, Sis. Glad you were able to stop by."

She frowned and contorted her lips as a grumpy face peered back at him. "I had to come over, otherwise you'd be calling me throughout the night with questions about all of these suspicious deaths."

"You sure know me. Can't help it. It's my inquisitive nature. You're graced with the same genetic trait in your body as do I. It's why you became a detective and I became a doctor."

Janet grinned. "Yeah. A Sherlock and Dr. Watson combo."

Michael sat at the kitchen table with Janet as she discussed the findings in the deaths of the three teenagers, something she couldn't say over the phone. Crystal watched TV in the living room. His children were in their bedrooms doing what teenagers do; communicating with friends on their electronic devices—an iPhone—and wouldn't be listening in on their parents and aunt's conversation. Young people and a growing number of middle-aged and older people were becoming addicted to their iPhones, iPads, tablets, laptops, desktop computers or a combination of them. Landline phones were becoming obsolete to all the generations, especially anyone born in the twenty-first century. If Carla or Matthew weren't talking to their friends, music from their electronic devices would be blaring out the latest song or tune into their ear buds.

Janet told Michael about the FBI's involvement.

"Does the FBI have any idea what had caused these deaths?"

"No. Not a clue. At least, this is what the agents said. Working with them in the past, they don't always give you full disclosure of information. It's a territorial thing. They like to be in charge. Their philosophy is, 'what latest information is ours and what information you get is ours,' if you know what I mean?"

"It's like what Crystal told me after we got married."

"What did she tell you?"

"What's mine is mine. And what's yours is mine." He chuckled. *Of course, she was kidding me.* He and Crystal had a good relationship and shared everything with one another. They didn't have any secrets between them. "It's not a one-sided marriage, as you already know."

Janet nodded, frowned. "You had to rub it in? Since you know my ex basically cared about himself, creating a one-sided marriage."

Michael's shoulders slumped, as he glanced away. "I'm really sorry, Sis. I didn't mean to bring up—"

"There's nothing to be sorry about, big brother," she interrupted. "My marriage to him wasn't your fault."

He raised his shoulders, nodded and sighed. She had divorced Rick about a year ago. Thank God his sister didn't have any kids with him. For sure, he wouldn't have given financial or emotional support to a family. Janet stated it right, *he cared about himself and no one else.*

"You told me before I married him, ten years ago, he wasn't the right guy for me. Of course, I didn't listen to you. And I let my emotions blind me for what he was…a selfish asshole." She got up from her chair, went to the kitchen counter and poured another cup of coffee from the coffee pot. The coffee was made by her sister-in-law earlier. She then turned around and added, "What was even worse, several years passed before I realized who and what I'd married. Toward the end of my marriage to him, I finally admitted to myself that I'd made a mistake in marrying him. I have a tough time even mentioning his name. Instead I refer to my ex as 'him' rather than Rick."

"I'm sure you'll find the right guy."

"Hum. Maybe."

"You're pretty and smart." Janet stood five-foot nine-inches tall with short, blonde hair. Her size twelve slacks with a belt containing her holstered nine-millimeter gun and a pair of handcuffs fit snugly around a slim waistline. A size twelve, grey sports coat fit comfortably on her, covering her handcuffs and weapon. Michael snickered to himself. *Unfortunately, she's probably intimidating to most men, either before or after they find out she's a sheriff detective.*

Janet smirked. "I've heard this line ten years ago and look where it got me. If you weren't my brother, I'd take your compliment about me as an ominous statement and prompting me to walk away from you and not look back."

After about an hour of discussion, Michael and Janet concluded the deaths of all these people occurring exactly at 11:58 in the morning was an act of terrorism by its definition: The use of violence to instill panic as a means of achieving some type of goal. If this scenario turned out to be true of why all these people had died—even though no group had come forward and claimed responsibility—then what was their goal or reason for this evil act? Who were the perpetrators behind this horrendous act? And another important question: How did they achieve killing eight people in different areas of Ocala at the same time? Michael suggested there had to be a network of malevolent militants using a chemical or device directed at their victims. The logistics of delivering their deadly outcome was monumental. Yet these possible unknown terrorists completed this evil act flawlessly. Michael and Janet dismissed the idea of one psychopath responsible for this heinous act, it would've been logistically impossible.

"These deaths were deliberate, instigated by evilness," Janet said.

"I agree." Michael got up, put their empty coffee cups into the dishwasher and turned off the coffee pot. He turned around and rubbed his chin as an ominous possibility flashed across his mind.

"You look as if you stepped on an explosive device ready to

explode, big brother."

"What if these deaths today were only the beginning? And possibly many more people will perish in the near future at another selected time."

The thought of this possibility frightened them.

Also by the Author
at
Rogue Phoenix Press

Strange

Frightening dreams night after night are afflicting the chief of pediatrics, Adam Stafford, at Ocala Regional Medical Center. Will there be a conclusion of his dreams or will he succumb to a death spiral before he can awake? At ORMC, Adam attempts to understand why deathbed children on the pediatric floor at ORMC awakened cured without any medical explanation? In a near-by town, an archeologist, Lisa Douglas, is searching for the meaning of ancient hieroglyphs on various Mayan relics recently discovered in a cave along Mexico's Yucatan peninsula. There seems to be a possibility that all these scenarios are intertwined with a twelve-year-old male patient, Arius Turner, at Ocala Regional Medical Center.

Frozen Death

Something is causing people to freeze to death in Florida during ninety-degree weather. Ancient Indian lore holds the answer to these mysterious medical aberrations. A newly constructed Florida male prison sits on ancient hallowed grounds called Forbidden Hill. Soon after the prison opens, two male inmates freeze to death without exposure to frigid temperatures. John Randall, a widowed prison doctor, meets Lena Windmaker, a single, off-duty sheriff detective at a local library. Their initial plutonic relationship soon kindles into a more amorous one. They hide a personal secret that could bring them together or destroy them. They uncover articles in local, post-Civil war newspapers describing residence succumbing to Frozen Death. John and Lena race to discover a cause before it chooses other victims.

Sudden Blindness

People in Ocala, a small city in Florida, face an epidemic of sudden blindness. The head of Ocala Regional Medical Center's emergency room, David Belmont, and his wife, Sarah, a high school science teacher, seek answers to what is causing the blindness, where did the blindness originate and why did it suddenly afflict people and animals without warning or other symptoms? Their son, a high school senior, is one of the victims. These questions are baffling an experienced investigative medical team from CDC whom arrive later in the day from Atlanta, Georgia. Unbeknownst to David, Sarah and the leader of the CDC's team, Russell Patton, has a mutual amorous secret.

Strange Appearance

Two hairless teenage bodies are found dead with ritual-type death masks on their faces in Ocala National Forest. Robert Jenson, a fourth-year medical student and Cynthia Davidson, a pathologist's assistant, join together to solve these unexplained mysterious deaths. Clandestine members of a secluded satanic cult adjacent to the national forest cross their paths. Shortly afterwards, Robert and Cynthia face deadly situations jeopardizing their own lives as they soon discover someone doesn't want them to know the truth behind the teenagers' deaths. Robert and Cynthia's initial platonic relationship evolves to amorous feelings and needs complicating their investigation. Evil touches the two medical sleuths. And they don't realize it until it's almost too late.

The Strange Horizon

The Strange Horizon ranges from stories less than a hundred words to over four thousand words. There isn't any profanity, gore or sexual innuendo in any of the short stories. The genre varies from mystery, suspense, contemporary, horror, science fiction and fantasy. You may smile, chuckle, express a tear or two, feel a sudden chill or feel warmth at the end of the story. Emotions are in the mind of the reader and the heart cuddles or rejects those emotions.